UNDER ATTACK

SGT. HAWK BOOK THREE

PATRICK CLAY

ROUGH
EDGES
PRESS

To Mr. and Mrs. N.B. Clay

UNDER ATTACK

UNDER ATTACK

FLAMES OF DEATH

Hawk stared wildly into the eyes of one of the Japanese gunners. The machine gun sputtered blinding flashes that registered deep within his retinas. A violent concussion filled his helmet, brilliant red oozed down over his eyes. He was deafened by a powerful ringing. He didn't realize it, but a slug had landed in his helmet and rolled around inside it, taking pieces of flesh with it. He pulled one of the flamethrower's triggers.

The world instantly divided in two. A red-orange world roared in front of the nozzle, and behind it was the only slightly less uncomfortable world that Hawk stood upon. The concussion of the ignition and the steady cushion of threatening heat caused Hawk to stagger back. He rallied his waning energy and pointed the nozzle higher. The machine gun stopped. He lapped the flame repeatedly across the mouth of the cave. Popping explosions came out of the volcanic gunpit as the ammunition went up. Cries screeched from within the hissing flame. Nine seconds of hell, and then it was over. Nine seconds was enough.

1

FOG SWIRLED AROUND THE TOPS OF THE MOUNTAINS, AND between them. Stark red explosions pulsated through the haze. Yellow smoke shimmered off the edges of the explosions. The grey fog inhaled the smoke, making it part of itself.

"I know I can't do it," said the tight-lipped young man. He shook his head. "No." His eyes were closed. Beside him crouched a second boy hugging his rifle and gently rocking himself. This one could say nothing. His eyes were open.

Sgt. Hawk slumped down with a tired groan. He didn't tell them that they had to go on. He didn't belittle them or plead with them. It was too serious for that. Either you would do it or you would not. He unsnapped his canteen and took a slow drink, staring all the while into the eyes of Joe Canlon below him on the slope. Joe's eyes were narrowed and twitching on each side of his warped nose. The nervous charges of energy that filled his body caused perpetual motion across his features.

He wanted to stay here on the slope with the others. He would go on, if Hawk did.

Between Hawk and Canlon lay Pharmacist's Mate George Simpson. He had felt the same way. His neck had taken an oversized, L-shaped piece of shrapnel. The L was still there, folding his head back on one blood-blackened shoulder. Joe Canlon turned away from this, looking over his own shoulder and back down the mountainside. Ray Neal with a bullet through his head. John Romano in several glistening pieces, scattered in a circle around Neal. He had known all these men. They had drunk coffee together this morning. They weren't ordinary men. They had all volunteered to do this. Some found out that they weren't up to the task. Most of them didn't live that long.

It was a little island off of the coast of New Guinea and World War II was only a year or so old. The island had a name but that would soon be forgotten. It was the island of the here and now. They were told to clear the cave-riddled hills of the Japanese invaders. Eventually, they—or someone—would. It was the type of assignment that took away all your friends, everyone you knew, all within a matter of minutes. It was a quick reorganization of the world as you knew it.

Hawk was fresh from a campaign of a different sort. It had been a long and costly affair, with the men disappearing at a slow and inevitable rate. It was grinding, demoralizing, easily capable of driving the best of men mad by the sheer length of time involved. This was different. This took your mind and spirit and hammered them flat, making it as difficult to function as it would be to play the piano with a mashed thumb. You were no longer human, no longer capable of being demoralized, no longer possessed of anything that could go mad. You had gone beyond all of that. Hawk replaced his canteen. Facts registered within his brain as he coldly filtered out the confusing run of feelings.

He ran his calloused hand along the sharp edge of his submachine gun's burnished surface. He attached a fifty-round drum to the Thompson. This was one of the times he would need that many rounds.

"You going, Joe?" he asked under his breath. He didn't look back at his friend.

"For a ways, I guess."

"Let's go."

They scrambled over the rocks, grabbing the wiry grass to steady themselves. The grass had a residue of smoke and ash sticking to it that blackened their hands. Hawk's shirt hung open as he climbed. An unbroken chain of funnel-shaped ricochets squealed between them. Canlon flattened and waited for the machine gun fire to subside. Hawk kept going. Bent at the waist, panting and climbing, he squinted at the gun-pits above him and held his fire. He thrust his heavy boot over the corpse of a marine and lay in the gravelly soil beside it. He would wait for Joe to catch up. He looked over at the face of the dead man. He had known him well. He too had been a veteran of Guadalcanal. He couldn't remember the last time he had spoken with the man, but it couldn't have been very long ago—probably about nothing important. He looked away and out to the sea behind him. The vision of the soulless face stayed with him.

He snapped his head around. His mouth was closed and angry now. His fiery blue eyes counted the machine guns above him. To the right, to the left, they stretched into infinity. He could see maybe ten. Some were closer than the others so that they might protect each other. They formed a coughing meat grinder with interlocking blades. Sweat ran from beneath the domed shadow of his helmet and down the side of his face. He clenched his teeth and swallowed. His bronze skin was flushed Choctaw red. Canlon's helmet bumped into the sole of his worn boot. He had finally made it up. Time to go on.

To the right he could see several other marines daring the climb. These were the bravest of the brave, the ones who would go on, no matter what. Two of them fell and rolled limply down the mountain. From where Hawk stood, it looked as if they had done so for no particular reason. He couldn't see what had struck them. A third man knelt and clutched at his face. His scream was high-pitched at first and then deep and bellowing on the wind.

The pounding of the machine guns increased until the hammering staccato reports blended into a single vibrating roar. The men in the caves swung their weapons back and forth, blanketing the mountainside with exploding fountains of lead. It must have been a magnificent spectacle from the elevated perspective of the Japanese, but the beauty of it was lost on the men struggling up the middle of the slope. They saw only the deadly fog, pushing the gunsmoke down into their ranks in great rolling swells. Hawk had gone farther than this. He could see the enemy gunners. He could see the ring-coiled barrels of their automatic weapons, the conical flash-guards on the muzzles of the guns and even the shadows they cast upon the rocks as they glided to and fro. The Japanese were pointing out targets and talking to one another. He watched in fascination. They didn't move like real men. The movements were quicker, more than real; the slightest gesture was dreadful and important. They were ghouls, insatiable monsters perched above him. His raging anger died. Anger no longer comforted him. Too many had died. His pupils shrank into his eyes as a dreamy daze overtook him. Sanity and the instinct of self-preservation evaporated from the remnants of his vicious spirit. *Keep going. Get them. Kill them. That's all you can do, now. Pay them back.*

Behind the mountaintop, the sky was a deep, rich black. Neon reflections of slashing machine gun fire splashed against it like heat lightning. The filthy air was heavy with a burning chemical odor. It was hard to breathe. Down below, Canlon gave hand signals. Men began climbing up to him from somewhere. He waited. Hawk didn't. He climbed on alone.

A snaking line of fire spewed down the slope in the direction of the sergeant. Hawk fell and let it dance over him. The burst of fire stopped, took a breath, and came after him again, pouncing on him and playing all around him. Chips of rock and metal splattered his face and rang off his helmet. When the fire ceased, he judged himself to still be in one piece. Holes like cigarette burns dotted his cloth helmet cover, where the hot pieces of metal had landed. He looked up at the Japanese, the muscles in his face strained as if he were looking into a strong wind. He raised his weapon and balanced it awkwardly on a stone. He squeezed the trigger and it leapt violently. A snow-white flash zigzagged from the Cutts compensator of the muzzle, glowing urgently, realistically against the dark brown of the earth. Spent casings shot from the breech, into the air, and plinked onto the rocks. If the Japanese minded his display of fury, they didn't let it show. Their fire never slackened.

Hawk lay behind a sheltering boulder and breathed deeply. His hairy chest heaved with exertion and flooding adrenalin. He muttered an obscenity and rummaged through his pockets for some chewing tobacco. Today they would get him. Soon. His time was up. Where in God's name did all that lead come from? Fire chewed and slapped at the stone around his ears. The battle had started less than two hours ago, and already grime and tiredness had worn their way into the marrow of his bones. Canlon dropped beside him in a fear-exhausted heap.

"Third platoon got over the top," Canlon shouted. "They say third platoon is on the other side of the mountain."

"Can't be," Hawk said. His eyes were aimed at the ocean far behind him. Naval guns thundered in the distance. Landing craft, followed by white wakes, continued to congregate on the shore at the foot of the slope. Hawk's eyes didn't blink. He chewed slowly on a plug of tobacco. "They couldn't get through this."

"Japs let 'em through." Canlon held onto his helmet with both hands. "Bait, I guess." Hawk nodded. Maybe it was true. The Japanese might have suckered them up there. They might be doing the same thing to Hawk. They certainly weren't being obvious about it. But then he hadn't run into any concentrations of artillery, or mortars. It could be true. Hawk spat.

"Wonder what them ships is shootin' at?" he asked Canlon.

"I don't know. Ain't doin' us no good."

"That's for goddam sure." Smoke still simmered off the Cutts compensator and it wafted between their faces. "How many left in the squad?"

"Our squad? None, I don't figure. There's some fellas comin' up behind me. They're from McGuiness's squad," Canlon stuttered. He was shaking. The front of his dungarees were wet where he had urinated and dust caked the damp spot.

Hawk spat again. "Crazy. Just crazy," he muttered in a strange tone. Where was McGuiness? McGuiness had told them that it was crazy. They didn't know it, but McGuiness had been vaporized, two hundred yards down the slope. He had a wife and three children.

Hawk's dead eyes watched the green gathering of marines below Canlon. He had seen the eyes of so many dead men that his own had taken on that all-knowing look they had. His ears were deaf to the roaring machine guns. The senses could handle only so much. He heard the closer sounds of the thousands of metal slugs cutting through the wind. Each one carried its own vibrating buzz. Collide with one of those buzzes and you were dead. That invisible whir could turn your face into a broken ketchup bottle, or your bones into scattered talcum powder. He could see the bullets streaming down from above in a veritable cascade. They looked like molten rocks being thrown down in angry disarray. But when they struck, it was in a pattern, in a line on the ground or across a human being.

Sgt. Hawk told them again that they would have to keep going. He didn't want to tell them that. It would have been easier to walk into a bullet and end his responsibilities. But he would fight to stay alive and make them do the same. He stood, and most of them followed his example, half standing, half crouching, nervously prepared to fall on the ground before being knocked onto it. He hoped that he was right and that it was all worth it. He was the sort of man who felt it was easier to die than to order another man to die. He would never be an officer. He never died, either. Or so it seemed. Everyone else did, and still he remained.

Then the first of the heavy mortar shelling began. Hawk's gullet tightened to the size of a pencil. Everyone fell to the earth.

"Looks like the good times are over," Hawk roared at Canlon. Little noises crawled out of Joe's throat, though his lips were welded tightly together. His clinging fingers were buried up to their second joints in the rocky soil.

* * *

THE ISLAND of New Guinea had been partially liberated, though the major portion as well as the surrounding waters were still hotly contested. The city of New Oss was one of the first freed of Japanese occupation by the U. S. Army. The Empire's southern outpost, the stronghold at Rabaul, was so close that the town would always be subject to recapture. Nevertheless, Sir Richard St. Cyr considered it a safe place. Since the Battle of the Coral Sea, it was as safe as Australia—if you considered Australia safe. And he did. He had an interest in all of this, a personal interest.

Sir Richard adjusted his dinner jacket as he looked about the tables in the Cafe Aoflt Bonte. A local merchant was seated at his table and that irritated him, but he didn't let on to his fiancée, Monica Asquith, that he was miffed. Sir

Richard allowed the maître d' to seat them at another table, toying nonchalantly with the wine list as the maître d' bowed and backed away. One would not have been able to tell from his outward appearance that he was upset. Miss Asquith certainly didn't notice.

An assortment of Indonesian musicians played Continental music quietly on the far side of the room, where the better tables were located. The people dining here did not come for local color or to hear strange island compositions. Most of them lived here and had had all the local color that one lifetime can tolerate. They came for a touch of the old country. Chandeliers hung in swaying dignity from the ceiling, elegant drapes covered the windows, blocking out the miserable exterior of New Oss. Everyone was dressed. One had to dress to be allowed into the Aoflt Bonte.

"It's lovely," Miss Asquith said, adjusting the white lace at her throat. "Isn't it exciting! It's quite a civilized place after all, I think."

"Of course, my dear," said Sir Richard.

"Do you think that such a thing could be done? The concept is so appalling. Your own nation," she laughed, shuddering with glee.

"Without a doubt. The empire passed away first and the commonwealth will follow, along with the colonies of its members. They're all things of the past. The war will take care of such anachronisms. I've always been accused of being a conservative, but I think that I'm actually quite progressive. Independence is the politics of the future. And I'll be there at the outset. I've already done it, in fact." He leaned forward across the table and whispered this with mock confidentiality.

Sir Richard wanted his own country, not a humble ambition, even if the nation were to be Malang on the coast of New Guinea. The astounding thing was, he *did* already have it. The Americans had liberated the ex-Australian territory and subsequently abandoned it to the primitive natives. The U.S. didn't really care if the Australians and the Dutch ever settled their endless squabbling over the worthless real estate, just so the Japanese didn't try to reclaim it. Sir Richard had stepped into the loose organization set up and left by the Japanese, declaring himself to be interim adminis-trator of the Malang territorial province. He gradually began calling himself governor, using the term inter-changeably with administrator, but was becoming more stubborn about leaving the word "territory" off the offi-cial title of Malang. "Territory" would be dropped, and "governor" would be replaced by "prime minister"—or perhaps even something else. He didn't need Australia. What had it ever done for the region? Private corpora-tions had taken all this risk and made all the advances here. What could Australia do? Send a gunboat? Against white settlers? Preposterous.

"Friends in high places, being in the proper situa-tion at an opportune moment—these are the things that history is made of." He smiled across his wine glass at her. Despite an irrational vein of ambition, he was a dashing fellow, with sleepy hazel eyes and a sparkling smile. He had once been handsome, and egotistical enough to make a fair living as an actor before he got into politics. His companion was half his age. She didn't seem to mind that as she touched her glass to his. The glasses clinked daintily. He poured some of his wine into her glass.

"It is such a beautiful place. I can't believe that you've done all this at such a young age," she said. "As you say, there is still the government, and the Dutch and the natives to contend with. I suppose the war will take care of all of them. Survival of the fittest and all that rot," she laughed.

"The war?" He laughed in return.

"Yes, you remember—the war?"

"Oh, yes, but that's in Europe, or some such uncivilized place, is it not?"

"I seem to have heard something like that."

How merry it all was! He smiled and put his well-manicured hand over hers. A cloud came over his happy eyes when he again spotted the insubordinate maître d'. We'll see how many more times he gives my table away, Sir Richard thought.

Across the Straights of Cavazo from New Oss, on a rocky little island in the Haarmeer Archipelago, things were not so pleasant, and the world was not so ordered. A truly unpleasant person was about to bring his horrible way of life across the Straits. Sgt. Hawk.

* * *

THE EARTH VOMITED black gushers of blazing shrapnel. The mortars shielded the enemy positions from view with an unholy shroud. The noise obliterated the sound of the chattering machine guns. Hawk went through it. He didn't know where the others were. His great courage served him well, for he ultimately got so close to the caves that he was inside the range of the mortars.

He couldn't get any closer. A lone man couldn't do anything more, except wait for a bullet or a grenade to stop him. He aimed his submachine gun up the craggy, bullet casing-covered slope, firing at the nearest of the machine gun nests. They must have been frantic with their inability to hit him. He drew fire from all along the enemy emplacements, taking what cover he could behind a serrated ledge. The bullets chipped great hunks of the brass-colored stone from the ledge, cutting their furious way down to him like a power saw. He rubbed his hand up and down the cooling ribs of the Thompson. Another man dropped beside him. Hawk had never seen this individual before.

He was a short man, broad shouldered, obviously in possession of unlimited nerve. He had carried a flamethrower up the slope with him. The sergeant may not have known him, but he was never more glad to see anyone. Seventy pounds of pure hell were strapped to the man's back, and it couldn't have been an easy task getting it up the mountain. Weaponry was going through an age of transition and Hawk wasn't entirely certain how the flamethrower operated. Without hesitation, he prepared to support and cover the other man's attack. He removed the gangster magazine from the Thompson and replaced it with a full clip.

The strategy was laid out in grunts and gestures. Hawk would pin the closest of the nests down with a burst of automatic fire, and the flamethrower would jump into the breach. It would have worked nicely, too, if a piece of shrapnel hadn't come flying from the rear and penetrated the helmet of the shorter man, draining his head of its brains. Hawk numbly tried to free the dead arms from the carrying sling. Machine gun bursts skidded across the rock behind him. His temper finally got the best of him. He ripped his knife from its sheath and severed the tangled straps. Sweat fell from his face and onto the smallest of the weapon's three tanks. Slinging his submachine gun, he studied the launcher for a moment. The launcher ended in a blunt, double-cupped nozzle, and it supported two hand grips with a trigger on each. Two triggers.

"Okay," he whispered to himself. A half dozen mortar shells crashed in a tightening circle around him. They fell almost simultaneously, the nearest landing within fifteen yards of him. Solid breakers of dust and stone washed over him. He didn't care if he understood the mechanism or not. He didn't care if they shot him. He held the two grips tightly, and leapt from behind the sheltering ledge. The rubber hose that connected the launcher to the fuel tanks dragged them along behind him. The tanks made hollow, metallic noises as they scraped along the stone. He operated involuntarily now. His brain was turned off. His spinal cord was directing all functions. *Go on, you mindless moving object!* Each step he took carried him deeper into Death's stinking throat.

Hawk stared wildly into the eyes of one of the Japanese gunners. The machine gun sputtered blinding flashes that registered deep within his retinas. Head-high geysers ran along the ground, down the slope and directly at him. A violent concussion filled his helmet, brilliant red oozed down over his eyes. He was deafened by a powerful ringing. He didn't realize it, but a slug had landed in his helmet and rolled around inside it, taking pieces of flesh with it. He pulled one of the launcher's triggers with his right hand. This released the fuel.

Nothing happened. He pulled the other trigger with his left hand, activating the ignition device.

The world instantly divided in two. A red-orange world roared in front of the nozzle, and behind it was the only slightly less uncomfortable world that he stood upon. The fuel had gone up in a vacuum-snapping *whumpf*. The concussion of the ignition and the steady cushion of threatening heat caused Hawk to stagger back. He rallied his waning energy and pointed the nozzle higher. The machine gun stopped.

"Suck it up, Jap," he half-sobbed, half-growled. He lapped the flame repeatedly across the mouth of the cave. Popping explosions came out of the volcanic gunpit as the ammunition went up. Cries screeched and warbled from within the hissing flames. A blazing helmet rolled down from above. Nine seconds of hell, and then it was over. Nine seconds was enough. The other machine guns came to life, no longer spellbound by the shocking spectacle. He heard bullets striking nearby. His fingers uncoiled from the grips of the launcher and it fell at his feet. He ran upward, running and yet moving slowly because of the steep ascent and his exhaustion.

Angrily twitching flames ringed the mouth of the stricken cave. A half dozen charred, mummified creatures sat foolishly around a black Nambu machine gun. He stepped over the barricade and into their midst. Jellied globs of fire dripped from the roof of the inferno. It didn't matter. This was the only place left for him to go. The Japanese bodies still burned. The odor of cooked human flesh caused the lines around his nose to jam upwards against his eyes.

Canlon led the men from McGuiness's squad up the

slope. Some of them outranked him, but he was the one with the guts to lead. At the point Hawk had broken through the enemy lines, the fire slackened. They charged forward, making great progress for a while. It wouldn't be that easy. Covering machine guns took their toll of the Americans, and then when that failed to stop the mad attack, the Japanese sprang enthusiastically from their holes. Offensive by nature, and fearing a breakthrough, the enemy abandoned their own invulnerable line. They wore flat helmets and grey uniforms. Leggings were wrapped up to their knees and they carried large rifles with long, savage bayonets.

Hawk watched from his vantage point in their own lines. He got off a short burst into their backs before they closed with the Americans below. The Japanese were adroit in the use of the bayonet; they had no inhibitions when it came to close combat. Their long knifes slid through several of the big marines. Hawk could see the faces of the Americans, distorted in disbelief at the proximity of their foes. The fearless enemy took advantage of their revulsion, falling on them with a passion. One man was clutching at a bayonet rammed into his stomach, slicing his hands to pieces. Anger washed away Hawk's paralyzing daze. He vaulted over the barricade and ran to join the fray. A machine gun fired behind him. He ducked and looked over his shoulder. Two little warriors were charging after him. At first he was relieved to see them. The machine gun would not fire at them. The relief was short-lived.

Jets of freezing adrenalin permeated his body as he turned to face them. Both of them leveled bayonets at him. They didn't shoot, they didn't slow up. He didn't know that they had long since run out of ammunition.

He barely turned himself around before they were upon him. He couldn't get his hand in place to fire his machine pistol. One of the men stopped and feinted with his long knife. The marine watched as his left elbow jerked this way and a right hand jerked that way. His own hands reflexively jerked in compensating motions. He had to fend off the weapon or die. The second man lunged at him. He batted the bayonet aside, its blunt side sliding harmlessly across his arm. The first man lunged and Hawk narrowly avoided the razor-sharp point. He avoided the knife but not the man. The two of them collided. Their arms tangled as they sought quick holds. Hawk tossed an arm over his head and the two of them went rolling down the mountainside.

When they stopped, they were among the countless others fighting the hand-to-hand battle on the slope. They sought each other's throats with their hands. Hawk's thick fingers encircled the little neck. His square-tipped thumbs dug into and beneath the man's windpipe, splitting open flesh and vital blood vessels, and spraying himself, his opponent and the ground with a terrifying red flood. The Japanese soldier released the marine's heavy neck and clawed upward for his eyes. But he was too late. Hawk lay over his twitching body, breathing heavily.

More Americans came up the slope, passing quickly by the wounded and dying. Minutes earlier, these wounded and dying were the only ones brave enough to occupy this ground. Hawk stood up at last and joined the throng of advancing men. He found Canlon, and walked along with him for a while unarmed, until he was able to retrieve his tommy gun from a scavenger.

The two of them crossed over the mountain together. They were no longer in the vanguard.

The company dug in on the reverse slope for the night. Hawk and Canlon walked down the slope and through the territory occupied by the legendary third platoon, the platoon that had first crossed the mountain. Only one machine gunner was still alive in the unit. They didn't find him until nightfall. He and his gun continued to face the crumbling enemy lines. Hawk cleared the dead from his foxhole and decided to stay with him. The machine gunner didn't help in the task.

Canlon made the three of them coffee. The machine gunner left his cup sitting next to the canned heat. He said he'd drink it later. Canlon glanced at Hawk as the silence of the third man became increasingly eerie. It didn't bother Hawk as much as it did Canlon, for he was rather quiet himself. The slug that rolled around in his helmet had seared a trail through his scalp and given him a headache. Dried blood drew crusted lines on his forehead.

"Must have been pretty tough up here today," Joe said to the machine gunner.

"You know it," the man answered. He had a nasal voice that marked him as a native of the Texas-Oklahoma-Arkansas region.

"Y'all managed to get over the top, though, huh?" Hawk grudgingly made conversation. The man deserved that much, regardless of any peculiarities he might have.

"Yep."

Another half hour of the night passed and the machine gunner didn't speak. Hawk suspected that the horrifying experiences of the day had left him a bit touched in the head. He felt more than a bit touched himself. Joe decided to go to sleep.

"If you're gonna sit there facin' the Japs all night, you might as well take the first watch," Canlon told the man from third platoon. His voice was tired and weak, but one could still detect the irritation in it "You ain't turned around once since we got here."

"No need. This is the way they'll be coming. It's fine with me if you want to sleep all night. I'll be here waitin' on 'em when they come."

"Okay," Joe answered and smiled sadly at Hawk. Nuts. He studied the machine gunner's back in the dark. Both of his hands were wrapped tensely around the Browning. He sat on an empty ammunition crate. Joe read insane determination in his bent posture. His legs were spread wide apart...his...Joe opened his eyes wider. He stared at the man's legs. He motioned to Hawk and pointed at the legs. Hawk looked over. His expression didn't change as he settled against the earthen wall of the hole. The man had no legs. Blood-soaked tourni- quets were attached to each knee.

Hawk figured he had to say something. "You...ready to go back to the aid station?"

"Not by a long shot," the man replied.

"Them legs'll need patchin' up," Canlon said. "Ain'tcha worried about 'em?"

The man turned his torn and eyeless face toward Joe. "Naw. I cain't see 'em."

2

THE HARSH GLARE BOUNCED ALONG THE PEAKED SURFACE of the ocean. A tiny landing craft, packed with men, lurched over each angry swell, thumping and shuddering as if a mighty fist were pounding at its belly. Joe Canlon stared ahead, out over the endless sea. Hawk stood beside him. He looked back at the mountain where so many of his friends had died. He knew that he would never see this place again. The Haarmeer Archipelago. Not that it mattered.

An immense LST glided past them. They squinted at the swift leviathan. It was filled with officers. The officers weren't riding with their men. The LST weaved through the smaller craft and outdistanced them. The officers were given the opportunity to make the brief passage on the larger craft and they took it. It was faster and smoother. A major, who was a chaplain, and a captain, named Howell Carlisle, were the only exceptions. They rode in the rear of Hawk's landing craft.

"Ain't that something, now?" Canlon asked rhetorically as the LST steamed by. "They put us out to the open sea on a thing like this. They know damn good and well we'll be heaving ourselves to death before we hit land."

"Ah..." Hawk spat black chewing tobacco over the side and shrugged.

"Sonofabitches! I'm gettin' pissed off. The whole First Division spends Christmas in New Hebrides or New Zealand or some goddam place, and then they get God knows how long down in Australia. Thirty day leaves. Liberty every other day. But what about Joe Canlon? Shit no! His ass has gotta go climb some Jap mountain!"

"Well, you're gettin' a break now, ain'tcha?" Hawk smiled at the rear of the passing LST.

"Yeah," Joe grumbled, "goin' into reserve...shit! In New Guinea. Ain't that nice? The place is crawling with Japs, there ain't a woman for a thousand miles—some reserve! If we was in the army, they'd call it front line duty. For us, it's a goddam vacation." Joe fumbled with a package of Japanese cigarettes. Lately, he couldn't control his fingers very well when it came to the finer movements. His nerves were bothering him. After he managed to get one into his mouth, the wind kept extinguishing his lighter. Anger overcame him; he screamed an obscenity and hurled the lighter out over the water at the departing LST. It dropped into the abysmal sea, covering only about a tenth of the distance between the two craft. "And then they stick us in the ocean in a tin can!"

Hawk was quiet for a few minutes before saying, "The Army's done cleared out New Guinea."

"I'll just bet they did!"

The South Pacific Ocean was no place to bound

about in a landing craft in 1943. The Japanese Navy still spoke with great authority in the region. The Americans, with considerable Australian support, had freed Malang Province, but the bulk of the northern part of the island remained in Japanese hands. It remained in their hands as much as it did anyone else's. New Guinea was the sort of land that defied ownership.

What was left of Hawk's battalion would garrison in New Oss on the shore of Malang. This protected the nearby oil fields from enemy reoccupation, and supported the Navy in its struggle against the mighty enemy fleet. The Navy would eventually need the port at New Oss. Enemy submarines were the greatest threat in all the waters around New Guinea—the Coral Sea, the Solomon Sea, the Arafura and the Bismarck. But the worst area of all, the one in which one was most likely to encounter this unseen menace, was the Straits of Cavazo.

The officers aboard the LST were in a festive mood. They had no business being all together like this. Some of them were passing around bottles. No bottles made any rounds on the enlisted men's transports. Boisterous voices carried over the waves from behind the LST's gargantuan walls. Since the ocean wasn't their problem, they didn't worry about attacks. They were just making a short little run to the mainland. No air cover. No escorts. A few little containers of men puttering peacefully along.

* * *

THE COMMANDER of the Imperial I-Boat muttered under his breath. He played his periscope along the school of helpless landing craft. Only one torpedo remained in his tubes. Just his luck! One torpedo and he hit the jackpot. He had already wasted the others in a game of tag with a worthless little American PT boat. He had won that game, but what he wouldn't give to have those torpedoes back! These fools were sitting ducks. He had to make the best of it. The LST probably had ammunition, supplies, possibly even tanks aboard. It also made the biggest target. This was something to consider, given the lackluster performance of his last few torpedoes.

He didn't consider it for very long. He knew his job, he had done this many times. In three minutes the LST was on the bottom of the ocean, all aboard lost before she even began to sink, and the I-Boat was on her way back to Rabaul.

The other craft continued on their way across the Straits of Cavazo. It was an odd predicament. They couldn't do anything but proceed on course and accept whatever punishment the incompetence of their superiors had laid them open to. The Americans had no way of knowing that the I-Boat was gone, and consequently there were a lot of grey hairs and soiled underwear before the survivors made New Oss. Most of the young men forgot even to get seasick. Death at sea is different from the variety found on terra firma. Like death in the air, it is cleaner. But it is often more sudden, with ominous unfriendly nature swallowing all traces of its passage. The I-Boat may have left, but the sea remained. Its great maw yawned beneath the few inches of steel decking, waiting to accommodate as many human beings as cared to fall into it.

Major Stephen Clemson was now the ranking officer. He was a chaplain. Captain Howell Carlisle was the only other officer. He had recently become battalion legal officer. The rest of the officers were dissolving on the sea bottom, along with a good number of the highest-ranking noncommissioned officers. Neither Major Clemson nor Capt. Carlisle had any orders. No one saw fit to give them any. The departure from the Haarmeer Archipelago had been done without any briefings. Presumably there had been a briefing aboard the LST, in transit, not that it mattered any more. The two officers didn't have the slightest idea of what they were doing in New Oss. The enlisted men knew even less about the matter. Most of them didn't know that they were in New Guinea, much less New Oss. New Guinea was Army territory, close to Australia. What was worse, a good part of their equipment had gone down with the LST.

Sir Richard St. Cyr knew what was going on, however. He was expecting the Americans. He had requested their presence. He reasoned that if marines occupied New Oss, he wouldn't be bothered with any crown or A.I.F. troops.

He knew that the Americans would leave when he was through using them, as they did everywhere else. The others would only be trouble. Australia still labored under the misconception that she owned Malang. Britain had always been the enemy of independence-minded men, such as himself. He met the new troops at the quay and invited the Major and the Captain to his mansion near the harbor. They walked the short distance, avoiding the tractor-drawn carts that formed the principal mode of transportation in New Oss. Sir Richard was preoccupied as they idly chatted. His thoughts were filled with the glory of independence. Or at least, a white-skinned version of it.

Hawk slouched impatiently among the men lounging on the wharf. The non-coms had them squared away as to units and equipment, but no one told them where to go or what to do. Dark-skinned natives moved among the crowd, offering their services to even the lowest-ranking of their number. Canlon hired a valet within a half hour of his arrival. He borrowed a container of C-rations from a boy named Harwood as payment. The native carried Joe's heavy pack, following the marine as he paced aimlessly up and down the dock. Sgt. Hawk lit a long thin cigar and sat against a hot tin boatshed. Canlon found him there. Joe smiled his ugly, black, gap-toothed smile. He could reach the point of complete mental collapse, and within the hour, be laughing at himself.

"Hey, Hawk, meet my man, Chives," Joe said. His voice was deep and husky, as if he had had some sort of throat injury. He laughed as he displayed the bowing native. His laugh was like the braying of a jackass. Hawk could tell that Joe had already forgotten the harrowing sea ride. Hawk hadn't been as worried about the I-Boat as Joe had. But he hadn't forgotten it either.

"Get rid of that sonofabitch," Hawk said without looking at either of them. Joe laughed again and sat beside the sergeant.

"What next?" he asked.

"I don't know. Ask MacArthur." Hawk's ferocious blue eyes stared at the row of empty landing craft. Joe knew that he was angry about something, but he wasn't going to leave him alone. That's the way Joe was.

"Where you from, Hawk? I thought you southerners

was supposed to be courteous and all that shit. Ain't you never heard of southern hospitality?"

"Why should I be courteous to a shitbag like you?" Hawk spat the words in his belligerent Delta accent. Then he reconsidered the harshness of the rebuff. "Mississippi."

"Yeah? I been there. All they talk about down there is the Civil War. They're still pissed off about the goddam Civil War!"

"Is that right?" Hawk looked over at him and back out to sea. He drew thoughtfully on his cigar. "What part of New York are you from?"

"Hey, how'd you know that?"

"Because you're a shitbag. Go find out what's goin' on, will you? Who's runnin, this show?"

Canlon nodded and his face became serious. "Yeah, I'll see what I can find out. We ain't got no BC or platoon leaders or nothin'. I'll see what they're gonna do here."

"I'd appreciate that. Find out who they are, too."

Canlon stood up. "Come on, Chives." The native picked up his pack. Joe looked over his shoulder and smiled at Hawk. The sergeant snorted. After the two of them had left, he continued staring at the weathered sides of his landing craft. "Sneaky Jap bastards," he whispered.

* * *

Capt. Carlisle told Canlon to bring Hawk up to the administrator's palace. The officer met his solemn noncom on the front porch of that august landmark. The porch had a fresh coat of white paint. It was freshly scrubbed, it sparkled. Labor, like life, was cheap in New

Oss. Hawk's dirty boots left a trail of mud across the sterile decking of the porch.

"Sergeant James Hawk reporting, sir."

"Hello, Sergeant. Here, sit down, sit down," said the captain nervously. He was a little shorter than Hawk, a little younger, and with an open, honest, less than rugged face. They sat in two freshly painted wicker chairs.

"I'm Captain Carlisle. I don't think we've met?"

"No, sir. I don't think so, sir." Hawk stretched his legs comfortably out across the porch. Clumps of mud fell all over the floor. He had seen Carlisle on the landing craft. The officer hadn't been interested in meeting him at that time.

"I'm kind of on a spot. Major Clemson is the ranking officer here. He's just told me that he's only going to minister to the men's spiritual needs," said the Captain. He was obviously upset. He spoke rapidly and his face showed his discomfort. "He's...he's...you see what I'm saying?"

"You're in charge, sir?"

"Exactly. Exactly. I'm in charge. I'm a battalion legal officer, Sergeant Hawk, I don't know what the hell is going on. I'm supposed to interview men who have gone AWOL and stuff like that. I haven't even done that yet. I don't know what to do here. No one told me anything about the program here. You see? You understand?"

"Yessir."

"You see? Here, want a cigarette?" Hawk took it and put it into his pocket. He would give it to somebody. "There's two officers in the whole city. I mean, my God, even if I knew what I was doing, it would be a mess!" Hawk nodded in agreement. "There's a Sergeant Major in the battalion, he's the ranking man under me. Then there's you. I need your help. I've never been in combat. I know the definition of a perimeter but I've never set one up or anything. They tell me that Japs are still wandering around out in the jungle. I mean, my God, they could come in here and kill us all!" Hawk found the way the man put this to be rather funny, but since it was true, he only allowed himself a somber half-smile.

"They been known to do that, yessir."

"Anyway...the Sergeant Major is an Endsworth or Densworth or something. Find him and you two get the whole thing set up. You know what I mean?"

"Well, yeah

"I mean, you know, dig some holes and put some men facing the jungle and then put some facing the sea. Make sure that they have ammunition and that kind of stuff. You see what I'm saying?"

"Yessir. I got the picture. You want me to..."

"I don't know. I don't know. You do it. The two of you do it all. I don't know anything about it. I'll rubber stamp anything that you do. You've been in combat since the war started so I know that you have a pretty good idea of what's going on."

"Okay. Aye, aye, sir."

"Good. Fine. Thank you." Hawk stood up to leave. "Oh, and Sergeant Hawk, the Sergeant Major was a little evasive on his experience, that's why I called for you. Everybody said to call you. Don't let him do anything that, you know, you would consider stupid or anything...you see what I'm saying? I mean, I'll overrule him, if you think he's doing anything dangerous or anything. I mean, we'll make you a master gunnery sergeant or some damn thing." Hawk nodded and started down the porch steps. "And let me know how it's going. I mean...when can I see you again?"

"Oh..." Hawk hesitated. He was used to being *told* how long he had to move mountains. "Pretty quick, I imagine, sir."

"Fine. Fine. And listen, we've got Regiment on the radio. They know what happened. They said the field grade officers should have been transported with the men. I mean, it's not *my* fault we're in this. They're sending line officers over here immediately. A couple of days at the most. Just cover for me until then. I don't want you to worry. We have good communications."

"That's a good deal, sir."

* * *

SGT. MAJOR WENTWORTH was the opposite of Capt. Carlisle. Words had to be pried out of his mouth. He still sat at the mouth of a landing craft, like a turtle with indigestion, waiting to be told what to do. He looked like a marine, with a hard-boned and seamed face. But as it turned out, he wasn't much of one, to Hawk's way of thinking. He might have been all right in his day, back before there was a war. He had been in supply for the last fifteen years. Here he was dead weight. This was a critical situation. His skills weren't particularly needed. He didn't offer to let Hawk run the show as the officer had done, though it was obvious that if the show was ever to run, Hawk would have to do it.

It was no big deal. The town wasn't under fire, they took their time and set up leisurely positions. Hawk put most of the weapons platoons facing the harbor. Most of the riflemen, however, were deployed in an arc west of the town, protecting it from the jungle. Everyone was set to stringing wire and digging in. At dark, Hawk informed Carlisle of the situation and the captain seemed more relaxed. The sergeant explained that the available men would not be enough to quell any major invasions. That was understood.

"I suspect that if we have any trouble, it will be with a few snipers holed up out in the wilds," said the captain. "Don't you think?" They were standing in the foyer of the administrator's palace. The gathering evening made it too dark in there to even see each other's faces. Carlisle motioned to the door and the two of them walked out onto the porch. The captain looked over his shoulder as he went through the door. He didn't wait for an answer to his first question. "Did Endsworth give you any trouble?"

"The Sergeant Major? No, sir. He's fulla...no, sir, he didn't."

"Good. That's one less problem. Listen...something's going on here. I can't quite put my finger on what it is. I told this colonial administrator, St. Cyr, that we could get some A.I.F.'s up here in a matter of hours...and he wouldn't do it. I mean, it's not my place to call them, is it? I mean, they're another country. I can call Americans in on the whole thing, but I can't go calling Canberra for relief and all...like I'm Roosevelt or something...can I? I mean, I can ask Regiment to do it, but it's not my place, is it?"

Hawk wasn't familiar with the protocol in such situations. "If it was a matter of an attack, I reckon I would, sir."

"Oh, I agree, I agree!"

"Problem is, we ain't got no reconnaissance, no kind

of air or sea reports to see what we're up against here. We got a non-com that's in intelligence, let him use the radio and see what he can find out from Regiment. See if the Japs got their eye on this place."

"Good idea. I should have done that. *You* should have done that. I turned everything over to you. I'm not criticizing you, you understand, but I *did* tell you that."

"Yessir. Now, I ain't never run no campaigns from the top down. I set up LP's and OP's along the perimeter and sent out a few scouts—regular infantry stuff. This other kinda business is a little outa my line."

"No. I know. No, I wasn't criticizing you on the whole thing. I mean, if the Japs hit us, I know that you'll give a good account of yourself. No, I know that you can't do everything, or know everything. Like me, for example. I don t know how to do anything." Carlisle gestured for Hawk to sit down. The white porch and the white chairs glowed in the dark. "What do you think of this situation here? I mean, why wouldn't a guy call his own government for help?"

Hawk took a deep breath, smelling the damp tropical air of Malang. "Hard to figure, sir. Mighta had a fallin' out with 'em of some kind."

"Maybe. Maybe so. I don't understand it." Carlisle looked into the darkness. Intense thought could be seen behind his smooth features. "There's less than a thousand whites here, maybe he figured it wasn't worth the bother."

"But it's worth bothering us?"

"Exactly. That's exactly the problem. He was all enthused about my finding us some line officers, but he doesn't want an A. I. F. package deal. That's strange, isn't it?"

"Maybe he's crooked. He's afraid of a government investigation or something."

"That's what I'm thinking. Maybe I'm getting carried away on the whole thing. I don't know. I just don't like being in the middle of a thing like this. We'll see what we're up against before we start worrying. We may never see a Jap." Nocturnal bird cries trembled from the ocean of jungle that surrounded New Oss.

"Yessir."

Hawk left Carlisle that night with a new respect for officers. He had previously considered them to be a useless nuisance. Now, he realized their purpose. A man couldn't fight a war and worry about things like supplies and reconnaissance reports. You needed them around for these nonessentials. Officers were sort of like women. He settled down for the night on the open dock, trying not to guess what new duty Carlisle would thrust upon him tomorrow.

Mosquitoes were bad in the low coastlands. Tonight was no exception.

More bad news arrived the following day. The Liberty Ship transporting the cargo of line officers went down with all aboard, somewhere in the Solomon Sea. An escort went down with her. Most of its crew were rescued. Japanese midget submarines were credited with the kills. They disappeared in the treacherous Straits of Cavazo. It was shocking to Carlisle, needless to say, but also to the Allied High Command. As far as they knew, Rabaul was the primary, the only, refueling station. Rabaul was on the northern tip of New Britain. The Army and Marines had taken the southern part of the island, and the Navy was doing a good job blockading the northern waters. Where were all the submarines coming from? This was a long way from Japan, about as far south as the Japanese Empire would ever get. The enemy had to have a base somewhere down in the contested seas around New Guinea. It could be a small base, but it was rapidly developing into a major one. Carlisle was told that his coast of New Guinea, Malang, was a suspected location for this possible sub pen.

The young captain managed to keep outwardly calm as he received this news from his superiors. They delivered the news calmly; he had to accept it calmly. When he left the radio, however, his mind whirled like a wagon wheel. He walked rapidly through the town and searched the perimeter for Sgt. Hawk. He looked with envy upon the lounging townsfolk. Because of the war, there was little trade and little to do. The natives were quite busy, of course, tending the gardens to feed these malingerers.

Hawk was ironing out one of those less exotic difficulties that plague a stationary force. First Sergeant Bupta was riding the men in Dog Company's First Platoon pretty hard. This was Hawk's old outfit, and Joe Canlon was still a part of it. He asked Hawk to intervene, to make Bupta leave the men alone. Hawk did just that, and in the process did a rather thoughtless thing. He humiliated Bupta in front of his men. Hawk was no psychologist, nor really very interested in the social graces. He attacked problems quickly and head on.

It was well known that the First Sergeant had been a D.I. back in the State. He had been a tough one, the kind that people who don't have to put up with such silliness call a "good" one. It had also became known, thanks to the men serving under him both at home and abroad, that he had performed poorly under fire on Guadalcanal. This was nothing to be ashamed of. Some men's nerves are less resilient than others. You could be a great shot, whip any man in the company, and still be terrified of having your guts blown out. As long as you could continue to function, it shouldn't be something that would be allowed to affect carrying out your duty for the rest of your life. Bupta didn't help matters any by reverting back to being a jerk as soon as the shooting stopped.

"*Marines* keep their boots shining like a mirror. You gotta see yourself in those boots," Bupta told Hawk when he was challenged about his harsh discipline. The particular boots that the men were wearing would never shine. They were some sort of leftover garbage shipped in from New Zealand while the battalion was in the Haarmeer Archipelago. Several men turned around in their foxholes to watch the confrontation. They had the usual amused smiles that spectators wear in such situations. Hawk had asked him nicely to take it easy, but that was about as far out of character as he could get. Bupta replied in a loud voice, for all the platoon to hear, "As long as they're my men, they'll be clean-shaven, bald-headed and shining from head to toe."

Bupta was used to having his way with his superiors. Some sergeants get away with that type of thing. Talking loud and authoritatively helped to pull it off. The timid usually acquiesced. "This ain't San Diego or New River or wherever in the goddam hell you come from, Bupta. We don't need your boot camp horseshit here. A man that looks like a woman fights like a woman," Hawk answered hotly. The anger in his voice, as well as the unorthodox, un-regulation message, took

Bupta aback. He was shy about physical violence nowadays, and he appeared to be very near to it. He stood tongue-tied for a period of time that was long enough to make him look foolish. From that day on, he was known as Sgt. Boot Camp, and he hated Hawk's innards. He never did get a chance to reply, if such were his intentions, because Carlisle came whimpering up and took Hawk away. If the commanding officer was taking counsel from Hawk, what could Bupta hope to accomplish? The platoon would never be shipshape. He didn't try to accomplish anything. For a while.

Carlisle told Hawk about losing his latest hope, the new shipment of officers. "My God, Hawk, they're saying that we're sitting on a Jap sub base over here somewhere! I can't handle this, I tell you. I don't know what to do about all of this."

Hawk's icy deep eyes stared at the ground. "No problem about that, sir. We're just ground forces. We ain't responsible for every goddam thing. We ain't found no sign of trouble yet. I'd quit worryin' about it. They'll get help here somehow, when we need it." Hawk knew better than that, but it sounded good. Worry was more counter-productive than excess optimism. "They're probably right about that sub base, we been eatin' an awful lot of torpedoes over that stretch of water.

"That's exactly the point. They asked me to check it out. I mean, My God, what can *I* do on the whole thing?"

"Probably not a damn shittin' thing. They gotta tell you something, though."

"Exactly. That's exactly right. And this St. Cyr guy, that crazy bastard still won't let me call the A.I.F. Regiment says I have to follow his lead on the whole thing. They don't want to rock any boats with our allies."

"Well, that kind of settles that then, don't it?" Hawk bit off a plug of chewing tobacco.

"Absolutely. But what kind of solution is that?"

"I tell ya, sir...there ain't gonna be no perfect solutions to nothin' out here. Like, say if the Japs hit us hard, a lot of us will get killed. It'll be stupid and messy and after it's over, everybody'll say, well, you shoulda done this and that and all—that's that way it is on the line. You just do what you can and shit on 'em. If you don't see their ugly ass out there on the line with you, it don't make a shit what they say."

Carlisle thought about that. "You're right, that's exactly right, what right does anybody have to criticize me, anyway? I'm here doing what I can."

Hawk spat angrily at the ground. "Goddam right." He slapped Carlisle on the shoulder and turned back to First Platoon. Carlisle walked off, mumbling to the nonresponsive ground.

The captain went back to the administrator's palace, where he met St. Cyr on the first floor, and after a few polite greetings, climbed the winding stairs toward the room that had been given him. Carlisle was thinking of a way to bring Hawk and St. Cyr together. Hawk would be able to handle him. The captain only dimly realized that he was relying too much on his sergeant. He saw nothing wrong with delegating authority. He wanted Hawk to meet St. Cyr and size him up. Then he would have a second opinion as to what was going on in New Oss. He could have merely asked around town; all the locals knew what was going on. But Carlisle spent a lot of time in his room. The heat made him sleepy. He decided upon a direct approach, sometime before dozing off for his early afternoon nap. He would invite Hawk to dinner tomorrow. The sergeant could meet the entire motley crew that lived here in the mansion.

Foremost among these was the administrator himself, Sir Richard, the self-styled figure of intrigue. He acted as if he had a great deal more power than your average backwater local official. He often spoke of "my nation," "my people" and "my obligation" to the same. It was kind of irritating to a man with both feet on the ground like Captain Carlisle. Carlisle knew his own limitations. He didn't act pompously about being an officer. He didn't know that St. Cyr considered him a bumbling ass.

Also living in the palace was Miss Asquith, the administrator's fiancée. Propriety had been loosened somewhat, due to wartime conditions, and she occupied chambers on the ground floor. She was a beautiful young blonde, and so it was that any quirks in her personality or character went unnoticed by the captain.

Mr. Starrett lived on the third floor, near the quarters of Sir Richard. St. Cyr referred to him as his chief adviser. Starrett was short, bald, deep-voiced and with a demeanor too belligerent to be British, in Carlisle's estimation. The American didn't have a clear distinction between British and Australians as of yet, which was just as well, because both Sir Richard and Starrett were British. Starrett's hooded eyes resembled those of some sort of morose amphibian, and the dewlaps jiggling over his starched collar added to this resemblance. The adviser was probably in his mid-fifties and was generally unfriendly.

The two St. Cyr children also lived in the palace.

Diana was in her early teens and Roger was several years younger. Roger was a large-eyed, sad-looking boy who was an exact duplicate of the portrait of his deceased mother that hung over the unused library fireplace. Diana looked like a female version of her father, a little colder, a little less vulnerable.

Carlisle didn't think much of her. He had inadvertently heard her making fun of him at one time. He had a nervous speech pattern that was easily imitated.

Others, servants for the most part, lived in the endless recesses of the old house. Carlisle would see them as he stumbled out of his room from his many naps. They thought that he drank, since he usually looked under the weather when he awakened. Mr. Plunkett operated the radio, and the captain had to see a lot of him. Plunkett became acquainted rather quickly with the officer's various flaws. He sat close by as the American received all his bad news over the radio. Plunkett was considered a civilian. He had deserted from the Royal Navy before the war ever started. Everyone knew that, it was no secret. He would never be prosecuted as long as he stayed in this forgotten place.

Certain allowances had to be made for the citizens of New Oss. Whites and their skills were in short supply. A carpenter or a mechanic was an important man here —indispensable, in fact, though everyone fancied himself a bit of both. A sizeable percentage of New Oss's European population had convoluted backgrounds that had led them to choose this rugged outpost as their residence. Australians were considered to be of the least questionable character, since Australia wasn't very far away. But the Indonesians and other Asians were considered more reliable than the other whites. A man had to have a pretty good reason for living in New Oss.

Plunkett had a cockney accent and often spoke familiarly about Sir Richard and his "attitude." The radio was housed in a storeroom off the porch, and Plunkett was similarly confined to this other-than-prestigious location.

Carlisle couldn't sleep that night. He paced the floor of his room and opened his screens a dozen times to look out on the primitive port of New Oss. At around 0400 he got dressed and went outside. The night was relieved by a spooky, stone-age New Guinea half-moon. Dark clouds blew across the moon, as if it were windy in the upper reaches of the universe. Down here it was perfectly still. The humidity was crushing, even in the depths of the night.

The jungle seemed to be poised around the town, ready to close a violent fist on the feeble little makeshift structures that man had erected against nature.

Hawk rolled over on the hard planks of the wharf. Mosquitoes were busily drilling through the netting he wore over his head. He usually took his atabrine and accepted insects as a minor inconvenience. He could sleep through a barrage of 88's without difficulty. Tonight was different; the little bastards were really cutting up. The night was muggy and irritating. Within his dozing subconscious, things languished that he could not control. Hellish dreams troubled him. The blinding, deafening, skin-numbing burst of a flamethrower seethed across these uncontrolled thoughts. Bodies; bullets; noises; limbs; faces and names—they were all there and gone in horrid repetition. He was on the wrong side of the flamethrower, tonight, in the unreal reality of his dreams. He was outside of himself, watching himself being turned into an odorous piece of offal. He sat up quickly and sighed. He took off his mosquito net and reached for a block of chewing tobacco.

Flamethrowers. He took a deep breath and blew it out. They were handy weapons, you had to admit that. He rubbed the chilly sweat off of his forehead. Fire. An awful way to die. He saw Carlisle walking down the quay. Above the officer's head, the naked masts of sailboats cast desolate silhouettes against the pale night sea. The captain walked softly past Hawk.

"You're up early, Cap'n." Hawk stopped him. He knew Carlisle was probably looking for him. The captain jumped at the sound of the harsh voice.

"Oh, yes, I am. I wanted to tell you something. I thought we ought to talk over a few things."

"Shoot."

He invited Hawk to dinner with the administrator that afternoon in the mansion. He wanted the sergeant to size the man up as he had been doing. "You won't believe this, but I've got some dress blues you can wear, if you want," Carlisle offered.

Hawk smiled solemnly. "Don't think I look neat enough? Reckon I need that much help?"

"Sure, sure. I mean, no, I wasn't criticizing you about your appearance or anything. I mean, I have some clean uniforms and I thought you could wear those and make a good impression and all. We want the guy to pay attention to any advice you give him and all, you know. I mean, I know this isn't Fifty-second Street, I didn't expect to catch you in your pajamas or anything."

"Supper, huh? Okay, if you want me to be there. I'll even shave and wear the fancy duds."

"Thanks, Hawk. I'll bring them over for you, later today. Take the day off, check out the bars."

"That sounds like you got something planned for me, sir."

"No, no, well, I mean, I just want you to talk to this guy. And...uh, well you know about those submarines and all?"

"Yessir."

"Air recon spotted three midget subs yesterday, just before dark. They said that they came from here."

"Yeah? Well, that's better than comin' *to* here, ain't it, Captain?"

"Is it? I don't know. Where do you think they're coming from?"

"Could be anywhere. It's a big world. We're on a big island in a big ocean."

"I know," said Carlisle. He expected some such casual response. Now he would try his latest idea out on the sergeant. "Here's what I'm thinking. Regiment doesn't consider us very important, to start with." The captain crouched beside Hawk and opened his hands as he spoke. "I honestly don't believe that they're going to waste any more time and men trying to cross that ocean with help for us. If they needed us somewhere, they would come get us, but they're not going to go out of their way to help us."

"Yeah..." Hawk chewed calmly as he listened.

"You see what I'm saying? I mean, it's logical, isn't it?" Hawk made the required bob of his head. He couldn't argue with the reasoning of it. He had long ago learned that everyone was more interested in using than in helping. He accepted that as a given postulate. The world kept turning on its axis.

"I don't like that," Carlisle continued. "It's driving me crazy. I don't have any business being here and doing this. So...look, they're just going to let the situation remain as it is. The status quo isn't at all upsetting to them. They never *act* on this type of thing, they *react*. If the Japs don't come charging into New Oss, they're just going to leave us here."

Hawk raised an eyebrow. "It's a peaceful enough spot."

"For now, sure. By the time it's *not* peaceful, we'll be in trouble. You see what I'm saying? We're forgotten over here. We've got to overcome this inertia at Regiment."

"I bet this is where I get to pay for my day off."

Carlisle smiled nervously. He liked Hawk. Hawk didn't throw his inexperience up to him. Hawk listened to his anxious complaints. "Yes, sort of. Listen, don't you think it would be a good idea to patrol the coast and see if you see any signs of the base? I mean, they asked me to check it out and all."

"Well..."

"I mean if we were to find the base, report its location and they go ahead and knock it out, we can get some kind of communications opened up with Regiment again. If nothing happens, the Japs are going to be bringing in support troops and all sorts of things, once they know we're just a bunch of suckers over here. Don't you think?"

"I'm inclined to sit here and let the Japs come marchin' their ass to us. But I know you're uncomfortable with the set-up, and I'll do what you want. Your idea sounds like a good plan, I'll go along with it." Hawk spat. The plan sounded like something an officer would dream up. That was what he was thinking. "This patrol, are we talking about doing it on foot or in the landing crafts? This is a hell of a country to go walking through."

"I'll leave it up to you. If you're going very far, you'll have to have the boats, of course. We'll work the whole thing out." Carlisle stood and took a deep breath of hot night air. He felt better now that a course of action had been chosen. "You meet this man tonight and see what you think of him. Maybe I'm all wrong about him, but I think he's going to get us into trouble." The captain rubbed his forehead and turned to look out over the dock. Bundles of sleeping men were strewn along it. "Did you ever..." Carlisle held out a hand to help him formulate his words, "ever feel like something terrible was about to happen? And you knew that you ought to do something about it, but you just didn't know where to start?"

"Sometimes." They looked at each other.

"I mean...did you ever wonder what the purpose for being alive is? I mean, here we are, and then all of sudden we're not here anymore, and what good was it even being here? Did you ever think about that?"

"Nah."

"Hell, I think I'll go sleep another couple of hours."

Hawk nodded and spat between his knees. He groaned and got to his feet. The sun had already punctured the horizon and leaked a line of orange light across the lower sky. He knew that he was up for the day. A man that slept past dawn wasn't much good for anything. Carlisle's boots clopped down the wharf.

* * *

AT 1800 HAWK looked like a recruiting poster. The war had put on him a few lines that a young man shouldn't have in his face. The angry, brooding eyes were clouded with a visible pain. Someone who didn't know him might have thought that there was a tragic, experience-instilled sensitivity behind the eyes. Carlisle's dress blues were a little short in the arms. He didn't notice. Government issue seldom fit right. Before wearing government issue, he had hardly ever worn new clothes. They looked pretty good to him.

After an extraordinary dinner of several varieties of seafood, Sir Richard attacked Hawk with a barrage of questions. The sergeant had remained silent up to this point, other than initially acknowledging the introductions. He was taking it all in.

"Captain Carlisle tells me that you are the individual responsible for most of the defenses we see here, Sergeant Hawk. Care for a cigar?"

"Thank you, sir. Yessir, that's about right."

"I'm sure you've done an excellent job of it. He tells me that you are quite skilled in the war arts."

"Been around a little, yessir."

"Is it your opinion that we would be able to repel another Japanese assault? You may know that we've already been occupied by a company of enemy marines. The U.S. Army and the A.I.F. pressured them to leave," St. Cyr said with a smile.

"If it's just a company comes, we won't have no trouble with 'em, no sir. Any more than that will be a problem, though. We're set up to meet a ground attack, mainly. I figure if it's gonna be a major attack, it'll come from the sea. That's just the way it looks. It'd be tough gettin' men through that back country. An amphibious assault would give us trouble. We're not fixed for that, not for standing on our ground, anyways."

St. Cyr ran his long fingers over the damask table cloth. He was thinking. Hawk lit a cigar and blew the smoke up into the ceiling fan. He decided to interrupt the Englishman's chain of thought. He didn't want to continue giving assurances where none could be given. If you were in combat, you were already in a bad situation. No amount of planning or precautions could guarantee your survival, or even temporary survival. He knew that St. Cyr would keep rephrasing the question until Hawk confessed that the marines would be able, beyond any doubt, to repulse fifty divisions of crack Japanese shock troops.

"Nice house," Hawk commented. That would get him off his back. People were vain about their houses. They couldn't resist talking about them.

"Oh, yes, isn't it? Seventy years old. The oldest thing in the country. Handed down from one administrator to the next."

Carlisle lifted his head and interrupted the exchange. "Is that right? I thought that I had heard of an old church in Port Moresby."

"I was referring to *my* country," Sir Richard smiled wisely, "Yes, it is the oldest structure in Malang. You see, the climate is a problem here for wooden buildings. I think that I shall construct something a bit more substantial once things settle a bit. We replace the roof here every year and a half, if a storm doesn't force us to do so sooner. There's no way around that. But we have a new church built of concrete that seems to be bearing up well." Carlisle glanced at Hawk. The sergeant's eyes met his. Hawk shrugged.

What the hell? Somebody might as well bring it all out into the open.

"So, you're settin' up your own country here, sir?" Hawk asked. Carlisle sat bolt upright. He wasn't prepared for an approach of such a direct nature.

"Yes, indeed," St. Cyr answered without hesitation. "The former province of the territory is now the nation of Malang. The Japs were kind enough to appoint some native toadies as councilmen to head the state divisions and I've assured them that they can stay in power. I have everyone's support, white and native alike. I think that we'll do very well here."

"What's Australia say about all that?" Hawk asked quietly. Carlisle felt like crawling under the table. He wanted to hear the answers, but he was squeamish about hearing the questions.

"Nothing, yet, sergeant. I don't see how they can do *anything* about it. They could use force against us; that's the only way they could bring us back under their control, and they won't do that."

A couple of Mississippi sheriffs could bring this dump back under control, Hawk thought. He noticed that St. Cyr enjoyed talking about the political situation. He wasn't at all bashful about it. "Now, there ain't none of that any of my business, sir," Hawk said, studying the intricate design of the tablecloth, "except maybe for the fact that you're puttin' this whole area in danger by refusing A.I.F. support."

"I haven't refused anything. We have you, Sergeant," St. Cyr replied politely. "We have our own militia, also. I've turned our sixty-man policing force into an army and impressed some of the older male citizens into the constabulary functions."

Hawk nodded. St. Cyr had that strange mixture of practicality and impracticality that could make a man successful.

All that was missing was a little luck, enough to keep these two components balanced. It was working so far. "We're just kinda concerned that we're gettin' used by you, sir," said the sergeant.

Carlisle cleared his throat. "That's...that's not *exactly* the case," the captain stuttered, "I mean, we were wondering what was going on on the whole thing...but, I mean, we're not *accusing* anybody of anything." Carlisle's face was red. "We...we're in an uproar ourselves, what with having no officers and all. We hate to get mixed up in something else." Carlisle managed to look over at St. Cyr. "You see what I'm saying?"

"I understand," St. Cyr raised a hand. "You owe me nothing. I ask no allegiance of you, or even any aid. You are perfectly free to go, so far as I am concerned. But I believe, and correct me if I'm wrong, that your superiors put you here of their own initiative and want you to stay here?" He knew that these two characters didn't know any better than that. They had no way of knowing about the strings he had to pull to get them here.

"Yeah," Hawk said abruptly, "yessir, they did. What we're gettin' at here is that things'd go a lot smoother with some Aussie troops in here—and you ain't lettin' us ask for 'em."

"I'm not stopping you from doing anything."

Hawk saw no reason to continue the conversation. He was only becoming angry. He had long ago learned that that was a luxury that he couldn't afford. Anger meant rage and rage had no limit for Sgt. Hawk. So he didn't get angry. St. Cyr was one of those fellows who had all of the answers. Or at least, he always had something clever to say after you said what you had to say. As far as Hawk was concerned, someone like that had to be either ignored or stomped into the floor.

"Well," Carlisle said, noticing the tension in the air, "you *are* sort of." He could barely speak. Emotion was cutting off his respiratory functions. "Our Regiment says we have to go along with you. *We* can't ask for the A.I.F., *you* have to. I mean, we're supposed to have a colonel here running this battalion, and even *he* couldn't do a thing like that. You see what I'm saying?"

"I will not ask for them, Captain Carlisle, and I have it upon good authority that they will not be coming under their own motion, either. This is a backward little nation, but it is going to be a rich one. We have oil fields, refineries, copra and rubber plantations, deposits of gold and silver...by calling myself an independent nation, I've suddenly become quite influential among the businessmen and politicians in Canberra. My supporters are strong and my opponents don't know that I'm here—if they exist at all."

Hawk slid his chair out. He could have told the administrator that he was going to get everyone sitting at the table hurt. But he would neither believe nor understand that. "Well, at least we all know where we stand." He smiled his grim, mocking smile as he stood. He felt entitled to that much, since he would be the first to feel the effects of this madness. Miss Asquith smiled back at him with a charm and enthusiasm that led him to believe that she had been deaf to the preceding conversation. None of these people really knew what they were up against. The Japanese Army wasn't something to fool around with. "It's good to get your cards on the table. I guess I'd best get some rest if I'm gonna find a sub base any time soon."

Carlisle remained seated and nodding to himself. He was still replaying the conversation in his mind. "I mean...we can get along on the whole thing," he said suddenly, "we just wanted to get an idea of the situation."

"I quite understand." Sir Richard stood. "I'm sorry to see you leave early, Sergeant. Won't you please stay for a drink? We have liqueur, brandy, wine..."

"Naw, I really gotta head out, sir. Thank you, though, I appreciate the offer. Ladies..." he bowed to Miss Asquith and Diana. St. Cyr's son, Roger, got up from his seat and scampered to Hawk's side.

"Would it be possible for me to visit your fortifications, Sergeant?" the boy asked.

"Uh..."

"Roger is enthralled with military matters, Sergeant," Sir Richard explained. "Don't let him make a nuisance of himself."

"Oh, uh, no, he won't bother me none. I'm kind of a nuisance myself. Yeah, kid, come on and we'll take a look around before we turn in."

The boy grinned and turned around. "Are you coming, Diana?"

His sister made a face. "I'm not interested in fortifications," she said.

He made a face back at her. "Not yet, you aren't," he replied as he walked Hawk to the door. "Have you killed many Japs, Sergeant?" Roger asked in a loud voice. His excitement caused the people sitting at the table to laugh. Hawk didn't laugh. He stopped at the door and looked back at the elegant scene. An awkward silence fell over the diners. Miss Asquith looked away.

"Yeah," Hawk answered finally, and turned and walked out of the room. Roger skipped happily behind him.

"May I fire your gun? What sort of gun do you have?" Roger questioned as they stepped off of the front porch.

"Tommy gun. Ever hear of a Tommy gun?"

"Certainly, like in Chicago, like Edward G. Robinson and James Cagney?"

Hawk held a match to the end of his cigar. "No, kid, a real one."

* * *

THE NEXT DAY, Hawk prepared a patrol for scouting along the coastline. He didn't want to do a very thorough job. He didn't want to do Sir Richard any favors, if he could help it. He knew he wasn't going to find any submarine bases, but he almost certainly would run across a few snipers, or even pockets of resistance. The less he ran into, the better. He was an American, not a Malangian. He owed Malang nothing, and neither did his men.

It wasn't his preference, but he chose to go on foot. It would be the easiest, and safest way to check a few miles of beachfront. He figured that if he got into a landing craft and went exploring for days, he would cover too much ground. More snipers, more casualties with the same net result of zero.

Roger St. Cyr was out early the next morning, too.

He forced Hawk to show him how a hand grenade works. He still wanted to fire the Tommy gun, but Hawk told him that ammunition was too low for that. Hawk sat against a rotting boathouse on the quay.

"Look, Roger, we ain't here to fart around, you know? What if I run into a bunch of goddam Japs out there? Am I gonna tell 'em I can't shoot 'em cause I let some kid fire off all my clips?"

"Just one shot? One shan't matter."

"No." Hawk chewed placidly on his tobacco as he filled the drum magazine with .45 caliber shells. "One shot ain't no fun." He spat through the boards of the dock. "We'll get some supplies in later and you can shoot off a whole goddam clip."

"Do you think so?"

"Shit, yeah."

Roger jumped to his feet and made his hands into a Tommy gun, shooting up the entire town in a matter of seconds. He was a delicate, cultured little boy, but he was still a boy. Adventure fascinated him.

"What would you do if there were a Jap in front of you and another one behind you, like this?"

"Probably get shot in the ass."

"You should shoot the one and duck, you see, like so, and turn quickly and shoot the other," Roger demonstrated.

"Uh huh." Hawk looked impatiently around the dock for a way to get rid of him. He could have booted him in the pants, but the boy probably knew how to swim. "Listen, would you settle for a souvenir?"

"Surely. Surely I would! What sort?"

Hawk reached into his webbing. "Here's a Jap grenade. Pretty hard to find. I got it on Guadalcanal.

Japs like to kill themselves with it. Killed themselves more than they killed us."

"*Really?* And you'll give it to me?"

"Said I would, didn't I? They're kinda dangerous, anyway. I been waitin' on the damn thing to blow me up. It's better that you have it." He winked at Roger. He wrapped his fingers around the firing pin holder and gave it a hard wrench. Then he screwed the detonator out of the body of the grenade and blew the powder off the fuzzy cotton fuse at its tip. "You can use it as a paperweight or hide your cigarettes in it," Hawk said absently as he poured the bursting charge through the top of the open shell. He replaced the fuse on the body and screwed it on. "It's got a percussion cap in the bottom, but it won't hurt you. There you go, now get lost, I'm busy as hell." He set the charge on one of the boards of the pier and got to his feet.

"Thank you, Sergeant Hawk," Roger said, looking over the prize. Hawk snorted. He ruffled the boy's hair. That's what you were supposed to do with kids. He walked down the quay without looking back. Roger scraped up the discarded powder charge and put it into his pocket.

That afternoon Roger showed the treasure to his sister, Diana. She held it, once assured that it was disarmed. They sat on the sundeck of the topmost floor's cupola.

"What do you want with this old thing?" she sneered and shoved it back into his hand.

"It will be quite valuable, some day," he told her. He loved to roll it about in his hand.

"You shouldn't play with that filthy American marine sergeant, you know."

"I wasn't playing. Why do you call him filthy? He's a nice fellow. He's killed thousands of Japs."

"He *says* he has," Diana sneered. "Being stupid doesn't make you a hero, Roger. He's nothing but a brute. He's no gentleman. He's a bad influence, I think. Soon you'll be talking dirty, and not bathing and behaving frantically, the way Americans do."

"Diana, you *are* absurd at times!" Roger studied his hand grenade with a new expression of hurt in his big eyes.

"I'm not, *you* are. Did you see the way he cross-examined Father at dinner? He has no manners whatsoever. He's crude and vulgar and Miss Asquith says that he seems devious to her."

"Miss Asquith." Roger twisted his mouth and looked away. He shook his head and looked at his hand grenade again. "Mother would have liked him. Mother didn't put on airs or judge people in that manner." Roger looked up at her with a challenge in his eyes. "I think Miss Asquith is a bad influence on you."

"Oh, Roger, not again! Let's not start that all over, please. Mother is gone. Miss Asquith is very nice. She's quite sophisticated. You can't expect a man Father's age to go through life unmarried. You'll understand that when you're older. Just as you'll understand men like Sergeant Hawk."

"He's very brave."

"Perhaps he is. We don't know. But he isn't brave in the way that a gentleman is brave. A gentleman is brave as a matter of honor; he's chivalrous and strong. If Sergeant Hawk is brave, it's because he's too stupid to be anything else."

"That's very unfair, Diana! He's knowledgeable

about military matters. That's the most important thing in the world right now. Besides, I understand Miss Asquith better than you, already. She's after Father's position more than anything else...you know, you're not *that* much older than I, Diana."

Diana shook her head. "I'm much more mature. Women mature much earlier than men. I would be more mature, even if we were the same age."

"You would not!"

"I would, too."

"If what you say is true, it's only because it's more difficult to become a man."

"Rubbish! You're just jealous of her. You're being selfish, the way children are. You can't have Mother back, so you don't want Father to have a wife."

Tears fell from Roger's eyes. Pain knifed across his chest and forced a sob from his throat, but he managed to say, "That's not true."

"It is! You should be developing gentlemanly qualities of kindness and understanding, instead of traipsing behind some half-witted killer. You should consider others and their feelings, rather than your own. You are going to hurt us all very much with your attitude, Roger, and I won't have it."

"I...I really don't want to discuss it any further," the boy said, getting up off of the sun-hot floor. He walked to the stairs and went down without another word.

"See that you don't," she called after him. A moment later, he came trudging back up the stairs like a captured prisoner of war. Miss Asquith was behind him.

"Did I hear raised voices?" Miss Asquith asked. "What's going on, my dears?" Roger looked at Diana with a disgusted expression.

"We were discussing Sergeant Hawk, weren't we, Roger? I believe Roger has taken some sort of fancy to him."

"Oh, is that true, Roger?" No answer. "He *was* a rough and tumble character, wasn't he?" Miss Asquith asked with feigned enthusiasm.

"Yes," Roger looked up with a sad smile. "Wasn't he?"

"I don't believe that I've ever heard a white man speak in that sort of accent," Miss Asquith commented as she adjusted her hair with one hand. "He sounds... oh...what is that Jack Benny man's name?"

"Rochester?" Diana helped her out. The two of them laughed uproariously in high-pitched giggles. Roger took a step toward the stairs. He had heard enough. This wasn't the sort of humor he was interested in.

"But he was very handsome," Miss Asquith said to the retreating boy. "He had the bluest eyes I've ever seen." Roger thundered down the stairs. "It's a shame that such good looks are wasted on that beast," she whispered to Diana. They laughed again and Diana covered her mouth with her hand. "I hope that we haven't upset little Roger."

"Nothing that could be said would agree with him," Diana assured her. "You must forgive him, he's still a child."

3

A SINGLE FILE OF MARINES FOLLOWED THE COASTLINE OF Malang several kilometers to the south. Leading them was the un-mannered Sgt. Hawk. He regretted having considered the idea of this patrol. The men had to walk in the sea; there was no beach. Choking vegetation grew right to the water's edge. Stumps of dead trees extended for yards into the ocean. It was the worst terrain any of them had ever experienced. If a submarine base did indeed exist, they would never find it this way. Hawk had known that all along, but he didn't expect the charade to be quite this much trouble. The best thing that could be expected to happen, using this method of reconnaissance, was someone being bitten by one of the brightly colored sea creatures that writhed about in the muck at the men's feet. Seeing no great advantage to such an occurrence, Hawk returned to New Oss.

He was met just outside of the perimeter by an agitated Capt. Carlisle. Carlisle was fitted out with a full pack, as were Major Clemson and Sergeant Major

Wentworth, who walked behind him. It was a rather comical sight, though no one laughed.

"Hawk, thank God you came back!" Carlisle shouted and struggled to get out of his pack. He walked quickly the sergeant's side. The men in the patrol looked curiously at each other. Most of them hadn't known the conditions at the top of the chain of command, until now.

Hawk delivered his prepared excuse. "Yeah...it seemed like a waste of time, Cap'n."

"Forget the sub base...needle in a haystack...you'll never guess what the hell's happened now...we're really in for it...St. Cyr's kid's been stolen...he's having a fit," Carlisle gasped the phrases; he wasn't used to carrying a pack." What do we do? Where can we look?"

"The boy or the girl?"

"The boy...uh, Richard or Roger or some damn thing!"

"Okay."

The returning patrol crossed through the gap in the pyramid of barbed wire that encircled the defensive perimeter. Carlisle continued to talk as he ran along beside Hawk. His running was odd, because Hawk was walking in his slow, dogged gait and they were somehow keeping abreast of one another. The late morning sun created intricate, frightening shadows as it wound through the barbed wire.

"Who did it? Did anybody see anything?"

"Yes, they did, yes. That's the worst part..." The Captain was on the verge of hysteria.

"The Japanese did it," said the church organ voice of Major Clemson. The preacher was bareheaded now and beads of sweat were visible on his scalp beneath his thinning red hair. The major was in full control of himself, or maybe he just seemed to be because the captain was so out of control. "The constable says that six of them were seen leaving the prime minister's palace with the boy bound and gagged."

"Japs, huh?" Hawk stopped and slid a cigar from his pocket. It was saturated with sweat and he had trouble lighting it. He could have claimed the problem was out of his jurisdiction, if the Japanese hadn't been involved. But he wouldn't have. "If they seen 'em, why didn't nobody do nothin' about it?"

"I don't know. It happened suddenly, I'm told, and not that many saw it," Clemson answered. "The police force is a group of old timers, and you really can't blame them; after all, the Japs had to get through *our* perimeter."

"I ain't blamin' nobody for nothing, Major. Japs been known to get through our perimeters without much trouble." He looked down at his wear-yellowed boots. This was getting complicated. Politics, revolutions, submarines, kidnappings and even Japanese. He knew that he didn't have any business trying to oversee all of this chaos, but he also knew that he could do a better job than any of the other available personnel. "Don't make sense," said Hawk, looking first at Clemson and then at Carlisle. His flashing eyes made them uneasy. "Why would some goddam Japs pull some shit like that?"

"Those sons of bitches would do anything, Hawk, you know that," the captain said. "I beg your pardon, Major."

"Quite all right. It has happened, Sergeant Hawk, that is the fact of the matter. Captain Carlisle thinks that you may be able to retrieve the boy. I, personally, don't see how. They've more than likely gone into the interior, and the jungle is impenetrable."

"Maybe." Hawk's cigar went out. He bit it in two and started chewing it. "Maybe not. If they's a sub base around here, like we been hearin', they could have come in from it and be anywhere by now."

The Sergeant Major interrupted. "I thought of that. I told Bupta to see if he could pick up a trail before they got to sea." Everyone looked at Wentworth for a moment. There was no need to look at him any longer than that. Then Hawk said, "Good."

"St. Cyr is beside himself. He says that he has some theories about it. He asked us to bring you back. He's counting on your finding the boy," Clemson said.

At least the bastard has that much sense, Hawk said to himself. "I'll do what I can," he said aloud. "Cute little fellow." He shook his head. "I can't believe it, to tell you the truth."

"Isn't it something?" Carlisle exclaimed. Hawk started walking again and they all followed him. "Maybe we can find the base and the boy, too. Boy, that would make us look good!" Carlisle had been transformed from anxious incompetent to enthusiastic glory-seeker in a matter of minutes.

Ignoring such naiveté, Hawk said, "They tell us the Japs are using midget subs across the Straits. That means they can't carry many torpedoes or haul much of a fuel supply. That base is right here, somewhere."

"I think so, too," Carlisle agreed.

"But for now, the boy comes first. We got to see what we can do before the trail gets too cold." They all nodded in agreement. Carlisle was glad that someone was doing something. Clemson and Wentworth were glad that they could go back to doing nothing. The weather was much too hot and humid for tramping about in this disease-infested edge of creation. They arrived at the palace shortly. Hawk and the two officers went inside and the rest of the entourage remained standing outside in the street.

The uproar inside the mansion made Carlisle's antics seem like sublime tranquility. The servants wailed. Sir Richard's hair stood straight up on his head, as if he had been running his hands through it. His eyes were wide and animated with distress. Diana and Miss Asquith clung supportively to one another. St. Cyr called Hawk into his private study to discuss the crisis. Even Carlisle was left out this time.

Neither man sat down as Sir Richard walked away from the closed door. He began pacing the room. "Can you find him?" he asked.

"I'll try, sir."

"Yes, I'm certain that you will. But what are the chances?"

"I'll have a better idea, once I get on it."

"Yes, yes of course. The boy has been...distant... lately. He was a trifle upset over my relationship with Miss Asquith. You see, his mother died of fever last year. She died in Australia, of all places. We've been strained, Roger and I. I...my God, I don't want us to part this way! If you could only do your very best, Sergeant."

"I'll guarantee that, sir. They told me you might have some ideas about where to start. I best be gettin' on it."

"Absolutely. You must interview Constable Powers. He saw the entire episode. The old fool! See what he can tell you, and then see if you can catch them. We mustn't waste any more time. Later, if we fail, I will tell you some other things that may have a bearing on this. There is more to this than meets the eye."

Hawk rocked back his helmet with a thumb. "That's kinda what I figure, sir. It's a odd thing. I'll try and pick up a trail and then we'll let you know." Sir Richard wasn't looking at him as the marine let himself out. St. Cyr stared silently out of the bay window of his study.

Powers had seen the Japanese leave the St. Cyr house with the boy. No one could imagine how they got into the town, much less the house. A few natives corroborated the constable's story, though they didn't appear to be unshakable in their convictions. The general tenor of their reports was that whatever Constable Powers said, was the way it happened. Powers said that he was the only one of any note seeing the incident, and by the time he set up an alarm, the enemy had disappeared in the direction of the weakly defended northern perimeter. They were armed with rifles. Powers didn't remember seeing any of the particular natives that chose to corroborate his story. He confided to Clemson that he thought they were just looking for a little attention. Powers, a tiny man of about seventy, was the only man in town unperturbed by the kidnapping. That may have been due to his being strongly fortified with alcohol. Hawk told Carlisle that he felt like Powers was full of shit. He also had to admit that he was stumped.

Dismissing for the present any thought of the kidnappers having gone into the interior, Carlisle proposed that a patrol be sent along the coast to the north. Since Hawk was patrolling the southern coast at the time of the capture, the Japanese had to have headed north, out to sea or into the interior. The north was the easiest possibility to check out. It was also the easiest way to make a getaway. Hawk went along with this, shrugged and took his old squad on the trip, telling Carlisle to inform Regiment about all of it. They could get some planes to fly over. The Japanese had rendered both of New Oss's biplanes useless during their occupation, and they had not yet been replaced.

While the journey to the south had been taken on foot by choice, the one to the north was taken by necessity. You couldn't trail someone by sea. Again the relentless vegetation grew right to the water's edge, forcing the men to wade in the sea. The cheeriest terrain passed was a gloomy mangrove swamp; the ocean lolled right up beneath the trees. Vicious-looking reptiles coiled about the bases of the trees in search of a dry, sunny lair. Evening was coming on and no trace of the quarry had been sighted.

"God, this an awful place!" Joe Canlon commented. "You know? Look at this shit! Even a goddam hill jack like you couldn't get by in this." Hawk smiled. To his left was a black mesh of plant life. He could see less than a yard into it. To his right was the ugly, ocher-colored sea. Shark fins swirled about in it, as far as the eye could see. They began on the horizon and extended to within thirty feet of where the men stood. A little spit of sand, about ten feet out, was the only barrier between their legs and the voracious monsters. "How the hell we gonna camp in this?" Joe asked in his most studied, pitiable voice. Mosquitoes the size of hummingbirds orbited his head.

"I don't plan to. I guess we'll turn around and go back. This ain't gettin' us nowhere. We'll try something else," Hawk surrendered grudgingly. The terrain was a factor to be considered more seriously in the next reassessment of strategy. As Hawk was turning around to return to New Oss, a gigantic white-muzzled shark surged out of the water and landed on the spit of sand. Everyone jumped back in surprise and several stumbled in the dirty water.

The evil eyes in the brainless head stared at Joe Canlon. The animal angrily whipped his tail about in an effort to reverse his body off the sand. Failing in that, he tried to come forward.

"Look at the *size* of that mother!" Canlon raised his rifle at the threatening spectacle.

"No shootin'. Stick him with your bayonet, if you got to kill him," Hawk said, smiling at his own wisdom. No one would be stupid enough to do that. He didn't like killing animals.

"No, thanks," Canlon lowered his rifle.

"I'll get him," said Harwood, the man behind Canlon, snapping his bayonet into place. He waded out to the sandbar with his bayonet cautiously poised in front of him. The men watched with breathless curiosity. Hawk started to say something, but he didn't. Harwood waded fearlessly up to the thing and reared back in order to land a thrust between the creature's eyes. The sandbar gave way and Harwood was sucked out of sight beneath the brackish water, his rifle going down on top of him. Nothing floated to the surface. Only swirling sand remained at the spot where he had been standing. He never made an outcry. He probably never realized the seriousness of his predicament.

The rest of the men looked dumbfounded. Hawk stared mutely at the shark. It was trying to reach

Harwood, but it was still hopelessly beached. A friend of Harwood's rushed from the file of men and toward the place where the marine had gone under. Before he reached it, the ocean bottom gave way, and he too was sucked under.

"Jesus!" Canlon jumped back against the thorny foliage of the forest.

"Everybody stay put," Hawk shouted. He raised an arm in front of the men as if protecting a bunch of children. The shark made one tremendous effort and cleared the sandbar, disappearing beneath the coffee brine where the two marines had gone under.

A mocking bird screeched loudly from above and behind them. A procession of circling sharks, moving as though they were on a carousel, edged closer to the sandbar. Other circles of man-eaters spun on every side of this circle, like the cogs in the wheels of a massive machine. Hawk swallowed as he watched the silent power of the display. He demonstrated no outward emotion over the irreversible accident.

"All right," he turned and faced the others, "that's it, let's go back." Two men gone. Just like that. For no reason whatsoever. The survivors each dealt with it silently, in their own way. Hawk had to keep them moving. Dark fell before they made it even halfway back. No one considered stopping. The terrifying jungle drove any thoughts of rest or camping from their minds.

After dark, they heard a rumbling in the distance. The ground shook and the black trees shivered. The earth seemed to belch far beneath them. Echoing cracks came on the tail of the rumble, they popped from far out to sea. The men listened stoically, certain that the end of the world had come and found them already in

Hell. Hawk knew by the echoes what was going on. Explosions, coming from New Oss. He could even tell what had caused them. They proceeded in silence.

The exhausted patrol made it back to a disorienting scene at dawn. The harbor at New Oss was aflame. Wind-angled columns of smoke were scattered randomly throughout the town. The first man Hawk met was Bupta. The first sergeant delivered the news: approximately fourteen marines had been killed or seriously wounded. Midget subs had cruised into the harbor and sunk all but a half dozen landing barges, and those remaining were disabled. A Japanese airstrike had dropped about a score of bombs on the town. Ten civilians, all Melanesian natives, were killed or wounded.

Carlisle was with St. Cyr in the latter's study when Hawk arrived. Hawk told them that he had found no trace of Roger and inquired about the reaction of Regiment to the attack on New Oss.

"They recorded the details," Carlisle said dejectedly. "They said that they can't risk the Straits of Cavazo for a while. We just have to stick it out. We're not worth what it would cost to get over here. But we're to defend the oil refinery at all costs, and if it looks hopeless, absolutely hopeless, we're to destroy it. We're also supposed to get off our duffs and find that sub base. They can't be bothered with Roger, they're combing the coastline with all available aircraft, trying to find the base. If they see anything, though, they'll let us know."

"Everything that could possibly go wrong has done so," Sir Richard said to Hawk. "They aren't being the least bit helpful. I won't give this nation up! Nothing can make me give it up. You can't destroy that refinery, it's all we have. Our source of revenues will disappear without it. The Asian workers will leave, the white technicians will go."

"Nobody's destroying nothing," Hawk said, disgusted with both of them. He turned and left the room. Carlisle jumped up and followed him.

"Wait, Hawk! What about the boy?" He caught the sergeant in the hall.

"What about him? It looks like I'm the only one interested in him, don't it? I'll find him."

Hawk kept walking. "Wait up, St. Cyr's got this theory," Carlisle called after him. "There's this German farmer across the peninsula that's been giving him trouble..."

"That's right," Sir Richard shuffled wearily out of the study. "And I'm afraid he has a rapport with some of the natives. On one occasion he as much as told me that he was going to take the government of Malang away from me."

"You ain't got it," Hawk replied gruffly.

"I *do* have it. Regardless of that, he killed one of my militiamen last month, when he went over that way to collect a few paltry taxes. He's slightly mad, you see."

"He ain't the only one."

"I don't care what you think of me, Sergeant Hawk. Please let me finish. If you want to help, fine. If you don't, fine. I think that he may be behind this, as a ploy to force me to turn the government over to him. And I think he may have had help from the servants, or someone here in the house. The militia came close to having a pitched battle with his hired native boys. He has quite a following out in the bush. He did it, and he had help, I'm certain of it."

"Yeah, and help from a half dozen Japs, too, let's don't forget them," Hawk reminded him.

"He could be harboring them. The Germans have an alliance with the Japanese. You may be able to find both my son and your submarine base out at his plantation."

Hawk didn't say anything to this revelation. He looked at Carlisle. The captain wore the same empty expression that he always had. Hawk shrugged. "Tell you what, Mr. St. Cyr, you best get the A.I.F. up here, quick, and quit shittin' around." He turned his back on the two men. They didn't stop him again. He felt sure St. Cyr would call Australia this time. The air and sea attack had surely knocked a little common sense into him.

Hawk returned to a foxhole on the northern perimeter. He liked the company better there. A child had been abducted, two men had been killed trying to find him, and no one was particularly concerned, including the child's father and the commanding officer of the men. That's the way he saw it. The contingent of Americans at New Oss was on the road to destruction; the air attack had shown him that. The town would ultimately be indefensible. He couldn't do anything about it. He would turn command over to Carlisle and spend all of his time trying to find Roger. That was the only way to accomplish anything of value. He settled into the hole for a nap. He had a headache from lack of sleep.

A little while later, Canlon awakened him. A little man in a vested suit stood over the hole. Hawk recognized Mr. Starrett, St. Cyr's adviser. "I've been informed that you intend to go to Herr Ranke's farm?" Mr. Starrett asked.

Hawk sat up groggily. "That's right."

"It's a good idea. I've a guide for you. A man named Charles Larsen. He's familiar with the bush. He's agreed to take you there. The interior is a dangerous place for the inexperienced. I have heard that you already have learned as much?"

"Yeah?"

"Yes. As you know, our airfield has been severely damaged, as have our two planes. Most of your landing barges were destroyed, and the five that you have left will never sail again. It would have been an easy matter to sail over to Ranke's, but that option is unquestionably closed. He lives on the rocky coast on the other side of the peninsula. You'll have to cross the peninsula on foot and by canoe."

Hawk sighed. He was a little aggravated by Mr. Starrett, though he didn't know exactly why and so he kept his feelings to himself. "This guide's an Aussie?"

"He's a Malangian of Australian descent, yes."

"Ah huh." Hawk had forgotten the local jargon. "Well...send him by. I'm taking a platoon into the jungle today. I can use any help that strays by. Come to think of it..." Hawk stood up. "Mr. Starrett, how well do you know this Constable Powers?"

"As well as anyone, I'm sure. Everyone knows everyone else in New Oss. Why do you ask?" Mr. Starrett took a pipe from his inside coat pocket. His smooth little face was cool as ice, in spite of his being overdressed for the oppressive climate.

"It strikes me as funny that nobody else seen six Japs walking through town and into the most important building in the...country. All we got to go on is his word that it happened that way, ain't it?"

"That is true, Mr. Hawk. He may have misperceptions common to a man his age. I've never doubted his honesty, if that is what you're hinting at." Mr. Starrett lit his pipe.

"Yessir. Sort of. Mr. St. Cyr tells me he's got enemies and all of this and I got to thinking that the kid might still be in town. I don't want to go back out there for *no* reason, seein' as how much trouble it's caused already."

"I understand. You are properly concerned. The back country here is like nothing that you've ever experienced. The peninsula is the stamping grounds of two vicious tribes of natives. As far as enemies...I must tell you that I am the brains here in New Oss, and Sir Richard supplies the ambition. He was an actor by trade and his ego is monumental. You may have noticed?" Starrett arched his eye-brows and puffed smoke like a steam engine. Hawk acknowledged the question with a snort. "Sometimes he becomes...oh, shall we say, overly concerned with his own importance. One might even say that he imagines others are overly concerned with him, too. Consequently, I can't fault your theory in principle, Mr. Hawk. But, for now, the only concrete evidence that we have to go on is the word of Constable Powers. And since we both want the child back, shouldn't we act on that?"

Hawk ran his hand through his sandy hair. "Yessir, I guess you're right."

"Good. I'll send Larsen by. If I can be of service in any other way, don't hesitate to call me. If something needs to be done you will find me to be your most active ally."

"Thank you, sir." Hawk watched the plump little figure step carefully through the rear area and proceed briskly back toward the town. Starrett seemed genuinely concerned, more concerned than the others. Maybe he just wanted Hawk out in the jungle for some reason. It didn't matter; in all good conscience, he had to check out Ranke first.

Hawk called for volunteers to cross the peninsula. Most of them came from first platoon, since these were the men who knew the sergeant well. He selected fifty men in all, some from all parts of the battalion. He helped Carlisle make the necessary casualty and damage reports after they picked up the pieces of the enemy attack. Larsen was sent over to the perimeter and the two of them mapped out the journey. It would begin on foot and then they would travel by pirogue to Ranke's. Slimy little bayous riddled the interior, and a great salt water swamp lay on the far side of the peninsula. Boats were indispensible.

Hawk liked Larsen at first. The guide was a rugged outdoorsman, past his prime, a little smelly but refreshing amidst this bunch of over-civilized, under-matured Malangians. Larsen spoke of the interior with authority, but he didn't preach on the subject as some lonely backwoods windbags are wont to do. He also left the impression that he had the loose morals of a man kicking about in the backwaters of the universe. Not that he was any looser than anyone else, just a bit more honest.

He let it be known that he was doing this for a hundred pounds and not out of any fondness for the well-being of children. He laughed lustily when he conveyed this sentiment to Hawk, indicating that maybe it was a joke and that there really was a heart of gold down there somewhere. He reminded Hawk of the comical villain in the movies, who turns out to be good in the end. But the sergeant was enough of a student of human nature not to rely on stereotyped impressions such as these. Something about Larsen bore watching.

Sgt. Hawk passed judgment on men quickly. He had earned that privilege. He had volunteered his life and limb to his country in a savage war for the simple reason that it was the right thing to do. The Marine Corps was filled with such men. They were some of the meanest, granted, but they were also some of the noblest. Men outside the Corps fell under a different set of standards and scrutiny. They were not always the noblest. But that was all right, because they weren't the meanest, either.

4

THE HAND-HEWN LOG PIROGUE HAD A GUNWALE NO MORE than three inches high. Its blunt prow separated the tender woven plants that matted the swamp's surface. Hawk sat in the front of the first canoe. An average-sized man, he still felt huge in the little boat. Green shadows tinted his expressionless face. Rough country, he thought. He spat an angry stream of black tobacco juice into the fathomless, creamy green water. They said that somewhere beneath this swamp lay the ocean. The marsh had no bottom. They were gliding over a motionless eternity. Above was the threatening black forest. It was midday, but it was as dark as dusk in here.

Jeff McGranger crouched behind Hawk in the first canoe. He was afraid. The silent forest was talking to him, saying, "You don't belong here." It was talking to all of them, but most of them were too insensitive to hear. Sgt. Hawk heard it, McGranger could tell that much by looking at his eyes...he heard but he was answering it back, "Kiss my ass!"

"Sergeant Hawk?"

"Yeah?"

"Could I talk to you? About something personal?"

Hawk had to look over his shoulder to see who it was talking to him. McGranger. Expert marksman, real young, real skinny. The kind that always got some kind of sickness. "What is it?" A bird of paradise flitted before their eyes, just in front of the canoe and low over the water. A splash came from behind them as Canlon missed a stroke. Chives was behind him.

"I had this girl friend, see, back in Akron..."

He's going to start whining about some woman, Hawk said to himself. It's going to really be stupid, too, because it won't be about a woman, it'll be about a kid.

"So what?"

"We were pretty close and I...really thought a lot of her, a whole lot. I thought she was pretty nice and everything. The other day I heard she was going with this other guy. An older guy—too old to even get drafted. It sounds like they *really* been going together, if you know what I mean?"

"Yeah?" Hawk didn't want to hear about any sniveling women. He sighed and listened patiently. Women always wanted something. Always griping. You couldn't knock the shit out of them.

"What do you think of that, Sergeant Hawk?"

"Uh...of what?"

"Could you like someone, after they had gone with someone else, like that, I mean?"

Hawk thought about it for a moment. The poignancy of the question touched him. He realized that deeply running emotions were surfacing here. Youth, looking for loyalty and faith and love and romance. It was so silly he couldn't even think of an appropriate reply. He decided to answer in the way that the boy wanted him to.

"Shit, no. Forget her. Don't put up with that shit. Half the people in the world are women. Get another one. Hell, after the war, they're gonna *all* be women—all the men'll be dead."

McGranger nodded his head sullenly. Stupid kid. Kids were so stupid. You couldn't tell them anything. Or you could *tell* them, but they had no experience with which to translate the words into reality. There was no sense talking to them, they always did what seemed like the fun thing to do at the moment. Like the brainless, whining thing back in Akron causing McGranger this pain. Hawk sighed. Romance was fun, it was good to be young, even when it hurt. It never hurt for long. Nothing was fun for Sergeant Hawk. There was only the serious and the inconsequential.

Canlon hit a stroke and looked over his shoulder. A line of canoes snaked behind him. It made him feel better to look at them. Being in front made it seem like you were alone. He hated this country, as he had hated most of the tropical islands he had seen. This one roused more fear than the others, more fear and more hatred. When he turned around he met the eyes of McGranger. McGranger's eyes said, "This is too evil, I'm not coming out of this." Canlon smiled stupidly at him, trying to blind himself to what he saw.

A cool breath of wind introduced a brief rainstorm. A violent outburst opened the canopy of green overhead, letting in large silver bullets of rain. Within minutes it was over, the boats were filled with water and everyone was thoroughly miserable. Helmets and ponchos kept the upper portions of the men's bodies dry, while their feet and hindquarters rested in cold, clear puddles of rainwater. It was important to keep your feet dry in the tropics. They had the damnedest tendency to rot right off of you. No dry feet today. Hawk took off his boots and let his socks dry on the gunwale. Canlon slung his over his helmet. Neither attempt worked. Once the storm had passed, the canopy of green fell back into place, effectively screening the warmth and light of the torrid sun.

Larsen, the last man in Hawk's canoe, took off his wet shirt and smeared himself with some foul-smelling, greasy form of insect repellant. Canlon coughed a couple of times, but made no mention of the odor.

The gloomy trance of the lost wilderness returned after the storm. Every stroke of his paddle made Canlon more certain that this time he had gone too far. The Japanese must be hard up for real estate to want something like this. He put his paddle across the gunwales and lit a cigarette. The acid in the Japanese cigarettes were causing ulcers on his lips. He had lost his cardboard holders for them. *Jap bastards!* he thought.

"Owwwshit!" someone grunted in the second canoe. It didn't sound critical. "What in the goddam..."Canlon and Larsen looked back. The man in front of the second canoe was only a few feet away from them. A long, thin stick jutted out of his upper arm. He knocked off his helmet and ripped at the stick. Canlon leaned back and noticed that the stick was painted and had feathers on it. Realizing that it was an arrow, he gasped and picked up his rifle, biting hard into his cigarette. "Hey, lookit this," the stricken marine was saying. He had pulled the arrow out and was holding it up for all to see. A red oval plastered his shirt to his wounded arm.

Hawk looked curiously back. The corner of his eye still watched the swamp before him. The stricken marine didn't seem to be upset. What was going on? Larsen hit a J-stroke, letting the second canoe catch up with him. He took the stick from the lead man in the other boat. "Hoonoomaroo," he announced with great authority.

Hawk turned around and looked over the blackish-green basin of slime in front of him. He rocked his helmet brim down over his eyes. "Watch your face, one of them sonofabitches could knock a eye out," he advised McGranger. The boy pulled his helmet down.

"They're usually harmless during the daytime," Larsen assured Hawk. He dropped the arrow into the bottom of the soggy canoe. "They're just showing off a bit, probably in the trees above us."

Hawk looked up cautiously. "What's so harmless about shootin' arrows into a man?" he asked with calm irritation.

"No harm done," Larsen insisted. "Get sulfa on it, lad. It's not tainted, just a sharpened stick. You lads have had your lockjaw inoculations, I'm sure. You can thank the Japs for that, you know, they developed that inoculation."

Hawk looked around at the green and brown foliage. Crazy bastard! Getting shot at was something that he didn't take casually. He couldn't see anything. The shadows were deep at the tops of the trees. If he saw anything, what he planned on doing to it would not be called harmless. "Hoonoomaroo are tribal outcasts, Sergeant Hawk. They rather fancy young men. They don't hurt you, usually, until you resist them. At night, however, they often get unruly." As Hawk didn't say anything, Larsen continued. "You see, there are no *women* Hoonoomaroo." The guide hit a stroke with his paddle. "White men are a special treat for them."

"You...mean they're *queer?*" Canlon asked as he watched them sprinkle sulfa on the injured man's arm.

"Fiercely," Larsen laughed loudly.

"For shit sakes!" Joe turned around and looked at Hawk. The sergeant shrugged. "Damn, I thought they minded their own business." Canlon left his paddle idle and fingered the bolt of his rifle. He swallowed as he looked about the quiet cavern of jungle that encased him."

"Ah, you're wrong there, laddy," Larsen told him. "I've had my fun with the native boys...but the Hoonoomaroo, now they're a different sort...not my cup of tea."

Joe looked straight ahead. After a minute or two, he leaned toward the front of the pirogue and said in a low voice, "Did you hear what this guy just said?"

Hawk shrugged again. He didn't know much about that kind of stuff. He was from Mississippi. He didn't really want to know, either. He had enough problems without worrying about someone else's. Violence, however, he understood. He also knew how to deal with it.

A hollow, mournful whoop slid through the trees somewhere in front of them. "They are serenading you," Larsen informed Canlon. Joe shifted uneasily.

"Kinda romantic," said Hawk, smiling as he spat over the prow of the boat.

"Yes. Wait till we see the blighters. You're certain to be charmed," Larsen joked. He seemed more amused than afraid of the unseen tribesmen.

"*See* 'em?" Joe asked, finally picking up his paddle. "We ain't gonna *see* 'em, are we?"

"Let's hope not," Larsen answered. "That would only mean trouble." They did not again feel the twang of Cupid's bow on that day.

Larsen hadn't expected to make the Ranke plantation by nightfall. He had planned on reaching a certain campsite, however. But it takes longer to move fifty men than it takes to move one or two. It was an hour after dark before they reached the muddy, overgrown island where he had planned on spending the night. The hour after dark was the longest of all. The darkness made the settling down difficult. A great deal of cursing and stumbling resulted as the fleet of canoes congregated in the close quarters. One man fell overboard, only a few feet from shore, but he went swiftly beneath the still, black waters. He didn't rise again and two of his friends jumped in after him. The first man had become tangled in the species of hyacinths that grew under the swamp. After a few gasping plunges, the other two managed to free him. They reported the swamp as having no bottom. Later in the night, they all three swelled up from head to toe. This discouraged anyone from considered a late swim.

Hawk forbade the building of fires. Larsen pooh-poohed this, saying it would be completely safe to do so. It was safer, in fact, than not doing so. Larsen knew about the wilds. Hawk knew about war. Therefore he allowed himself to be overruled. Three pitiful orange campfires pierced the vacuum of the evil night.

Larsen sat beside Hawk, leaning against a canoe that had been dragged up onto the overgrown island .The sergeant drank coffee from a folding cup. He didn't like coffee, but he had developed a taste for it since the start of the war. Individual preferences get lost in a war and you take whatever luxuries are offered. He didn't say anything to the guide. Larsen finally spoke.

"We'll get there early tomorrow," Larsen said, extending his lips far out over the top of his cup. He sipped loudly at the brew. "I'm looking forward to seeing old Ranke. It's been a while."

Hawk sniffed and looked out past the playful dance of the firelight. "These cannibals and such go out much at night?"

"To be sure. Love the night. Anything to be appearing supernatural and scare the pants off a bloke. They won't bother us. We're too many for them. There's two tribes to watch out for, mainly. The Cahwey are the cannibals and the Nodu are the headhunters. Fortunately, they like to fight one another and generally leave us alone. They even trade with us for cargo at times. See 'em in town every now and then. They've complained about the Japs," Larsen laughed, "claim they're uncivilized." Hawk snorted and sipped his coffee. "No, they're pretty good to us sometimes and they don't like the Japs. If a blighter gets off by himself, now that's another story. They're not afraid of whites, just being sensible. We used to mow them down quite regularly. They respect us. But they'll overpower a small party and do their business on 'em, yessir, that they will, to be sure." Larsen sipped some more coffee.

"I used to work on patrol for the government," he began again. "We went through a string of Nodu villages —about twenty kilometers from here, near the mountains. We were looking for a lost missionary. This was five or six years ago, mind you. I saw his head on a pole in one of the biggest hamlets. I only had a couple of bearers with me. I thought it would be bad manners to call the head to the attention of the local chief," Larsen laughed.

Hawk laughed. "Yeah, I can understand that."

"They lops off the head and takes out the bone and shrink it down. Quite the art to it. Make good souvenirs for the city folk; it's still legal to trade in 'em, too. Lot of caterwauling about it before the war. The little old ladies in Canberra are more worried about Japs and their own heads right now." Larsen reeled his anteater lips out over the steaming coffee and took another sip. "I won't mention what they do with the rest of you, once they got your head. The Cahwaey, well, I guess they can be the worst. They have some filthy customs. The Hoonoomaroo aren't really a tribe as such, but they'll sure give you some trouble at night. You already know about their specialty."

"At night, huh?" Hawk folded his empty cup and stuck it into his pocket. He looked out into the darkness. "Well, that's half the time, ain't it?"

Larsen laughed heartily. "That it is, that it is! No cause for alarm, mind you, there's too damned many of us for any of these monkeys. They like to get ahold of small parties and scare old Willy-Hell out of 'em."

Hawk yawned. Ghost stories didn't worry him. He had been through too much genuine horror for that. The Nodus and the Cahweys were amateurs; the Japanese were professionals. And so was he.

He was right about the Japanese, of course. Where he made his mistake was in thinking of them in terms of the long ago and far away. He should have known that fifty armed men meant very little to an Imperial soldier.

The shots awakened him at midnight. He knew when he heard them that they were Japanese. Light cracking noises, twenty-five caliber sniper rifles, that put little holes in one side of you and big ones in the other side.

He sat up, momentarily disoriented by the opaque darkness. The fires were out. Which way had the water been? More cracking noises. Each crack had its own echo, like when you hear someone hammering at a distance, *crack-uh. Crack-uh.* American voices could be heard in the night. Confused voices, angry voices, and mostly, just frightened voices.

"Fook you, marine!" A scream came out of the hideous night. "Fook you! Die! Die! Drink you blood, marine!" Hawk heard the angry, vibrating buzz of the bullets, but he couldn't see a thing.

"Flare," Hawk bellowed.

A pop could be heard on the other end of the island. The spewing flare went up about fifty feet, where it met with a screen of vines and tree limbs. Luckily, its little parachute fouled on a branch and it hung over the island like a light bulb. A BAR rattled low and angrily by the boats.

"Grenade!" someone screamed. Everyone was up and running now. They didn't know where to run, but instinct told them to run somewhere. The sizzling flare doused their backs and helmets with silver illumination, making them look even more helpless than they had in the dark. A grenade went off in the middle of the island. Dust blew through the flare-light. The noise shut off Hawk's auditory functions, as if a switch had been thrown.

"Get in the water! By the boats!" he yelled. The men

scrambled into the swamp, lying on the shore between the beached canoes, with their legs in the water. The marines were pouring rounds into the dark, even though the targets were invisible.

"Drink you blood—Die—Die!" the deep-throated cry lashed out at them. Another grenade hit on the far side of the island. Someone screamed in pain, *"Ahhoooo!"* Someone else screamed, "They got the goddam boat!"

"Corpsman! Corpsman!"

"Get some shit goin' the other way," Hawk screamed.

"They're over there, goddamnit!"

"I'm hit! I'm shot!"

Crack-uh. Crack-uh. Crack-crack-crack-uh.

"They're over *here*! Help me!"

"Corpsman!"

"Fook you, marine!"

Hawk's deafness numbed his brain. "Shit," he muttered, "what the goddam hell's goin' on?" He bellowed loud enough to hear himself, "Where are they?" Larsen crawled beside him and lay under the cover of a canoe. He was taking it well. He didn't have to direct any operations, all he had to do was survive. He had that certain grace under pressure that men a little past their prime are possessed of, having reached the age where one realizes that death is the least of life's little hardships; but he had not yet reached the age where one learns what is bullshit.

"They've got to be in boats," Larsen contributed.

"My God!" McGranger exclaimed. "There they are!" He was on the other side of Hawk. "I see them! They're on the island." Hawk squinted into the dark leafy undergrowth. He saw a long, white loincloth on a short, fat man. The man carried a rifle and bayonet and he was charging the marines stretched out along the water's edge. It was the old Japanese strategy: don't shoot when you can kill yourself by closing with the enemy. Sometimes it even worked. It always scared the hell out of you.

"Banzai! Banzai!" the man screamed. McGranger flinched, shrinking back a foot or so, though he was far from the danger. It was as if he feared for the safety of the enemy soldier. A score of yellow, electric muzzles blazed away at the figure. It went flying backwards as if a wire had been drawn taut around its neck. Hawk stood. He went from man to man, walking in a crouch, stepping over the canoes and equipment. He felt fairly certain that he had not been targeted. The other marines, not as experienced as he, did not understand this and thought he'd lost his mind. Had they understood it, they might well have still thought the same.

"Take it easy, let 'em come to us. Take it easy, let 'em come to us. We're okay. Stay put. Take it easy, let' em come to us," he kept the refrain up as he maneuvered along the line. Bullets scattered the muddy sod at his feet. An occasional resonant *thwock* could be heard when one of the canoes absorbed a slug. He made it to the end of the line. Two men had been hit down there. He was concerned for the flank, but when he saw it, it appeared to be in no more danger than the rest of the line. The other side was probably just as disoriented as were the marines.

One of the stricken Americans had been hit by a grenade. The other was dead of a bullet wound in the groin. Hawk lay half in the water, near where the corpsman worked over the wounded boy. He was satisfied that an attack was not underway. If they wanted to shoot it out, that was fine. The flare went out.

The rifle fire intensified in the darkness. After-images of the silver foliage blinked in Hawk's eyes when the island became dark again. As he lay listening, and searching for something to shoot at, he realized that only the Americans were firing. "Hold your fire! Hold that fire, goddamnit!"

He knelt in the mud, holding his Thompson awkwardly in his left hand and rubbing his right anxiously up and down his sand-coated thigh. "Flare!" he cried. This flare didn't do as well as the first. It hit a tree limb about twenty feet up and plopped hissing into the water. The wounded man began to scream, "Give me something! Morphine! For *Go-o-d's sake! Do* something!" Hawk looked over at him. Between himself and the wounded man was the dead one.

His lifeless eyes glowed in the dark, staring at Hawk, accusing him. His hips rested in a hole in the mud. The hole was filled with blood. "I...I'm dyin'," the other man screamed, and then he wailed something incoherent. The corpsman worked feverishly in the dark.

"Jesus Christ, what's going on?" Hawk asked, crawling over to them. He looked out at the darkness again, his eyes narrowed and his lips parted. When he looked down again, he noticed that somehow, the dead man was still staring at him. He swallowed and was about to reach for him to make sure he was dead when the corpsman asked for help with the other man.

"Hold him up a second, Sarge, would you?" The corpsman's voice was high and choked. He was either repulsed by what he was doing or very much afraid. Hawk put a hand behind the wounded man and pulled him up. His heavy hand sank into the back. The back was a wet sponge of stringy flesh.

"It's his back," Hawk whispered.

"I know," said the corpsman.

"Ah...ahhh...help me..."

Hawk felt air coming out of the man's back as he labored to breath. "It's...his lung, I think. I can feel it sucking wind in the back," Hawk told the corpsman. He was having trouble breathing himself, all of a sudden. It was the same reaction McGranger had had when he saw the plight of the Japanese attacker; the feeling that what happens to one man, happens to all of humanity.

"I know," said the corpsman. The firing had stopped. Hawk rubbed his bloody forearm across his eyes. "He's gone," the corpsman said in an odd tone, as if he had just finished a grueling accomplishment.

Hawk nodded and let him down easily. He watched him for a moment, hoping that maybe the corpsman was wrong, or maybe waiting for the man to say one last thing. Or maybe waiting for God to part the clouds and say, "This is ridiculous, get up, man." None of that happened. It never did. Hawk reached a red hand into his wet shirt pocket and pulled out some chewing tobacco. He bit off a plug and looked up across the stilled island. Blue swirls of smoke glided along the ground. "Son of a goddam bitch," he sighed.

"Hell of a way to wake a man up, ain't it?" the corpsman asked. He was crying.

Hawk hung his head and spat. "Yeah."

"He was only a boy...he was just a baby..."the corpsman sobbed louder.

"I know it." Hawk left them together there.

Some of the men had entrenching tools. Metal

could be heard sliding against metal as they unfolded them. They scraped fighting holes along the edge of the water and passed the shovels along to their comrades. The night remained calm and dark. It seemed that the human pupil was incapable of enlarging enough to see anything in the gruesome night. No one heard the enemy. That didn't mean they were absent.

It wasn't the way a man would have chosen to spend the night following the rigorous inland trek. Hawk had spent worse. He took a strange sort of pleasure in hardship, when it was mere hardship. When hardship descended into death and horror, his feelings were much the same as any other man's. But he accepted discomfort as his lot in life. It didn't seem right to him that a man should be comfortable. He didn't care for contrived discomfort, such as the sterile disciplinary nonsense of a boot camp. There had to be a purpose for it. He liked the dirty, dangerous sort of necessary misery. He was ashamed to admit it, but he also liked the fighting. Most men like having once fought. Afterwards you can boast and swagger and scorn those who haven't done the things you've done. But he liked *doing* it. The action, the revenge and the ruthlessness all erupted naturally from his dark spirit. The appearance of a truly merciless foe, as the Japanese were, was a godsend to him.

He became aware of this as the months of warfare dragged on. Other men became more fearful, less physically capable of functioning in combat situations. It was like an addiction to drugs or alcohol for others. The more they went through, the easier it was to get enough. One taste of combat made them drunk. The backfiring of a truck would snap them back into a reliving of the worst of their experiences. It never bothered Hawk, while he was awake. He became less cautious, more numb, more efficient. It hurt him to see men killed. His stomach knotted as easily as that of a child first experiencing the passing of a favorite puppy. Then his temper took over, anger overwhelming the grief. When others cried, Enough, stop this madness, he cried out for revenge. *Pay them back. Kill them. Kill more of them and kill them better.* That would do it, that would make the pain go away. He didn't realize that just as the others were addicted to fear, killing was his addiction. It was a destructive addiction—where could it end? You could overwhelm fear someday, but never this other dark thing. He never thought about any of it. He acted on nerve and instinct. But sometimes he dreamed.

Some of the men passed up the opportunity to dig holes. They preferred lying in the water to the further exposure required by digging. These were the ones left open to the next of the night's shocks. They were fortunate in that Sgt. Hawk was himself a swamp creature. He was sitting in a hole, facing the swamp, when he saw them: shining little orbs on the surface of the black slush, homing in on the shore at a rapid rate of speed.

"Gators! Get your ass outa the water!" he warned. The blood spilled by the conflict had attracted the devilish local crocodiles. Marines in the water scrambled up onto the land, fully exposed to enemy marksmen. No shots were fired, and neither did the little orbs slow nor veer from their course. "Them's some mean sonofabitches," Hawk told Canlon as they watched the chase. These weren't the sluggish, passive monsters from the Gulf Coast that he was familiar with. These sharp-snouted fellows wanted meat, and they were going to have it immediately. As he watched, he became convinced that the giant salt water beasts were coming ashore. He fired a burst into one of the submerged heads. A great liquid thrashing followed. The other animals continued forward. Thousands of razor sharp teeth in machine-strong jaws glided unerringly down on the position. Everyone opened fire in mindless panic. The orbs disappeared beneath the splashes of the bullets. Once the muzzle flashes ceased, the angry darkness again swallowed the men. They weren't sure if the reptiles were gone. They weren't sure if the Japanese were gone. This made a difficult night even more so.

A nervous watcher fired into the swamp a little before daylight. He probably thought he was shooting at a crocodile, was probably shooting at nothing, and that was what he hit. In the flash of yellow light, Hawk saw something suspicious. Others saw it, too. A shadow was on the murky water. Without warning, he squeezed the trigger of his submachine gun. The prolonged blaze of fire framed the overhanging foliage and the surface of the marsh with a corona of shimmering blue light. Beast-like screams blended into the shattering fire, causing the drowsing men to jump to attention. The screams were followed by elaborate wails and the excited, guttural voices of the enemy. Other weapons hammered away at the relentless darkness. Hundreds of splashes could be heard out on the water.

"Hold your fire!" the sergeant ordered. Moans came out of the silence that ensued. Several minutes later, a canoe with three dead Japanese snipers thumped into the stern of one of the marine canoes. The men near it fled from the vicinity. They feared the enemy had rigged explosives to the boat. Hawk tapped Canlon and

McGranger on the shoulder. He led them in a cautious approach to the death boat. McGranger lagged behind, wading in the wake of the other two. Hawk looked over the dead and slung his machine pistol, the muzzle pointed toward the surface of the water. He nodded.

"Man, them bastards stink," Canlon said in a trembling whisper. "They musta been rollin' in dead fish." Hawk unsheathed his hunting knife.

"You don't smell so good, yourself," he answered. "We gotta finish 'em off. Dead Japs kill more people than live ones."

The other two chose to ignore his exhortation. Even though they shared his respect for the tenacity of the enemy, they wanted no part of what he had planned. Hawk was cold when it came to this. He had seen too many of them come back to life. He wasn't going to lie cooped up with these three until morning without some insurance. He wasn't going to be nice about it. He rammed his blade home, repeatedly, without the slightest tremor of revulsion. "That ought to hold 'em," he told the other two calmly, once he had finished. He put a boot on the bow of the boat and shoved it away from the shore. It didn't float far on the still water. He slid the bloody knife back into its scabbard and took a deep breath. "Okay, get on back."

Dawn sort of sneaked up on the marines. The light in the

spaces between the leaves of the trees became more distinct. It was pitch black, and then it was just black, and then they realized that nearly black was as light as it was going to get until midday, when the tropical sun bored straight through the tops of the enshrouding trees.

The body of an enemy soldier lay within twenty feet of Canlon's fighting hole. Worms and flies already were at work on it. Hawk had heard the insects humming like a sewing machine in the dark, though he hadn't deduced a cause. Two more corpses floated face down in the water. One had lost his legs, either to a crocodile or a grenade. Streamers of flesh fanned out across the water where the legs had been.

Hawk walked to the other side of the little mud-hump island. There he found a place where boats had been dragged ashore. Another body lay over here; its throat was torn open and its shaved head was half buried in mud. It looked like it might have been carried over there. The enemy had apparently pulled out right after the firing stopped for the first time. A few diehards came back and tried the abortive rear attack. Hawk lit a cigar. Canlon and Larsen came up beside him! He didn't say anything to them, and finally, they all three turned around and went back to the canoes.

When they got back to the boats, McGranger called Hawk's attention to the metal strapping nailed around the bottom of the enemy canoe containing the three dead men. Explosives were probably attached to the bottom of the pirogue. The boat floated aimlessly about with its grim cargo. It could easily strike a submerged tree limb or other flotsam.

Hawk watched the pilotless boat and drew on his cigar. " Wonder if them Japs was followin' us or if the fires drawed them to us," he said to Canlon.

"The main thing is that they're gone," Canlon answered. His eyes were red and puffy from lack of sleep. His bare feet were swollen due to the magical effect of the vile swamp water.

"No, the main thing is, where did they come from?" Hawk shook his head. "There might be a bigger base here than we figured. Course, they coulda just been holed up since New Oss fell."

"Even a Jap wouldn't hole up in something like this," Canlon disagreed. Hawk shook his head again. He wanted to get onto some dry ground. They gathered up their dead.

The party reached dry ground before they reached any sign of Ranke's plantation. The land became rockier and more sparsely forested. The ground rose abruptly. In the distance, a line of toothy blue mountains tantalized the powers of vision. More forest lay somewhere in between, but it was a true forest and not the congested sludge they had spent the night in. Larsen said that the faraway peaks jutted up directly from the shore of the peninsula. They were in fact only rocks, and not mountains at all.

The weary column came to a plain blanketed with pit-pit grass, and there it was that they buried their two casualties. Looking around at the aged young faces glaring at the graves, Hawk wished that he had Clemson, the chaplain, with him. Hawk didn't know what to say about any of it. "Go through all this shit and end up like that," a particularly cynical teen-aged marine commented. It was the only eulogy.

As the march resumed, Canlon noticed that this teenaged marine, named Ned Albert, had several bloody ears on a wire necklace. The grisly thing bounced against his hairless, bare chest as he walked. "Why'd you do something like that?" Canlon asked, without passing judgment.

The slight boy shrugged. "I don't know," he

muttered. "It made me feel better. I felt like I had to do something." Canlon shook his head. He wouldn't do anything like that. But he felt that way, too.

"Something up ahead. Shelvin, take the point," Hawk called down the line. He ordered the flankers to spread out farther from the column. A dark rope of smoke rose above the grass-fringed horizon. It spiraled upwards and flattened out into a T-shaped cap high in the dark blue sky. Shelvin, a newly appointed scout, trotted ahead to investigate. The others proceeded at an unhurried pace in the same direction.

"That's Ranke," Larsen confided in Hawk. "He's had a time of it, I'll wager."

"Yeah, probably so," Hawk agreed. He scanned the horizon, then ordered Canlon to guard the rear and waved the flankers even farther out. The grass slapped at his pants legs. This was a good place to get hit with mortars. It was a good place to get hit with anything: perfectly flat and only blades of grass for cover. Hawk clenched his teeth and moved his head from one side to the other. The straps of his helmet creaked as they swayed in and out. Shelvin came running back with his report. His boots pounded heavily on the earth and his legs tore through the whispering grass. He and the sergeant squatted on the ground. Bupta halted the column.

"There's a little shed on fire. I saw some bodies in a plowed field. It's all quiet right now, nothing moving. There's a bigger house five or six hundred yards from the shed. Looks like a crowd of people around it. Most of 'em were black-looking." Shelvin wasn't excited. He lit a cigarette.

"And the dead ones?" Hawk asked.

"Only saw one of 'em very good. He was black-looking."

Hawk motioned to Larsen. The guide crouched in the grass with them. They traded speculations, ranging from enemy attack to native uprising. "Let's look her over," the guide suggested. "It's Ranke's place, to be sure. He has native boys working for him. They're probably just his, although it's the time of year for the Hoonoomaroo's little...gatherings."

"All right," Hawk cut him off. He didn't want to hear any more of the local lore. He went through new lands like a bulldozer, damn the history and the customs. He stood and got the men into a skirmish line. The line moved cautiously forward in the direction of the smoke. Hawk walked in front of the scythe of men, throwing one boot before the other in his characteristic shrugging swagger. He occasionally held his machine pistol in one hand and gestured back at the line with the other. Everyone watched him and took his directions religiously. They trusted him in matters such as these. The clanking of their equipment and the swishing of the grass combined to make the sound of an irresistible threat. The marines glared angrily ahead. They had lost two men last night. Their movements were determined. Those deaths made them dangerous. Had it been twenty, they would have been shaky and probably in no mood for revenge.

Hawk's face was expressionless. He was always in the mood for revenge, regardless of the odds. They passed a body on the edge of the plowed field. A Melanesian native lay face down in the soft black dirt. He looked comfortable there in the cool soil. He wore khaki shorts and was without a shirt. Not the dress of a wild tribesman. No wound was visible, but you could tell from the limber bend of his arms and legs that he was dead. Hawk kept the line moving. He stepped over the dead man, split the line in two and went around the burning shed. The shed was on an unplowed island in the field.

As he passed the shed, the wicked flames were reflected in Hawk's squinting eyes. Fire. He remembered the flamethrower. Of all of the good men dead, of all the selfless souls he had seen reduced to inanimate heaps, he remembered those he had killed in the cave on the Haarmeer Archipelago most vividly. Death at his hands. Fire. An awful way to die. The sight, the sound, the smell and the taste of it still assaulted him. He had wallowed in it. Drops of sweat fell from his nose and chin.

There at his feet lay another corpse. The reality swirled away the ghastly flashback. This one was Japanese and it lay face up. The forehead was one massive hole. The edges of the hole looked like melted plastic; inside it was red, gray and white. One eye was relocated down around the bottom of the nose. It was open and intact. Hawk glanced at it and looked away. Just another dead Jap, he thought. He wouldn't remember that one. Those were a dime a dozen. The dead man wore a fundoshi loincloth. *Goddam Japs run around naked like a bunch of animals.* He stepped over the body without breaking his stride. He wasn't worried about that one getting up and shooting him in the back.

Hawk's jaw muscles tightened as they neared the plantation house. Larsen came running behind him. Hawk continued looking forward. He wasn't going to die with a bullet in the back of his head. He would go out like that Japanese lying in the field. "I see Ranke," said Larsen. "Those are his boys with him. It appears that they've beaten off a Jap attack." Larsen was breathing heavily. He was a bit overweight and short-winded. Maybe he had been a little afraid. "They probably hit him at the same time they were hitting us."

"I reckon we'll find out," Hawk told him. The marines moved more quickly now, marching right up to the plantation house. Neatly kept palm trees ringed a plaza in front of the building. Hummocks of dirt-covered roots lifted the bases of these trees several feet from the ground. Sago palms grew in a neat arrangement on two sides of the house. The sago was an important food source for the natives. A white man and about thirty natives were gathered in the plaza. Hawk saw three or four old bolt-action rifles.

Larsen walked ahead of the Americans and shouted a greeting. The German raised his rifle, and not in a friendly manner. Hawk raised the muzzle of his Thompson a trifle and tightened his finger on its trigger.

"That's far enough, Larsen. Collect your taxes from the Japs," said Ranke.

"Ah, you've got me all wrong, sir," Larsen kept walking toward the rifle muzzle with a big smile. "I've brought you some Yanks, to look out for your welfare."

"Get your stinking ass off of my land, you maggot-eyed carrion eater!" Ranke replied in an increasingly angry tone. Hawk followed Larsen, a little nonplussed by the warm reception. He didn't know whether he should continue trusting Larsen's judgment of the situation. Larsen only laughed at the vicious words, walked past the rifle and clapped the plantation owner on the shoulder.

"Looks like you had a time of it, old friend, eh?" Larsen asked in a sincere voice. A remarkably meaningful look of hate shot from Ranke's eyes. The German was several shades darker than even the sun-bronzed Sgt. Hawk, and yet his eyes were the pale blue of a fair-skinned individual. It was a striking contrast. Ranke towered over everyone there and spoke English with only a slight accent.

"How do you do, sir?" Hawk intervened. "I'm Sgt. James Hawk, United States Marine Corps."

"Get out of here."

"Ah, listen, Otto, you need these boys," Larsen consoled. "What's happened here? We lost a few lads ourselves, last night."

"Never mind what happened. I told you to get out of here and that's exactly what I meant."

The marines gathered around, leaning on their rifles. Some of them were joking. The natives looked them over, grunting to each other and staying out of the way of the Americans.

"There's a Jap base somewhere in this area, sir," said Hawk. "We'd appreciate any help you could give us in finding it." Ranke looked Hawk over. He knew the American wasn't going to just go away. Hawk was a serious-looking individual with several days' growth of beard on his uncompromising features. His moldy shirt was open, exposing a chestful of hair. His rotted sleeves were rolled up past heavy biceps that had veins as thick as pencils coiled around them. Not the sort of fellow to kick sand on.

Hawk stared back without expression. He judged the German to be a hothead. Ranke seemed capable of taking Roger. By all indications, however, he was not in league with the Japanese.

"You have my services in any way needed to rid the country of the Japs, Yank. If you have any notion of my declaring loyalty to St. Cyr, you can leave right now. This is not the nation of Malang, it's an Australian territory. And if it ever becomes Malang, St. Cyr won't be the man running it."

Hawk winced at the word "Yank." He never did get used to being called that. In the midst of the rather heated conversation, this was the only thing that really irritated him. "That don't mean shit to me, sir," he drawled slowly. "There's a Jap sub base been supportin' some heavy kind of operations out in the Straits of Cavazo. We got it figured to be somewhere in a fifty or hundred mile radius of New Oss. We done made some contact with ground troops, too. Now, St. Cyr does figure into all of this, in a roundabout way, and I'd like to talk to you about that, if I could." Ranke and the Sergeant stared at each other for a moment longer. Ranke knew it was best not to resist. Something about Hawk's eyes made you think he was contemplating the best way to burn down your house.

"Come inside. *You,* come inside," said the plantation owner, turning his back on the idle concourse that filled his plaza. Larsen chuckled and nudged Hawk. He began to follow him inside.

"Stay put," Hawk stopped him. "He ain't too crazy about you, for some reason." Larsen growled as if it were all nonsense, but he didn't go in. Ranke led the marine into an airy, central room of the house. Lattice-work surrounded the tops of the outer walls of the place, letting in light and a refreshing breeze. Mosquito nets were tacked up behind the screens and there were no fans. The lattice made up the upper quarter of the walls and it cast shaky, diamond-shadows on the planking of the floor. The two men sat at a spartan table, neither of them speaking at first.

"Drink?"

"No, thank you, sir."

"And so there is a Jap sub base out here?"

"That's what we figure, yessir."

"I've noticed that your planes go over every five minutes and they tell me patrol boats are roaming the sea out along the coast. I knew that they must be after something like that. What does that bastard St. Cyr have to do with any of it?"

"Well, nothin'. His kid was stole a couple days ago. He told us to come over here and see if you have him. He said you was in with the Japs and against him and all that sh...stuff." Hawk felt a little embarrassed. The subject of the nation of Malang was kind of ridiculous.

"Did he say that, now?" Ranke roared. "He's a madman! The little yellow bastards have been stealing food from me for weeks. Last night they made off with all of my hogs and a wagonload of flour. We cornered one setting fire to the outhouse and I killed him. One of their snipers got one of my boys after that. I'm the last man to side with those monkeys. Have you ever heard of a European siding with Japs, Sergeant?"

"No, sir. Not yet, I ain't. You see...I expect that the sub base is gonna turn up. Things like that always do. There's a lot of folks interested in finding it. What I'm concerned about is the kid."

"That would be little Roger?"

"Yessir. They say the Japs got him. Came right into

New Oss and took him, it was kind of a funny deal. St. Cyr figures the Japs had to have some kind of help, and he suggested you. I 'ain't found no clue on where he might be and we've lost a few men looking."

"And so here you are, after me? I don't have the boy. That's not my way of conducting business. I tend to my own affairs, and when someone wants to cross paths with me, I deal roughly with him. Ask St. Cyr what I did to one of his little tax collectors. I could have rounded up the natives and mounted a war against him, too, if it hadn't been for all the talk about the Japs coming back. I'm not part of his country. I personally favor the Netherlands claim to the land, but if they can't enforce their rights, then Australia can—and if she can't, the natives can and I'll help them. No crazy fool like St. Cyr is going to take over without a fight. I can manage the natives better than he, I've lived here all my life. We'll bide our time and let him pretend he's a god over in New Oss."

"Yessir. I ain't much one to get into the politics of this. I reckon the Japs are eventually gonna take St. Cyr off your hands. He ain't got a whole lot of common sense. What it is, though, I kinda liked the kid and I'd like to bring him back, if I can." Hawk draped an arm over the table.

"I understand. You're wasting your time. St. Cyr breeds enemies like this land breeds mosquitoes. Any of the lunatics in his so-called government could have done something like that. You don't really believe that the Japs went into New Oss, kidnapped one boy and left, do you?"

"I ain't sure, but..."

"In fact, my prime suspect would be that overstuffed

mongrel that brought you here. Larsen would sell his grandmother for five pounds. I could tell you stories about him, but you wouldn't believe them. You should investigate him closely where there is a young boy involved." Hawk smiled and Ranke let out a great roar of spiteful laughter. "I see you know him. Watch that one."

"Yessir. He does his job." Hawk studied the empty tabletop. He decided that Roger wasn't here. Ranke wasn't the type for that, just as he had said. He would settle any differences that he had with you right to your face. "Well, how about that base, sir? You know this country. Have you seen any kind of odd activity around here lately?"

Ranke reared back in his chair and let his arms hang at his side. He frowned. "That's the *only* kind of activity there is around here. But, yes, yes I have," he said in a low voice. Then he shouted, "Mellie, Mellie, come in here!" He lowered his voice and said, "My foreman," by way of explanation. A small, bald black man entered the front door. His body was horribly encircled with six-inch-wide striped scars, giving him a serpentine appearance. This tribal tattoo was further enhanced by large unsightly bumps in his skin between the stripes. The foreman bowed and smiled jovially at the marine.

"How do you do?" Hawk said and looked quizzically at Ranke.

"Tell the Sergeant about the young people's *omat*, Mellie. *Omat* is a little ceremony the local domestic tribes have for their young men and women. They had a sacred rock that the couples used to go to out on the coast. We call it Hollow Mountain, they call it something unpronounceable. Tell him, Mellie."

Mellie bowed again. "No *omat,* two moons. Two men-fellas no come back. Two women, no come back. People of these say-say Sap-fellas kill them. Say-say Sap-fellas let no fella go Hollow Mountain," Mellie reported with a sincere furrow in his brow. "Bad things happen at Hollow Mountain. My people, these people no go there. No *omat* until white mens kill all Sap-fellas across the big water."

Hawk leaned forward to get a better grasp of all of this. "You're sayin' you seen Japs fartin' around this place?"

"No see. No go. Mellie too old for *omat.* I tell you-fella what I hear. Sap-fellas there. I hear," Mellie smiled and pulled at his ear so that this dense listener could better understand.

"Thanks, Mellie." Ranke waved the foreman away. He bowed and left. "Evidently the Japs are at Hollow Mountain, Sergeant. The locals wouldn't let anything else disturb their tradition. They make no allowances for Hoonoomaroo or Nodus. The Japs are there, and they can have it, as far as I'm concerned. But you see, it *is* on the coast."

"I see." Hawk pulled a cigar out of his pocket and lit it. "Maybe something big. Maybe not."

"True. Is it worth investigating?"

Hawk drew thoughtfully on his cigar. "No, probably not. Probably just some stragglers. I guess, since it's on the coast, that I'll have to, though. It might lead to something."

"For my own reasons, I agree. Perhaps these Japs that have been harassing me are camped there. You can exterminate them, can't you? That's why you're here, isn't it?"

"Yeah."

"I have something else to show you here." He reached over to a stack of books and papers on the floor. He took a folded newspaper from the top of the pile and slid it across the table to the marine. It was a Brisbane paper. The headline on the editorial was, "The Emperor's New Clothes in Malang." It read:

Sir Richard St. Cyr, an unorthodox man whose views defy respect...has declared himself the Prime Minister of the "nation" of Malang... A British subject, transplanted to the shores of our poor northern neighbor, St. Cyr has long been a sympathizer with fascist causes, ranging from Spain to Italy... He has now taken the ultimate step for a true reactionary, declared himself the king of a nonexistent nation... The world situation seems to be to his advantage.

Hawk slid the paper back to the German. "I get the drift, sir."

"Everyone knows he's mad. He has money backing him, I'll grant you that, and he's in an out-of-the-way enough spot. Sure, I feel sorry for the child, too. But I'll advise you here and now not to do any favors for that pig of a father of his. He'll use you until you drop and then he'll throw you away. Believe me, I know these kinds of people. I'm German, you know. You know what's going on in Germany."

"I know. But it's gettin' to where the job is more important than the people. I ain't gonna forget about that kid. It ain't his fault that his Dad is a sonofabitch, is it?"

"No." A silence followed.

Hawk shifted about in his chair. "Have you got a radio, sir?"

"Yes, you may use it if you like."

"Thank you. Where is it?" Ranke led him to the rear of the house. A massive antediluvian radio took up one entire wall of one room. "I'll help you; let me get Mellie to operate the generator." Mellie ultimately sent someone else to turn the hand-over-hand crank of the generator. "Press this bar to transmit," Ranke instructed him. "They can't hear you while you hold it down."

"Yes sir." Hawk accepted the help graciously, even though he had run across a few radios in his day. "Thank you, sir." He took the transmitter and held the headset to one ear, then pushed the transmission bar. "Mr. Plunkett...Mr. Plunkett, this is Colonel Hawk calling for General Carlisle, come in Mr. Plunkett..." This went on for a minute or two. The native continued to crank the generator, looking contentedly out into space. Finally a voice crackled over the receiver.

"This is, uh, Carlisle, go ahead, Hawk."

"General, I'm at the destination. Over."

"Oh...yes, Colonel, did you find out anything?"

" Yessir." Hawk paused for a minute; he knew the enemy might be monitoring the conversation. "I have one of the divisions bivouacked in the swamp. We're still bringing in the tanks and artillery. Over."

"Uh...yes, good. I'm...uh...sending more tanks and another division as soon as we can make them available...uh...do you have any operations reports? Over."

"Yes sir. A small patrol of my boys got isolated and were attacked by a party of Japs. They were under the command of some green sergeant. Two of us dead, no wounded. Got more of them. I am at the destination. Over."

"Good...what about your priority one and priority two objectives?"

"There's a...no Roger on priority one, sir. I'm checking out a rumor on priority two that might develop into something. Over."

"You say no Roger?"

"That's right. Priority two will have to be reported in person, after further investigatin'."

"Do it, then. Listen, Hawk, this guy's getting worse. He read in the paper about the Germans kidnapping Stalin's son to make the Russians surrender and he's telling me that's why the Japs...uh...you know, I mean it's working on his mind, I think."

"No sense talkin' about it this way, sir. Put the bastard in a strait jacket. Any other trouble?"

"No, except that I'm still getting a lot of questions about priority two. Priority two is still giving our forces trouble. Hurry back with some good news."

"Roger and out."

The native stopped cranking without having to be told. Hawk placed the headset on top of the radio. Ranke was still in the room.

"How far to this Hollow Mountain, Mr. Ranke?"

"Maybe two hours."

"I'm going to check it out after dark. I don't want the Japs givin' us no shit like they did on the way over."

"That would be a good idea, except for one thing. Tonight is...well, have you heard of the Hoonoomaroo?"

"Yessir."

"Tonight begins their month-long *tambaran* cere-monies. They roam the jungle protected by spirits or some such nonsense. No one travels at night during the *tambaran* of the Hoonoomaroo."

"They supposed to be dangerous or something? You know, we ain't exactly Little Red Riding Hood."

"They are *very* dangerous. They are liable to attack you any night, but they are drugged with particular enthusiasm during the month of their *tambaran*. I'm afraid that tonight, the first night, is virtually out of the question. That stretch of jungle is their sacred stamping grounds. I wouldn't take two hundred men through there."

"They more dangerous than Japs?"

"Well, of course not, but..."

"Then I'm afraid we're going, sir. I'll just take a few of the men and we'll travel light and fast and be back before morning. I want to get this Hollow Mountain checked out."

"I don't think you understand, Sergeant. I'm telling you about several thousand stone-age savages on the rampage. Going out there would be foolhardy. They are human by resemblance only. If you survive, it will be at the expense of considerable bloodshed. If you don't—I'll let you use your imagination."

"Sorry, Mr. Ranke. I ain't got no imagination. I gotta go tonight. I ain't saying that I don't respect all this here jungle shit, I'm just telling you that there's a lot riding on me. I'll be able to handle a few spears and arrows and such."

"I warn you Sergeant, don't go. I promise you that you won't be back here in the morning. I will bet everything I own on that and I'm not a poor man. I don't know how to make it any more clear. I could sit here all day telling you horror stories, but I won't. I ask you to trust me and use your common sense when I tell you that it is accepted custom *not* to travel tonight."

"Thank you, sir. I appreciate your concern. I ain't a bettin' man or I'd take you up on all that."

Hawk shook hands with Ranke, then went outside and called together the men he wanted to take with him, and Bupta. Bupta would be in charge while he was gone. Can-Ion, McGranger, Shelvin, Ned Albert, a corpsman named Calloway, and Larsen sat around him in a circle in the plaza. Canlon fingered the ulcers on his lower lip.

"Got a lead on this sub base, " Hawk told them. "I figure we better check it out tonight, on account of if it's true, we could run into a whole crock of Japs."

"Where?" Larsen asked with caution in his voice. He had been paid to come over and see Ranke, not downtown Tokyo.

"Hollow Mountain. Heard of it?"

"Sure," said Larsen, covering his caution better now. "It bears consideration. It might be dangerous tonight, though..." Larsen leaned confidentially toward Hawk.

"I know, I know," Hawk stopped him, "trick-or-treat night. You men be ready at dark, or a little before, I guess. Get some sleep, now. We'll be back at daylight and have to go back to New Oss with some kind of report. That's a lot of walking."

Larsen stayed after the others had left. "I'm not going," he said.

"Why not?" Hawk was surprised. Larsen seemed fairly adventurous.

"The Hoonoomaroo."

Hawk shrugged. He didn't protest. "Then don't. Get me somebody that knows the way," was all he said about it. Larsen talked Mellie into leading them. It must have taken a great deal of courage on the part of the foreman to do such a thing, since he had the local's supernatural fear of both the Hoonoomaroo and the Japanese.

The seven men left a little before dark. The trail was easy at first. The ground was hard and rocky with little vegetation. After a while they entered a forbidding, lightless and airless jungle. There, dark hit them. The existence of a trail made it easier, but it was no consolation to Hawk. Trails attracted trouble. His misgivings made him no less willing to use the path this time. It was unthinkable to avoid the easy passage. Were he upon an aimless search-and-destroy mission, he would have avoided it. Tonight, he wanted to get to his destination as quickly as possible.

The trail had once been well-traveled. It led to the coast and a small loading dock, where the plantation had received its supplies and shipped its wares. The war had stopped most of the trade. Hollow Mountain was taboo. As a result, the road was pretty much off limits. Hardy plants had already reclaimed patches of it. The marines moved soundlessly down the winding corridor. The forest was close, like a subterranean chamber. The faintest smell of the sea could occasionally be detected. Mellie, the guide, was in the front at the point. A hollow whoop gurgled from the darkness, playing its warning up and down the spine of Joe Canlon. Mellie stopped.

He turned around in the darkness and whispered loudly to Hawk. "Hoonoomaroo." Canlon trotted up to Hawk from the rear. "What's that?" he asked.

"Them Hooners," Hawk answered. He had trouble with foreign words.

"That's them guys," said Canlon. No one had filled him in on the *tambaran*. Hawk unslung his submachine gun and pulled his helmet down over his eyes. He didn't say anything else. He motioned for Mellie to come forward. After a few more cautious paces, another urgent whoop sliced out of the blackness at them. Canlon felt it slice into his chest. It was a primitive and demanding scream and it frightened him. They stopped. Hawk judged it to be overhead and behind them. He gestured with the muzzle of his gun for Mellie to keep going. It would take more than noise to stop him. Canlon walked backwards, now, his rifle aimed at the eternal, blind void behind the patrol. McGranger, the man next to him, also walked backwards. McGranger was shaking. He got closer to Canlon. Canlon's rugged features made him look fearless, though this was not always the case.

The cry was louder the next time. An answering cry came from in front of the marines. Mellie didn't look back at Hawk this time for instructions. He kept walking slowly into the night. Hawk looked impatiently from one side to the next. He didn't want to be bothered with natives. He had business to take care of. He was confident that he could handle whatever might appear. He had to admit to a certain amount of curiosity, however.

From all sides, a blood-curdling din of primeval noise erupted. Canlon fell to one knee, as if the noise had pushed him down. He searched the night frantically for the source of the sound.

"All right, get some cover," Hawk shouted over the racket. He motioned the men to the side of the trail. It became obvious that the Hoonoomaroo were not going to go away. They had targeted the Americans.

An eerie surge of music jarred the earth. It began suddenly, as if an electronically amplified orchestra of madmen had been switched on. The marines huddled against the large trees that grew along the trail. Canlon was alone at the end of the column; McGranger shrank toward the others, hugging the sweaty bark of a rot-smelling tree. He wanted out of here.

The music droned on in a haunting, perpetual moan, punctuated by high-pitched horns and frightful screams. The strange rhythm hung on the black leaves and dripped into their collective subconscious. The men looked at one another frequently to make sure that the one next to him had not yet been hypnotized by the effects. The black hands of the jungle leaves reached from the darkness. Canlon turned around and put his back to his tree. The dark soul of evil had surrounded them and encaged them. All was chaotic and yet all was still.

Hawk chewed solemnly on a plug of tobacco. He spat out into the trail. He couldn't wait here forever. There was no telling how long this show would last. "Don't shoot unless you got to," he told McGranger and indicated that the message should be passed along. It seemed to McGranger that Hawk was deaf to what was going on around him. When Canlon got the message, he clicked his safety back on. He didn't trust his strained nerves. His finger pulled hard on the frozen trigger.

Hawk stood. He knew he was encircled by between fifty and maybe two hundred natives. But he was in a hurry. "Let's go!" he drawled loud enough for all of them to hear. The others stood slowly. The music seemed to weaken their muscles and destroy their will to move. Hawk stepped out into the trail and they followed him.

They took their strength from him. Had he faltered, they all would have.

No visible sign of their tormentors manifested itself. Again they moved along the trail and it sounded as if the Hoonoomaroo were gathered inches away; beside them, in the trees above them and under the very earth at their feet. The noise arched over them and permeated their thin ranks, demonstrating its unseen power to be greater than their own. They couldn't turn back. It would do no good to run. Mellie was pallid. It required the hand of Sgt. Hawk in the middle of his back for him to keeping taking short forward steps. Canlon faced forward again; it did no good to watch the back, they were everywhere. They were between himself and McGranger. He snapped off his safety. It felt as if the rhythm were going to snap his sanity. He waited for the rush, wishing that it would come at last and be done.

The music stopped. Hawk kept them moving. A great rustling noise followed. The tearing of foliage and vibrating of the ground caused the Americans to stop. The jungle was about to close in on the trail.

Canlon felt a hand on his ankle, and then another on his arm. The grips were powerful and unbreakable. The viselike hands, if indeed that is what they were, felt as large as his whole arm. He dropped his rifle and bellowed all of his panic out into the terrible night. "Jesus! Jesus God!"

Hawk turned around. "No shootin'," his voice cut through the darkness and the sound of the thrashing; still calm, still in control. In an instant, he was at the rear of the column, swinging his Thompson like an ax at the writhing shadows that were grappling over Joe. It fell quite solidly into flesh and bone, and he knew that these were mere men. Then the trail burst into flame.

Torches had somehow been ignited and thrown onto the ground before and behind the column. The marines saw one another in the daylight glare, but their attackers remained out of sight. Canlon lay on the ground beside his rifle. He was breathing heavily, his fatigues were torn and his eyes were wide open.

Hawk glanced upwards at the trees. Nothing up there. He studied the torches that blocked his path. "Okay," he said, a little out of breath, "I guess we'll have to shoot our way out." He didn't want to but he had no choice. The others looked at his sweat-drenched face. It was stubbornly set with the red-orange glow of the fires highlighting the bone structure. He reached down and helped Canlon to his feet. "Get that rifle, Joe." The Hoonoomaroo glided into the trail in front of them, on the far side of the torches. Mellie and Calloway gasped simultaneously at the sight.

Even more appeared behind them, almost at Canlon's elbow and just beyond the pyre of torches at the rear. Joe shrank back against Hawk. He made no attempt at looking defiant. Hawk spat a stream of chewing tobacco into the fire. "Them's goddam sure some ugly-lookin' shitpiles," he commented. And he was literally correct. Great conical helmets of dung were fastened to and covered the entire heads of the natives. Only eye and mouth holes let in air. Humming swarms of blue and green flies clung to the dung like orna-mental jewels. The well-muscled bodies of the tribesmen were smeared with white ash that made them glow in the dark. The crowd was endless, both before and behind them, as if all the white ghosts of the dead had risen from their graves and met here.

Each one carried a spear in one hand, and in the other a short stick, with, it was to be hoped, what was only the genitalia of some animal dangling ludicrously from the end. Mellie fell to his knees and refused to look up. The jungle became absolutely silent. The odor of the repressing throng was overwhelming. It was a smothering and revolting smell that the marines had noticed to a lesser extent during the musical barrage.

One of the hellish figures, identical to his fellows, stepped from the pack at the rear of the column. He spoke a few words incomprehensible to the Americans. Then he pointed at McGranger. Mellie looked up. He translated in a quivering voice. "Him say-say him take this fella," Mellie pointed at McGranger, "and let all rest fella go. No fella get hurt. This fella go to sing-sing tonight and come back to you alive next day."

Hawk spat. "Tell him no deal."

Mellie nodded. "Yes, yes. You give him this fella, he come back in short time and want next fella. Better we stay together. I tell him."

"Let's start shootin'," Canlon said in a low voice to Hawk.

"Settle down."

"Settle down, my ass! Do you know what these things got planned for us?"

"Nobody's hurt yet."

"Shit no, they want us alive," Canlon answered. He looked in horrible fascination at the monsters on the far side of the fire. They were waiting patiently.

"Tell him what I said, Mellie," Hawk raised his voice.

Then in a lower voice he said to Joe, "For shit sakes, man, all they got is sticks. Take it easy, will you?"

"You think this is a joke, don't you, Hawk? You'll be sayin' 'take it easy' when they're crammin' them sticks up my ass." Joe was losing control. His revulsion had outdistanced his discipline.

Hawk looked over his shoulder at the mass of natives that barred his way. He noticed that the faces of his men were more ashen than the decorated bodies of the Hoonoomaroo. He cursed them silently to himself. All the Hallowe'en tricks worked. Six men who had fought their way through hell were scared of some noise and pig shit. "They don't want you," he angrily told Canlon. "They threw your ass back. You're about the only thing uglier than they are."

The spokesman for the Hoonoomaroo began grunting an unhappy message before Mellie could finish his own. "He say-say put down all guns. All fella come with him. No fella be apart from other fella. No hurt any fella. He very mad, say-say come *now*." Mellie put a great deal of expression in the translation.

Hawk felt his temper slipping away from him. He lifted the spoon of a grenade from his belt. He knew that he was being too extreme, but after a point, he couldn't even control himself.

"Ask him if he knows what this is?" He held up the little pineapple in the firelight. Mellie did as he was told, evidently going into an explanation of what it was. He spread his hands and made childish explosion noises with his mouth. The spokesman stepped back among his comrades and excited conversation followed. It was impossible to tell whether excited facial expressions accompanied the talking.

"Him know what bomb is," said Mellie. He had gotten up off the ground and stood at Hawk's side. The loss of confidence displayed by the Hoonoomaroo gave his own a boost. "Him hear you fellas and Saps fight all time."

"Tell him he's gonna hear it close up if he don't get these sonofabitches out of the goddam way!"

Mellie relayed the message. The spokesman stepped forward again, his eyes unseen behind the thick mask. The playful insects that covered the mask made his face appear to be in constant motion, like the flickering lights of some sort of electronic gadget. "Him say him change mind and will take just one fella," Mellie translated a long, monotone speech. "Rest fella can go."

"Nobody. Nobody goes. Clear the trail," Hawk ordered. Ned Albert stepped toward the torches at the head of the column. He began shoving them aside with his rifle muzzle.

The tribesmen watched this for a few moments. They were somewhat confused by this show of resistance. Hawk held up his grenade, that they might all see it and have yet something else to think about. The individual speaking for the Hoonoomaroo shouted a single word and the tribesmen responded by lunging for the torches. After they had picked them up, they remained standing in place, holding the flaming sticks over their heads. They made no move toward letting the Americans pass. The marines stood poised for a rush, but nothing happened. Hawk's patience ran out, He didn't want the Japanese alerted to his presence, but he didn't want to spend the rest of his life here, either. In the dangerous silence, where the only sound was the flapping of the torch flames, he stalked to the front of the column and up to one of the tribesmen blocking his way. He put the grenade back onto his shirt pocket and raised his machine pistol at the man. The personal nature of the situation didn't affect the Hoonoomaroo. He stood his ground. Hawk kicked him viciously in the groin, his boot hitting with a frightful thump.

The man screamed and fell to the ground, dropping his torch at Hawk's feet. His cries were muffled in the mask. Hawk took a step back to check the reaction of the others. No reaction. They remained staring at him from the eyeless helmets of dung. The flies leapt and darted away from the fallen man's mask. This presumably detracted from his cosmetic appeal.

"Move your goddam ass!" Hawk raged at them. The roar echoed through the jungle. The sergeant's voice was ungentle at its best; when he was angry, it was awesome. The tribesmen realized that this man was crazier than they were, but it was difficult for them to arrive at a unified course of action under the circumstances. He helped them out by kicking another one of them. This time they lunged at him and he disappeared behind a circle of them. They were not dull-witted enough to let him cripple each one of them at his leisure.

The marines watched the jostling circle of natives in paralyzed terror. Without Hawk, they were lost. Had the other natives attacked, they would have surrendered with little or no resistance. A gyrating muzzle flash lit up the circle of Hoonoomaroo as the Americans heard the muffled rip of Hawk's Thompson. The circle of attackers fell away, with the raging marine in pursuit. He swung his gun at their retreating backs, chopping into them without mercy. The blows came down with a snapping hardness as if they intended to sever heads from bodies, in the way that only a man with a true killer instinct can deliver them. Those that fell went under his boots and were stomped with the thoroughness of a wild stallion.

And yet the Hoonoomaroo did not panic. They dispersed quietly into the forest at the sides of the trail, leaving the dead and injured. Those at the rear of the column did not move at all. They stood watching and motionless, as if they were deaf and blind.

Hawk picked up the helmet that had fallen from his head. He gave another kick to a moaning victim and gestured Mellie forward to take up the march again. Mellie hesitated until Hawk came out with a stream of terrifyingly blasphemous obscenities that set everyone into motion. The Hoonoomaroo now seemed like the lesser of two evils. Mellie took halting steps and stayed beside Hawk, still too frightened to put himself in the forefront. Canlon was left in the uncomfortable rear position, facing an enormous crowd of the silent, hideous tribesmen. They shuffled sullenly behind him, only inches away. He stepped over the one Hawk had shot to death. The sergeant had purposely buried the muzzle tightly against the native's body to silence the loud report. It was difficult to tell how well the burst had been muffled. It was easy to tell it had been made at point-blank range.

"See that?" Canlon squeaked to the horde following him. "You see that?" No answer. The torchlight slithered hauntingly along the close leaves. Pungent smoke clouded the catacomb of a trail. The strange procession went on this way for half an hour, until the torches burned themselves out. The ash-covered Hoonoomaroo looked more than ever like ghosts in the darkness, following relentlessly behind Canlon. He noticed after a while, however, that they were dropping off from the rear of the crowd, and finally the last of them evaporated into the eternal forest. Canlon took this as a good sign, but he continued walking backwards for the most part.

Hawk ignored this little drama in the rear. "How far to this Hollow Mountain?" he asked Mellie in a low voice.

"Not far. Not far, now. You see." The woods eased a bit. Trees no longer blocked the sky. The trail widened. Canlon blew out a sigh that he had been holding in reserve. As he did, an arrow swished through the night and burrowed into Calloway's back. The Corpsman fell to one knee and uttered a surprised, "Oh!"

"Hit the deck!" Hawk ordered the men at the side of the trail. McGranger helped the wounded man to get under the cover of the trees. He didn't seem seriously injured. Hawk crawled over to them. "Hold still," he told Calloway, "I'll get it." He pulled the arrow out, using two hands and a knee in the other's back. The arrow had no head; it was only a sharpened stick.

"It burns like hell," Calloway said, contorting his narrow face.

"Put some of this on it." Hawk handed McGranger an envelope and the boy tore it open and sprinkled the contents into the small black hole in Calloway's upper shoulder.

Mellie crawled beside them. "We stay here till daylight. Hoonoomaroo maybe go away in daylight."

"Nope," Hawk replied as he handed McGranger a bandage marked "This side up."

"I gotta check this Jap place out in the dark." Fifteen minutes went by without a sound from the forest. Hawk was content to trade a little time for a little peace. He kept the men under the thick trees and hoped that his nocturnal hunters were waning in their determination. Hawk, Mellie and Canlon sat together with their backs against the trunk of a gigantic tree. Calloway and McGranger sat against a tree nearby.

"We shoulda brought that crazy guide with us," said Canlon. "That old Larsen guy. We could'a throwed him to these bastards and been on our way."

Hawk thought about that for a moment. "That's probably why he ain't here," he said.

Canlon snarled. "Yeah, he'd have both sides against him. He wasn't so dumb. Wonder what makes a guy that way?"

"Why don't you ask him?"

Canlon laughed. "I don't know. He's a big old bastard, you know."

"That must be why," McGranger called from the next tree. They all laughed at Joe and he joined in. They were forgetting their fears, things were returning to normal. Mellie leaned over and whispered confidentially to Hawk. He had the answer to their question. "Man hit with Hoonoomaroo arrow becomes Hoonoomaroo." Canlon overheard this. He repeated it loudly in his foghorn voice, "Hey, Calloway, a guy that's plugged with a Hooner arrow turns into one!" He brayed out his incredibly stupid laugh with great gusto, releasing all of his pent-up tensions.

"Superstition." Calloway answered seriously. He was a serious fellow. Jokes always went over his head. "The natives believe that stuff and then when they get hit with an arrow, they convince themselves that they're Hoonoomaroo."

Canlon nodded. Logic always impressed him. "Yeah," he said thoughtfully, "I bet that's true. I bet most of 'em ain't that way at all, they just *think* they are."

"Sure," said Calloway. "And then their old tribe thinks they are, too, so they got no choice but to throw in with the Hoonoomaroo." Calloway rubbed his shoulder. It was starting to hurt a little more. He turned his pained face toward the others. They were looking at him curiously.

5

Mr. Starrett, barrister and chief adviser to the Prime Minister of Malang, walked into the grimy office of Mr. Plunkett, the radio operator. He asked for a full report on Hawk's conversation with Carlisle and received a word for word account.

"The sergeant told the captain that Roger wasn't there, then?"

"That's right, Mr. Starrett. They talked of Sir Richard a bit, and the Hawk feller said he oughta be put in a strait jacket."

Starrett smiled. "A view that he alone holds, Mr. Plunkett?" Plunkett smiled. "This Hawk would be a valuable asset to our country. We could use a practical fellow such as that to keep the natives and the townspeople in line. He would make an excellent chief of staff for our military. He's ruthless enough to do the job, and yet too ignorant to be ambitious."

"I don't know, sir." Plunkett seemed skeptical. "He might be a pretty nice feller. He went after the boy and all and you know he didn't have to do that."

"Of course he did, Plunkett. Are you implying that a chief of staff should be without any moral character"

"No, sir. I'm just sayin' that I don't think he'd do it—and he *ain't* the sort of man to go openin' up your heart to with a bunch of stories. Another thing the captain mentioned...he tole me this Hawk has his doubts about the Japs stealing the boy at all."

Mr. Starrett raised his eyebrows. "Oh, really?"

"Yes sir. Says it don't make sense."

"I'll grant him that," Starrett said quietly. "I'll meet with Constable Powers and we'll go over his version of the story once again."

* * *

HAWK JUDGED there to be only a couple hours of darkness left. He had to get them moving. Calloway had long since got over the shock of his minor injury. Mellie went along without objection. He knew that it was getting too late for the Hoonoomaroo to attack and have a complete ceremony before dawn. They sometimes took prisoners for the following night's festivities, but that was rare; it usually happened when the victims had put up little show of resistance. He figured that the Hoonoomaroo had returned to their village and gone ahead with tonight's carrying on before it became too late. They wouldn't want the first night of the *tambaran* to go by without a little action.

Joe Canlon would have liked to have known all of this. He walked backwards until they came out of the forest. The trail forked at this point, one path going to the dock and the other to Hollow Mountain. The sea could be heard in the distance. The dark mountains rose against the deep rich blue of the morning's pre-dawn sky. A thick mist was in the air, and before long they all became soaked by it. It was cold, being wet in the dark that way. They came to a stream of salt water flowing away from the ocean. Failing to note this as anything remarkable, they slogged wordlessly along its course, with Mellie still in the lead. The forest was behind them, but thick, scraggly brush covered the rocky earth. The high rocks that were between them and the sea towered overhead. The ocean roared unusually loud on the far side of the rocks.

"Hollow Mountain," Mellie shouted and pointed at one of the shorter and wider of the rocks. A little waterfall spilled right out of its slope that faced them. The water looked white in the dim light. It emanated from an irregular hole in the so-called mountain. The waterfall was the source of the little stream that had led them here.

"That's it?" Hawk looked incredulously at the massive blue-black rock. "It's deader than hell around here. Where's all the goddam Japs?"

"Mellie no say see Saps. Mellie say what his people say. Mellie say no fella come back from inside Hollow Mountain for two moons."

Hawk looked at the gurgling waterfall, part of the way up the side of the slope. "Yeah, well, I'd say not comin' back from this country is pretty normal. What do you mean, inside? How do you get inside that rock?"

"Go through falling water. Big water ocean is inside mountain. Big water ocean leaks through hole in back of mountain."

Hawk's skepticism bordered on anger now. "Yeah?"

"Yes. Ocean is on other side of mountain. Way over our heads."

Hawk looked up at the top of the rock. Mellie was indicating that the ring of high rocks along the coast served as a natural levee, holding the ocean back from the below sea-level land behind it. "The ocean is up there?" Hawk pointed at the summit of Hollow Mountain. The guide nodded. "Let's climb on up there. I gotta see this shit!" Mellie cheerfully led the ascent. He wasn't worried. He might even go inside. White men knew how far they could push evil spirits. They should know, of course, since they were really spirits themselves from the afterlife, and were in fact the ancestors of Mellie's own people. He trusted this fellow.

A residue of slick salt adhered to the steep slope of Hollow Mountain. They lost their handholds several times and had to help each other in the climb. Mellie finally clambered onto the summit, huffing and puffing. Hawk trudged up after him and rolled onto the flat top of the peak. "You see? Big water ocean!" Mellie shouted into the wind.

"Kiss my ass, if it ain't!" The ocean spread magnificently before them. It was daylight out on its vast expanse, and yet still dark behind the mountain. It met the seaward slope of Hollow Mountain at a point five to ten yards below them. This was in spite of the fact that the earth was over a hundred feet below them on the back slope, and there it was ground. Hawk walked sideways down the slope and stepped into the lapping waves. Mellie latched onto his arm.

" You-fella don't walk in big water ocean. Mountain drop very fast on this side. You fall." He made a sucking noise with his mouth, indicating that the ocean was deep and that there was a powerful undertow.

"Yeah? I imagine so. Is this high tide or low or what?"

Mellie shrugged. "This high as water gets. Come right to top of mountain and stop, never go over. Just like beer in glass, eh?" Mellie laughed.

"Hmmph." Hawk looked off to the east. For a half mile, a ring of similar rock formations held back the sea from the low ground behind them. The other rocks were higher than Hollow Mountain. He would later assume that the rock had therefore been subjected to greater pressure and that was why it had been hollowed out.

Beyond the bastion of coastal rocks, the low ground rose gradually to the level of the ocean and a normal shoreline formed. He couldn't see how the coastline developed on the west due to the height of a neighboring mountain. He looked out at the sea. It was unspeakably intimidating to see and feel the awesome body of water up here on a mountaintop, and to know that he had been so far beneath it only a short while before. "Ain't that some shit, now?" he commented. "Show me where these people been disappearing."

Mellie led him back down the tricky slope. The others waited for them at the waterfall. The spot was so desolate, no one gave a thought to any danger of detection. Everyone seriously doubted that the Japanese would come to this absolute end of the earth. "Come," said Mellie, "in here is the place of the *omat*." Hawk looked at the flood of water blasting its way through the fissure in the rock.

"How could a man go inside that?" Hawk shouted

over the noise. Mellie, with great exaggeration, held his breath. "But that's the ocean leaking out that hole, right?"

"Yes," Mellie smiled gleefully, proud of his superior knowledge. The white man was probably testing him, to see how worthy he was of the next life. They did that sometimes. But Mellie was old and crafty and the white spirit was young. The only time the white spirits didn't play stupid was in the trading for cargo. White men were very serious about cargo. It was possible that the nether world was populated only by the rich.

"And so this mountain's full of water? It has to be, right?"

"Yes," Mellie answered.

"I don't know, Mellie. It'd be pretty crazy to go into something like that, wouldn't it? Wouldn't you get sucked out to sea or something?"

"Mellie *show* you-fella the place of the *omat*. We climb up, inside mountain to this place. Many years since Mellie go there. Never forget way. Last time Mellie come here, no ladder. We were much greater men in those days. Young people now very weak. You see. Hold breath." Hawk

looked over his shoulder. Joe Canlon was looking back at him.

"You wanta go, Joe?"

"Shit *no*, are you outa your mind?"

Hawk looked at the waterfall. He wasn't overly fond of water. The guide referred to a ladder. Maybe he wouldn't have to swim much. He stepped into the rushing cataract, which nearly knocked him over. "*Dogshit!* I...don't know, Mellie," he said skeptically as he regained his balance.

"You see. Come with me." Mellie waved away his doubts with a hand.

Hawk took off his shirt and helmet. "Awright, then. Let's do it." Mellie dove forcefully against the column of water and disappeared through the rock. Hawk looked back at Canlon. "I guess this is just about the dumbest thing I've ever done," he said, and with that, imitated his instructor. Canlon shook his head and looked at McGranger.

"That stupid bastard! He's gonna find out why people been disappearin', all right. What does he expect? I can see from here what would happen to a sonofabitch crazy enough to do that."

As soon as he ducked under the waterfall and cleared the thick rock wall of the mountainside, the great force of the current pushed down on Hawk's head, neck and shoulders. He managed to stand up in the dark interior without being cast back out through the waterfall. The water was around his waist, where it flowed through the wall and into the dawn of the outside world. He felt Mellie's hand on his wrist, pulling from above and guiding him toward something. He let his hand be placed on what he guessed to be a railroad spike driven into the rock wall of the inside of the slope. This must be the first rung of the ladder the native had spoken of. He pulled up against the crushing weight of the current and latched onto a second spike, some three feet above the first.

Hawk couldn't conceive of climbing to the top of the mountain and back in this manner, all on one breath of air. The exertion, not to mention the distance, was too great. But Mellie was doing it. The ocean was black around him, save for the shaft of shimmering light below, where it poured out into the salt water stream. He fought hand over hand, straining mightily until he had progressed high enough to utilize his feet and leg muscles on the spike ladder. After a few rungs, the downward pressure on his shoulders decreased, as if someone had deflated an elephant he had been carrying. He climbed easily and quickly, starkly aware that his lungs contained only a limited supply of air. After a few more feet, the current began rushing from below, pushing him upwards now, instead of down. The pushing wasn't gentle. The uplifting force became urgent and insistent, it was more difficult to resist than the downward pressure. This was irresistible by the sheer gravity and balance of the circumstances. His feet were torn free of the spikes. His hands hung onto them and the water lifted him into a horizontal position, and finally lifted his feet over his head and his hands. He let the shock of the predicament sink in for a few precious seconds. If he survived this, he vowed to never go into the water again. He could not climb through the enormous stretch of water, upside down, on his remaining air. He had to admit that he couldn't even get back down safely. Where was Mellie? So this was the end. Goddamn water. *Goddammit!*

Acting out of stubbornness, more than anything else, he reached awkwardly up for one last rung of the ladder. Instead of a spike, he felt a pipe embedded in the rock. He ran his fingers blindly along it and latched onto it with his other hand in a fit of panic. Silent death. Nothing peaceful about it, really. Trapped in the middle of somewhere. Struggling against the all-powerful. Both hands closed tightly around the pipe, a vertical one, running parallel to the rock wall and set about six inches out from it. Evidently, he was supposed to climb the pipe from this point on. That was interesting, but it wasn't going to do him any good. It was sort of like hearing on your deathbed who was elected president.

But as soon as both hands closed on the pipe and the spikes were left behind, the current lifted him rapidly up. The pipe whirred through his fingers, he couldn't stop himself. It was a natural elevator and he slid upwards much like a fireman slides down a pole. The uncontrolled exhilaration of the flight took his breath away. Water seeped through the gasket of his tightly closed lips. He shot skyward, knowing that at last he had taken that final journey of the truly foolhardy. His head popped above the surface of the water. Stale air choked with chemical fumes filled his lungs and he drank it in. Mellie was beside him in the water. They both clung to the pipe in defense against a surface current.

Hawk put a hand to his eyes and rubbed the salty water from his lids. Light was coming from somewhere. He saw Mellie, his fingers to his lips. They were inside the very top of Hollow Mountain, at the level where the sea lapped against the outside slope. A cavern with a ceiling at least twenty feet high arched overhead above the water. The cavern wasn't empty. In the middle of it was a little island. Hawk thought at first that it must be a man-made, floating island. Upon longer study, he noticed the smooth stone along its banks. The boiling of the current had polished its rock shore into a shiny gem. Apparently, some sort of rock formation reached from down below on the floor of Hollow Mountain and right up to the water's surface, creating the island.

The wonder of all this was necessarily subdued by

the observation of more threatening matters. Men dressed in fundoshi were strutting about on the island, talking loudly to one another, their voices reverberating wildly off the grotto's stone walls.

On one end of the rock island were racks of torpedoes, stacked liked bunkbeds on top of one another. On the other end, massive fuel tanks rested in their wooden supports. Beside these were batteries, chargers and generators, some hooked up and in operation. Several of the men formed a line handing torpedoes to each other to be loaded onto a midget submarine that lay contentedly on the top of the water. This was the manufacturing plant for all the death and grief that plagued Allied shipping in the Straits of Cavazo. Families in Liverpool, in Amsterdam, in Columbus and in Portland would wait in vain for their sons to return because of this place. Hawk felt the impact of this immediately, upon first sight of the clever little operation. The idea of being in the presence of such goings-on made him want to strike out and destroy the laborers, so safe and snug here beneath the world. Instead he clung quietly to the pipe, his head just above the water, doing and saying nothing. The laborers were either Japanese or Korean. The submarines were definitely Japanese.

An arc light was bolted into the rock over their heads. It lit the entire cavern, though there were shadows around its edges. The air stank with carbon monoxide and fishy odors. The ventilation system, wherever it was, was a poor one. On the island's polished bank, a chair faced the water where the two intruders bobbed in the dark current. This was evidence that at some point a lookout had been posted there, watching that side of the cave where the natives normally entered; and thus it was that they had perished upon unwittingly stumbling across him. Through some stroke of luck, the guard was absent.

The bustling diligence of the enemy aroused Hawk's vicious temper. The little submarine that they were loading right this minute would kill an untold number of unwary men on the high seas. And he could do nothing about it. Kiss those suckers goodbye. All he could do would be to alert the air liaison. A couple of blockbusters ought to blow this rock to hell, and flood the jungle behind it. Every second wasted was costing someone his life. And yet he wanted *that* sub. He wanted to save the men *it* would kill. Common sense told him he couldn't have it. And that hurt.

As they watched, a second submarine emerged from the sinister current like some deadly reptile. This one, almost twice the length of the first, was still only a midget. A glass window was in its little conning tower, right in front of the periscope. Three fins were visible at its stern and in the bow were two torpedo tubes, one on top of the other like an over and under shotgun. Its tiny U-shaped hatch flopped open with an echoing clank. A man dressed in a wilted naval uniform climbed half way out of it. The size of this second craft made Hawk question the capacity of the Hollow Mountain depot. While there might have been room enough for an I-Boat along the side of the loading pier, and the cavern was spacious enough to accommodate it, it seemed that there would be a problem in maneuvering the larger underwater boats. He wasn't sure of this. He had never driven a submarine. He knew submariners, especially Japanese submariners, were an imaginative and fearless lot. Such a thing was not entirely out of the question. One factor important to the entering of larger craft could be the size of the opening on the seaward slope of the mountain. This was the gateway to the Pacific Ocean, as well as being the source of intake for the water that filled the rock. He would ask his guide later how big this hole was. Getting out of here alive was the critical problem of the moment. Getting *in* alive hadn't been easy, and he expected the exit to be even worse.

Hawk searched the walls and ceiling for an easy way out. Solid rock. It would be impossible to dive against the tremendous upward flow of the current. He felt like a cat that has climbed a tree and can't come down. His mind was so preoccupied with this difficulty that he lost all interest in observing his enemies. He just wanted out. He pointed downward. Mellie shook his head. Hawk stared at him. Mellie pointed to the far side of the cavern, the one bordering the ocean. Hawk deduced that a special way down must be on the other side of the island. That was logical. The current probably ran in a strong undertow on that side, just as it flowed upward on this side. The water flooded into the mountain and left it in a frantic circular swirl of currents.

Mellie edged along the side of the cave, keeping to the unlighted shadows. Spikes were driven into the walls of the cavern, just beneath the churning water. Had they not been, the current probably would have snatched Hawk up, drowned him and spat his crushed body out God knows where. Entry into Hollow Mountain was extremely risky, even for an avid and skilled diver such as Mellie. The Japanese were probably all divers. Hawk was not.

Circumnavigating the grotto gave Hawk an excellent view of the enemy submarines. The larger of them had a fierce rising sun with rays stenciled on its bow. The loading docks could service several boats of this size simultaneously. Throwing his head over his shoulder at nervous intervals, Hawk counted at least ten laborers on the island. Other Japanese milled about in white uniforms. Some of them wore black caps with abrupt visors that jutted straight down over their foreheads. On the ocean side of the base was a cramped recreation area. Two men sat smoking in canvas folding chairs. The white in Hawk's eyes grew larger as he watched his dread foe from this ringside seat. Their innocent smiles were mocking and cruel to him. Their voices were bestial. They were talking about him. He knew that was ridiculous, but he couldn't help but feel that way. Every time a new voice barked, he looked again over his shoulder. "Goddam Japs," he whispered.

He took some comfort from the assumption that if they did discover him, they would have to shoot him. They wouldn't risk trying to capture him in the treacherous waters. He bumped into Mellie. The native had stopped, he was pointing down toward the floor of Hollow Mountain. Hawk nodded. He reached under the water for the next handhold, that he might start down.

He felt nothing. Really nothing. The wall of the cave was gone. The ravenous current pulled so strongly at his legs, that he feared the spike he clung to would be torn from the rock. It took all his strength to hold his head above the water. Mellie broke his silence in order to explain what was to follow. He struggled to get closer to the marine. He spoke in a low voice, barely audible above the blaring hush of the rushing current. "You must let go," Mellie told him.

"I'll drown."

"No drown. Water take you down to bottom, very fast. Get on bottom and find holds in rock. Move toward light, that is way out."

"Why ain't there no wall here?"

"This side is big hole. Whole front of mountain is big hole."

Hawk contemplated that. He looked at the interwoven seams of the current that coiled around him. Before he knew it, Mellie had taken a deep breath and released his spike. The sea sucked him under in a fraction of a second. Hawk stared at the ominous sight. He looked up at the Japanese. They were going about their tasks in comparative safety. He envied them.

He was all alone now. "Sonofabitch," he growled and loosened his grasp. There wasn't a chance for any second thoughts. The undertow grabbed him and lashed him beneath the surface. The crushing pressure felt like a huge hand squeezing his entire body. He had a sensation of rapid movement as he shot through the black void. He abandoned himself to the whims of the undertow. The great squeezing fist relented after a surprisingly short period of time, turning instead into fingers, gentle but firm, twirling him about and finally depositing him on the bottom of Hollow Mountain. His feet bounced off the rocky floor of the sea-bottom. He found himself totally disoriented. He reached out for a wall or a handhold, daring not to try any bold swimming strokes, lest they cast him out into the Pacific that lay outside the mountain. He floated about for a few seconds, until his outstretched hand brushed stone. He opened his eyes and hugged the rock. The current was virtually nonexistent down here. The oppressive darkness was relieved by a faint light in the distance ahead of him. He could make out a line of spikes in the stone, leading to the shaft of light. Using the spikes, he walked spirit-like on the calm water of this mysterious world. When he stepped into the shaft of light, he felt the water pushing him through the hole in the wall. He let it. He burst through the waterfall and into the welcome air of the dank New Guinea morning.

Mellie stood in the stream below him. Farther behind him were the other men. Mellie smiled broadly. Hawk took a deep breath and smiled weakly back at him. Canlon jogged up to them. "I thought you two lost your ass for sure. What happened?" he asked.

"We found it," Hawk said quietly.

"You're shittin' me! The subs?"

"That's right. Right up there." Hawk gave him an abbreviated version of the story. Calloway walked up from along the bank and suggested that the enemy might have guards in the vicinity. No one paid much attention to him. Hawk went over to his shirt and took a cigar out of it. "We gotta get back now and tell 'em about this. This is pretty important shit here."

"Crap," Canlon shook his head, "I'm too tired to go all that way back." Hawk sat on the bank near the falls and lit his cigar.

"Well it'd take a lotta time and trouble to go back the way we come here," he said.

"Yeah," Canlon agreed, "we got the Japs and the other guys to wade through again."

Hawk called Mellie over and questioned him about alternate routes to New Oss. Mellie felt that the way through the swamp was the fastest way back, because boats could be used to cross it. But one could also follow the coastline and get back to the town in only a slightly longer period of time. There would be no Hoonoomaroo along the coast, and so far as anyone knew, no Japanese.

"But," Mellie added, "Nodu maybe on coast. They say Saps push them out of forest. Nodu bad fellas. You better with Hoonoomaroo than Nodu."

Hawk sighed. He just wanted to go back by the fastest route, he didn't care about the danger. "What do you think?" he asked Canlon.

"When you get right down to it," Canlon said, "I'd rather risk running up against anything but Japs. And them Japs gave us some kind of shit back in that swamp."

"Okay," Hawk nodded and dragged on his cigar. The Japanese could slow them up a lot more than natives. They could slow them up permanently and in short order.

The men sluggishly prepared for the return along the coast. The heat was stifling. One factor that no one had stopped to consider was that when they crossed the swamp, they had had fifty men. Seven would be returning along the coast. Hawk didn't worry about it. The kidnapping of Roger once more occupied his thoughts. In the overall analysis, he considered one-third of his problems solved. He had found the submarine base, and someone else would have to destroy it; if, that is, he, or any of the others, lived to tell the story back in New Oss. After surviving the entry into Hollow Mountain, he felt that this was a minor detail.

He was no closer, however, to solving the mystery of Roger's whereabouts than he was on the day of the abduction. He walked along quietly, thinking. He decided to go over Constable Powers's story more thoroughly upon reaching town. That was all he could do on that score for the time being. He came to realize that if a new lead didn't fall out of the sky, the case of Roger St. Cyr was as good as closed. In which instance, two-thirds of his problems might already be as solved as ever they could be.

The last third was the situation in New Oss. The garrison wasn't enough to meet the type of force that the Japanese indicated they were willing to use on the town. The enemy had demonstrated that they were interested in taking the port. The Allies were not responding. They were willing to let them have it. Richard St. Cyr wasn't helping any. That was all fine, except that Hawk and part of a battalion would be there when the end came. He could see it all developing clearly, inevitably, like a train wreck. This should have been the easiest of the problems to solve. For some perplexing reason, it wasn't. And it was the problem with the most disastrous consequences if left unsolved.

The return trip was a fated affair from the beginning. The coastal route turned out to be fraught with nameless perils. After the trip through the swamp to Ranke's, Hawk was convinced that the coastal route could be no worse. He had learned very little of the temperament of the jungles of Malang.

The first obstacle encountered was common enough. When they left the rocky region near Hollow Mountain, they came to a sandy beach, the first they had seen in New Guinea. Strewn across the narrow strip were half-buried Japanese mines. The tides had partially excavated most of them. The pattern in which the mines had been laid was easily deciphered by inspecting those exposed. They were arranged similarly to the dots on a dice roll of five. Satisfied that he understood this grim code, Hawk chose to walk through the minefield, rather than trying to skirt it. He led the way, trusting his own powers of deduction. They followed by stepping in his footprints.

The field was put there, obviously, to protect the submarine base from surprise visitors. Minefields probably ringed the whole Hollow Mountain area. Providence had somehow guided them through this barrier. No purpose could be served by marking the field, it would only tip off the enemy that someone was aware of their base. Hawk stood at the far end of the field and watched the others cross it. His cigar was tucked defiantly into the corner of his mouth. Cowardly weapon, the mine. But war was cowardly. Invariably it exterminated or maimed the best of a generation and left the less bold to procreate. Oddly enough, that thought actually occurred to dimwitted Sgt. Hawk as he watched his weathered men sweat their way through the mines.

The next obstacle was an even more familiar one. The beach tapered away and once again the savage forest grew right into the sea. It defied any attempt at hacking a path through it. The woody vines were woven into an impenetrable network, as strong as meshed steel cables, with thorns as forbidding as barbed wire. Once a vine was severed, twenty more fell into its place. Tall, gloomy trees hung out over the ocean, cutting off the light and harboring the hungriest brood of filthy mosquitoes that ever plagued mankind. They were so numerous that their long, translucent legs touched those of their swarming fellows, as if they were all holding hands. The men had to blow them out of their mouths and eyes every few steps.

As he fought these common difficulties, Hawk suffered from a private malady. He felt lightheaded. His limbs were weak from dizziness and he had trouble breathing and swallowing. He thought at first that this was caused by breathing and swallowing the mosquitoes. As the affliction wore on, however, he became certain that it was malaria. He was the only man he knew without at least a touch of the disease. When the requisite chills and fever failed to appear, he didn't know what to think. It went away at last, and he dismissed it as a passing weakness. He was too young to consider it being anything serious. He never gave the bends a thought. Neither did anyone else, because he didn't complain.

They slogged along the muddy shoals under the vile trees until the glare out on the ocean died and they knew night was coming. They began preparations for camp well before dark, in order to avoid the confusion that accompanies the sudden and violent fall of a tropical night. Calloway was weak from the hike and the wound in his shoulder. He didn't help them hack out a campsite. Mellie encouraged all of them with his estimate of reaching New Oss before noon of the following day.

Hawk took the first watch. He wanted to stay up a while and make sure his dizziness had left for good. The thought of dying out here in his sleep was sort of degrading. Calloway's shoulder was hurting him and he couldn't sleep. So far as anyone knew, he hadn't turned into a Hoonoomaroo. He got up and walked over to Hawk to pass the time. The sergeant was in a shallow hole covered with mosquito netting, idly watching the husky insects as they bounced forcefully off the net.

Calloway sat down, outside the net. He gingerly touched his shoulder. "This thing's getting infected, I think," he said.

"Think the arrow was poisoned or something?"

"No, but it wasn't the cleanest thing I've ever been stuck with."

"Yeah," Hawk snorted. "You oughta wash it in the salt water. That would help."

"Ah, I don't know. That water's like a toilet. No telling what-all I'd catch splashing around in that stuff. That's if the sharks and mosquitoes didn't haul me off."

"I guess you're right."

"I ain't ready to die yet."

"No," said Hawk.

Calloway eventually got too exhausted to stay awake and wandered back to his own hole. He slept a little closer to the forest than the others. He felt exposed near the water. Hawk was relieved by McGranger, and fell asleep immediately, completely forgetting about his illness. He wasn't much of a worrier. He was awakened at midnight.

"Hawk! Get up!" Canlon whispered. The sergeant opened his eyes, his hand on the trigger guard of his submachine gun. Joe's tone alerted him to the fact that all was not well. Canlon was crouching over him, his eyes large and white. He was greatly distraught and couldn't seem to say anything. McGranger was with him. Evidently the danger wasn't too pressing, or one or the other of them would have the presence of mind to say the word "Japs!" Hawk sat up. No, this was something strange.

"I didn't see a thing. I didn't hear anything. I don't see how it could've happened," said McGranger. He was on watch. He sounded like a sobbing child. Hawk was getting tired of playing father.

"What's goin' on?" he asked gruffly.

"You better take a look...you better go see," Canlon choked. Hawk slapped his net out of the way with angry impatience, but he stood up cautiously. Mellie ran up to him. He put his bony fingers on Hawk's wrist. "Nodu," he said. Shelvin came and stood behind Mellie. Hawk sensed that they were all gathering around him for protection or reassurance. Somebody was missing. Ned Albert was out in the water, looking down the coast toward the east. Somebody else was missing.

"What's up?" Hawk insisted.

"They...uh...got Calloway...I...well, see what you think...I don't know." Canlon started crying. Canlon was no kid. Hawk looked long and hard at him. Joe never met his eyes. Hawk looked away.

"Well, where are they?" the sergeant snarled at Mellie. He didn't see any arrows flying. What were all the dramatics for?

"Not here. Gone," the guide answered.

Hawk sighed. "All right. Where's Calloway? Did they leave the body?"

Canlon pointed toward Albert. "There," he said, "there he is." Hawk walked out into the water. He saw the reflections of flames on the sea before he saw the grisly reality. About a hundred feet down the shoreline, a headless torso was fastened to a dead tree by means of a stake driven through its chest. A low fire lapped at its legs, which had been reduced to black powder. Where the head had been was a sprig of brush. The right hand was reaching for the absent head. The two wrist bones were bared and partially burned, though the reaching hand was still fleshed and intact. The most arresting aspect of all was that the hand was opening and closing, spasmodically trying to grab the sprig that replaced the head.

Hawk couldn't suppress a gasp. As insensitive as barbed wire, he was still visibly shaken by the obscenity. He didn't say anything. It spoke for itself. He couldn't tear his eyes from the handiwork of the Nodu. The others couldn't look at it. He looked from beneath his brows at the threatening jungle. A dark, primitive and fearful passion swelled in his chest. It was madness. Madness on a string. He fought to hold it, to control it.

A human voice came from far away, from reality, from the tunnel on the other side of his insane rage. "Do...do you think he's...alive? I mean, should we help him, it looks like he's trying to..." Canlon lapsed into fitful babbling.

Hawk took a long deep breath. "Jesus Christ! His head's gone, Joe. He's dead! You can't help him. That's just reflexes, or a drug or they stabbed a nerve or something...but he couldn't be alive." Talking helped Hawk control himself. Canlon faced Calloway again.

Joe wanted to help the corpse, but he was too repulsed by it. McGranger had already thrown up and he was about to do it again. "God!" Joe said and walked back to his hole. Ned Albert and McGranger faced the nearby forest with their rifles locked and loaded.

Hawk slid a cigar from his shirt pocket and jammed it between his teeth. He lit it, holding the match up until it burned itself out. He desperately hoped that this would attract the Nodu. He longed for them. "They'll die for this," he told Mellie under his breath. "I'll kill every one of the sonofabitches." His eyes bored into the horrible image until Mellie thought that the mad gaze would make the torso disappear in an explosion of angry white man's magic. But it didn't. Pay them back, Hawk thought more rationally now. Pay them back. Yes, that was what you were supposed to do. Ah, yes. I forgot what to do there, for a moment. Fire. An awful way to die.

"Bad fellas," Mellie whimpered.

6

THE NIGHT OOZED BY LIKE A SNAKE. NO ONE SLEPT. THEY lived in the waking nightmare. It was Hawk's fault that the patrol didn't make it to New Oss by noon. He abandoned all his responsibilities and went off into the bush with Mellie to get a fix on the Nodu village. It took a total of five hours to go there and back to the coast. Mellie took him to the shores of a lake covered with a layer of scum icing. He made a crude map of the filthy hamlet's location. It could barely be seen on the far side of the lake. Mellie was afraid of the mere sight of the hut roofs in the distance. Hawk hoped for trouble, and though he made himself available for it by his bold reconnaissance, none developed. He was certain that he was being observed, even if his five senses told him otherwise. They went back to the coast and the patrol returned to New Oss before dark.

"I'll never get used to the killing," McGranger confided to Hawk as they entered the safety of the town.

Hawk looked at his feet as he walked. "There's a

trick to it," he said. "Don't look at dead people. Not till you start to liking it. Then it don't matter no more."

The sergeant took Canlon with him over to St. Cyr's mansion. About an hour of daylight remained. He figured he better let Carlisle know what was going on. When they got there, they were told that the captain was eating and had asked to not be disturbed. The two marines walked back out into the street and waited there. They could have made a big show and burst in with the urgent message, but Hawk wasn't that way. His mean streak extended even to the social side of life. Carlisle thought he was being cute by making himself inaccessible. Let him wait for the information. Maybe he would change his ways when he found out what he'd done. Maybe he wouldn't. Hawk didn't care.

Miss Asquith stood by the closed door of the second floor veranda. Through its many glass panes she could see the coming of evening to the street below. Diana St. Cyr stood beside her. Miss Asquith put her arm around Diana's shoulder. On the ground before them they could see the two marines waiting in front of the mansion. Miss Asquith decided to cheer Diana up with a bit of joking.

"Can Captain Carlisle come out and play?" she said, Diana laughed. She liked Miss Asquith. Some day she would be just like her. They stared at the two men with a sort of disgusted interest. A green glow surrounded the marines. They were covered with foliage stains, slime, and the fungus mold that grew on anything that entered the damp jungle for any period of time. Hawk spat a stream of black chewing tobacco into the street. Canlon was innocently blowing his nose with his thumb and without the aid of a handkerchief.

"There are two fine specimens of manhood," Miss Asquith took the opportunity to observe, "an extraordinary mixture of manners, culture and intelligence."

"Chewing tobacco must be the dirtiest thing a person could do," said Diana.

"Oh, I'm certain that clearing one's nose with one's finger ranks in there somewhere," Miss Asquith said light-heartedly.

"Are all Americans that crude?" Diana asked.

"Heavens, no! They *are* all crude, but not *that* crude. Take Captain Carlisle. He has some manners, and even some exposure to culture. I'm told that he's fairly well educated. Too excitable. That's the way Americans are, for the most part. Too emotional. They don't mature until midlife, I'm afraid. Their lives are too easy and they shirk responsibility. They either master a task quickly or give it up. Poor Captain Carlisle. How bright could he be if he takes advice from that animal down there in the street?"

"It's their cross-breeding, Father says. The classes mix too readily in America. The lower class traits always dominate in their offspring." Miss Asquith put her thumbs impatiently in the pockets of her riding breeches at this.

"You mustn't take all of your father's views seriously, dear. It's rather obvious that Sergeant Hawk's ancestors have never mixed with any class higher than his own. His bloodline is thoroughbred peasant, untainted since his relatives first slithered from beneath the rocks. You can rest assured that they came to America chained in the hold of a prison ship. That's how Americans in the southern part of the country got there, you know, much the same as Australians. And they don't associate with the Americans in the north."

"Yes," said Diana. "Of course, one would think that he had possibilities, were he to clean himself up a bit. He looked quite different in his uniform. He's rather attractive—in a crude sort of way," she hastened to add. Diana looked to Miss Asquith for confirmation.

"Isn't he, though?"

* * *

HAWK AND CANLON were finally granted the privilege of an interview with the captain. The officer commandeered the use of Sir Richard's study for the meeting. Hawk dropped the first bombshell before sitting down.

"Pharmacist's Mate Calloway's dead, sir. Killed by natives." The sergeant slumped into Sir Richard's favorite easy chair. Canlon stood uneasily at the door. Carlisle sat at the desk, turned away from it and toward Hawk. "How terrible," said the captain.

"Yeah. It was."

"Did you find out...anything?"

"Yeah. I found it, all right."

"You're kidding! Splendid!" Carlisle stood up with a big smile. He walked toward the stretched-out reporter in the chair. "Where is it, Sergeant?" Carlisle seemed a little more formal to Hawk since he had been on his own for a couple of days.

"Place called Hollow Mountain. An underwater cave." Hawk's taciturn methods of communication prevented him from going into the remarkable set of natural phenomena that had made the secrecy of the base possible. "Tell 'em to bomb the shit out of it," the sergeant said authoritatively. He lit a cigar. "Something else," he blew out the smoke and leveled his dark gaze on the captain. "I thought about telling you that this Nodu village was a Jap hideout, so's you'd call an airstrike on it. But I'm gonna play it straight. Them bastards killed an American. They...uh...what'd you say they call that, Joe?"

"Desecrated?" Joe rasped quietly in his boxer's voice.

"That's right, they desecrated the body. Made us madder'n shit. You tell the air liaison or the Army Air Force that them sonofabitches been harassin' us. Tell 'em they're a menace to the war effort and all that kind of dogshit. I want you to get 'em to bomb the goddam place flat." He reached into the pocket of his grime-stiffened shirt. "Here's a map of it."

"Sure. Sure, Hawk." Carlisle still wore his smile of jubilation. "What about the base? What are the coordinates and all? Boy, is this going to make us look good!"

Hawk got up slowly and walked over to an enormous map on the southern wall of the room. Sir Richard had purchased it from a printer in Sydney. It had "Republic of Malang" written in Gothic letters across the top of it. He had to have a lot of the maps printed up, and it wasn't cheap, but it was worth it to the Prime Minister. In spite of this little bit of petty history behind the chart, it was a good one; the best ever made of Malang. Hawk ran his finger along the coast, where the elevation was below sea level. This was marked with a dark green color on the map.

"Damn good map," Hawk mumbled. "It's in these rocks right here, sir," he said pointing to the unmarked location of Hollow Mountain. Ranke's dock was clearly marked. It was to the west of the rocks. Carlisle came over and scribbled down the coordinates as best he could figure them to be. He used a home-made overlay sketched on a sheet of wax paper.

"Excellent. I'll get a coded message and we'll radio it to Regiment. Boy, I bet they never thought we'd pull this off when they abandoned us in this hell hole!"

"Naw. Probably not." Hawk looked down the map for the Nodu village. Their lake was well marked on the map. "Don't forget this shitpile over here, sir. The Nodu village. Here it is."

"Oh, yes. You bet." Carlisle made a great show of writing down the coordinates. "We'll teach those buggers a lesson," he said. "What about the boy?" Carlisle asked, still working over the map.

"I'm gonna start over on that one, sir."

"Good. Okay, I'll send this now. I can't wait to hear what they say. You guys can stretch out in here, if you want. Turn on that other fan, if you like. I'll have some food sent up. It might take a while to get a response."

"Thanks, Captain," Canlon said with a sheepish grin. He found it hard to talk since the corpsman's death. He found himself thinking a lot and not paying attention to the outside world. Hawk threw himself back into his chair after the officer left and finished his cigar. It was dark outside and heavy rain was beating on the windows. An Indonesian servant brought the dinner a little later. It was an elaborate meal, but neither one of them finished it. Their appetites were gone.

Canlon lay back on the immaculate sofa and tried to take a nap. He hung his boots over the side. He felt odd about taking them off. Even in New Oss, he felt unprepared with his boots off. Some men could sleep naked on the front line, but not Joe Canlon. He finally began to spout a fitful chorus of snores. The snores were inter-rupted by wails and moans from the depths of his unruly nightmares.

"Shit." Hawk grumbled at the noise. He was tired but he'd been thinking. He got up and went outside. The rain had stopped. People were coming back onto the streets, resuming the tasks that the rain had inter-rupted. A few people had already turned in for the night, but the town seemed unusually active. He directed his steps to the office of Constable Powers. He was intercepted in the middle of the main street by Mr. Starrett, the adviser.

"How are you, Mr. Starrett?"

"Fine, just fine, my boy. I've heard that Ranke denies any knowledge of the boy. Is that correct?"

"Yessir, that's the way it is."

"Do you believe him?"

"Yessir."

"I don't."

Hawk stopped in front of Powers's office. It had an electric light bulb dangling over the front door. Gener-ally, the houses in New Oss had one generator for about three homes. Powers's office was in an area where five businesses were connected to one decrepit unit. His office was an uncommonly run-down building with a wild animal cage sitting on the wooden sidewalk out in front of it. Two natives sat sullenly inside the cage, staring through the bars at the white men. "Why not?" Hawk asked, taking a second glance at the two prisoners huddled in the dark. What a place. "I don't think the Japs done it, myself. It don't make no sense at all. I know that the German ain't in with the Japs, he's been fightin' 'em. I know he's a German and all, but it'd take a pretty low crock of piss to side with them bastards."

Constable Powers walked out of his opened door when he heard voices. A stomach-turning scent of alcohol accompanied him. He'd aged another sixty years since Hawk had seen him last.

Mr. Starrett put a friendly hand on Hawk's dirty shoulder. "But something has come to light in your absence that will dispense with all your suspicions," Starrett smiled triumphantly. Hawk looked into his little eyes for a moment and said, "What's that?" The single light bulb reflected as a white dot on each little eyeball. "Show him, Constable Powers," said Starrett.

The old man took a hand grenade out of his pocket. "The constable neglected to tell you that he saw the kidnappers drop this. Proof positive that they were Japs. You will notice that it is Japanese in make—I'm sure that you've encountered them before?"

"Mmm hmm." Hawk looked at the grenade and then at the two men. He had a strange feeling that these two birds were up to something. That something might even be kidnapping. Starrett's motive probably had something to do with the takeover of the worthless government of Malang from St. Cyr. Crazy, greedy bastards! Haul a kid off somewhere for this cheap hole in the ground. They may have even killed him. His face showed no change of expression. He had carried that grenade for four months. It was the one he had given to Roger. Or was it? Thousands of them had been manufactured. It was scratched and smudged. Any grenade would be in a similar condition after having been carried for a while. No, it was the same one, he was pretty sure. Roger himself could have dropped it.

"You seen a Jap drop this—I mean you seen a *real* Jap drop this in the street on that day, with your own eyes?"

"I did," Powers insisted. That covered that.

"And why is this just comin' out now?" Hawk asked, betraying no emotion, other than his characteristic crankiness.

"I figured my word was good enough around here," croaked the constable. "Didn't know I was being thought of as daft—or a damned liar." The crusty old-timer looked at Starrett. Starrett nodded consolingly at him. "Besides, that's a collector's item, that is. Some so-and-so is sure to steal it, if word got out that I got it."

Hawk pulled at his straight, narrow nose. "Mind if I take a look at it?" Powers handed it to the American. The marine weighed it in his hand. The body of that type of grenade made up the bulk of its weight. The body's exploding is where its shrapnel came from; there was none inside, only powder. It was difficult to tell by holding it whether there was a charge inside. He knew that Roger's had no charge, he had removed it himself. The other two looked blankly at Hawk. They had no idea of what he was up to. "Mind if I keep this?" he asked them.

"I sure do," Powers squawked. "You see there, what did I tell you? You're already trying to lift it off me!"

Hawk's lips tightened. If he handed the grenade back to Powers, he would never see it again. He didn't want to, but he had to play his hand right here and now. He was tired. He wasn't in the mood for this. But he had to know. He screwed the fuse off the little bomb.

The two observers took a step back. "He's blowin' her!" Powers cried. The two native prisoners stood up in their squalid cage. Starrett didn't say anything. He knew that a man wouldn't intentionally do something to jeopardize his own life. He had never been in the United Sates Marine Corps, or fought Japanese.

"Take it easy, you goddam old fossil," Hawk growled. He lifted out the detonator. The interior of the shell was packed with a black bursting charge. Hawk's eyebrows flinched. Wrong again. It wasn't Roger's. Roger's was disarmed. He screwed the detonator back. "Be careful with this thing," he advised, tossing it back to Powers. "It's a good one. Take the charge out of it if you're gonna go fartin' around with it."

Mr. Starrett made no attempt to understand what that little ceremony was all about. He saw Hawk's confused expression. "I know it seems unusual," Starrett smiled, "but I think the sooner you admit to yourself that the Japanese are behind this, the sooner you will be able to find Roger. We are all distressed by this. I was a second father to the boy. His own was a trifle addled, as you know..." Mr. Starrett cleared his throat. He knew that he had gone too far. He restated that. "Well, I meant that...being so preoccupied as he is with government and world affairs, a man cannot devote proper attention to his personal life." Starrett rocked on his heels. "One can either be a good public figure or a good family man, but seldom both."

"Yeah." Hawk stared at Powers. The constable shuffled anxiously. "So, six Japs, you say?"

"Right you are. Big as you please," said Powers.

"Okay. We'll probably need some air recon to find the kid. I don't know, any more. I'll keep y'all posted. I gotta get back to the captain."

Back at the mansion, Canlon was still asleep. Hawk

sat down and dozed for about an hour before Carlisle returned. He opened his eyes when the captain came into the study. His hand was on his submachine gun. It was a habit.

Carlisle looked over at Canlon's open mouth. "How can you sleep with all that racket going on?" he asked.

"We ain't sleepin'," Hawk shook his head groggily. "What'd they say?"

"Well, you're going to like some of it and some of it, you won't. I'll give you the good news first."

Hawk rubbed his forehead. He didn't like games. "Fair enough," he said.

"General Neatz of the Army Air Force says he'll personally see to it that the Nodu village is, and I quote, 'reduced to ashes.'"

"That is good news."

"But, he says it'll have to wait until the sub base is knocked out. He doesn't want to endanger the strike or let the Japs know we've been into the area."

"Humph. They been flyin' over that coast like a bunch of bastards for the past couple weeks. The Japs don't give a shit about that. Is this general from Europe or something? We ain't dealin' with real people here, you know."

Carlisle shrugged. "That's what he says, anyway." Neither man realized that the general had no intention of destroying a village of civilians. In order to be true to his word, he might send warning planes over it, to fake a strafing, and once the natives had been alerted and evacuated, only then would he bomb the vacant dwellings. Hawk most certainly would not have liked that. He was callous. Right and wrong were muddled for him. He considered the killing of the corpsman to be an act of war, deserving a just retribution. General Neatz saw extermination of a tribe as a great sin. The crime of the natives was merely one of ignorance. Hawk, on the other hand, had little tolerance for ignorance. He was ignorant, and he hadn't noticed anyone tolerating him. Tolerance was hard to come by in his profession.

"Anyway, it gets a little worse," Carlisle said. "They aren't going to bomb the sub base either. He says they've flown all over that coast without spotting a thing. They want the target marked by men on the ground, so they can do some heavy pinpoint bombing. They want white phosphorous on Hollow Mountain, before they do anything." Carlisle looked up. He didn't think Hawk would like that.

"That don't matter. Bupta's over there. He can do it," said Hawk.

"Does he have the willie peter?"

"No, but he can build a fire on it or any damn thing. The Japs ain't guarding the outside of it. That's why it's so hard to find. And ground troops can't get at the thing, so it's safe for them anyway. Artillery can't get into the area, mortars couldn't crack it. Planes or ships'll have to do it."

Carlisle nodded and shrugged. He wasn't worried. He didn't have to go back through that country. "There's more, Hawk. They want it marked and they want some charges planted so that it's sure to crack. You'll have to go back. They want to observe it for a couple of days. They say it's the logical location for the hits on the Straits of Cavazo, but they want to confirm that."

Hawk hung his head and looked at the carpet on the floor. He *knew* that *somehow* that was going to happen. He honestly did not want to go back. "All right," he sighed. Maybe he could delegate some of this misery to someone else. He knew better than that, too.

"Another thing." Carlisle guiltily knitted his brow, but Hawk wasn't looking at him. "I sort of let them think that...well, that I, *personally*, had found the thing. I mean I didn't *say* that, but they kind of got that idea and I didn't correct them...I...I'm sorry, I mean, I'll straighten it all out."

Hawk put his chin in his hand. "It don't matter. Forget it. Where are these charges gonna be planted?"

"Uh...RDX on the outside and some straight gelatin on the inside," Carlisle answered, looking at his notes. He was relieved at Hawk's reaction. He wouldn't even have to correct anything. Hawk didn't care.

"The inside?" Hawk hung his head again. They wanted a charge on the inside of Hollow Mountain. That meant *he* would have to do it. He was the only man who had ever been into the cave.

"Yes. And a few last details here that I overlooked. While you're in there, look for any evidence that they're shipping ground troops through the base. They've spotted over a company of Japs on the edge of the swamp, moving around over there," said Carlisle.

"Did you tell Bupta?"

"Not yet."

"Goddam! Alert him. If they're that close to Ranke's, they're bound to hit him."

"Plunkett won't let me call him." It was the captain's turn to hang his head. He was more ashamed of this than lying to Regiment. "He said St. Cyr doesn't allow transmissions to Ranke." Hawk looked incredulous.

"We're United States government men, we don't take

that kinda shit. Besides," he added impatiently, "it ain't a message to Ranke, it's to that asshole Bupta."

"It's to benefit Ranke. They say he's a revolutionary."

"This is where we butt heads with St. Cyr, sir." Hawk had been patient long enough. He felt the coming of a great tragedy. It was to be so gruesome that this was more than a premonition or a guess. He was *certain* that they would suffer greatly at the hands of the enemy. The vibrations of a shocking fall at New Oss reached to him from somewhere in the future. "I got forty men out there and they're entitled to know about an enemy concentration of that size. They won't be expectin' it. Ranke's used to gettin' shot at by two or three Japs. He won't know what the hell hit him."

"We're St. Cyr's guests. Hawk, I can't just throw orders around."

"You're gonna have to throw that one around, or be responsible for the casualties. We gotta quit shittin' around with these sonofabitches. Just like this town sittin' herewith nobody but us to guard it, and the whole goddam Jap army is parked up at Rabaul. Now they think the Nips are shippin' 'em in over *here*. You start payin' attention to what that crazy bastard says and a lot of people are gonna get killed: the lucky ones, that is."

"All right, all right, Hawk. You're probably right. And it means something else, too."

"What?"

"Those Japs are operating out of a ground base somewhere. Wherever that is, Roger is probably there. Unless they took him out on a sub. And I don't think that they could get him through this Hollow Mountain place."

Hawk sat back pensively. "Maybe," he said. Good

point, Carlisle, you dumb shitass. Damn good point. He could still get to Roger before a Japanese buildup took place. He would have to act reasonably fast, while their camp was still small—and before New Oss underwent a massacre, with Hawk in the middle of it. "When do we mark Hollow Mountain?"

"When they tell us. It sounded like a couple of days, but you know how they are," said Carlisle. Hawk shifted in his chair. Okay, Roger, he thought, hang on kid, and I'll find you. His thoughts were interrupted by an outcry outside. It sounded as if a crowd of people were shouting on the other side of the house. Canlon stirred.

"Let's check that out," said Hawk, standing. He feared the worst. He wouldn't have been surprised to see Japanese tanks rolling down the main street. "Get up, Joe!" He booted Canlon as he and the captain rushed out of the room.

"Huh?" Joe raised his head and dropped it back onto the couch. He was snoring again before his head touched the velvet pillow.

The shouting stopped as they made their way down the hall to the rear of the house. They now heard the voice of Sir Richard ahead of them. It sounded like he was giving a speech. The two marines stopped when they saw his back; he stood upon a rear balcony. Below him they could see an assemblage of the Asian and European populations of New Oss. They looked like wax statues in the odd and fluid torchlight.

"I want to express my deepest gratitude for this touching show of support," he was saying in projected tones. "I feel as if we are all one great family, undergoing this sad event together. You are my strength and what-ever happens, I want you to know that I shall not let you down. I shall never betray your trust or forget the concern that you have shown me."

The crowd cheered mightily.

"Now let us pray for little Roger...my dear son, Roger." St. Cyr bowed his head.

"It *is* kind of sad, isn't it?" Carlisle whispered to Hawk. Hawk nodded in agreement. He couldn't waste any compassion on St. Cyr. It was in short supply. He was allowed to feel no grief for the deaths of his own men, so he sure as hell wasn't going to feel anything for this fellow, who was setting them up for a magnificent blunder. Hawk was forced to function at maximum efficiency, regardless of the circumstances. If his compassion was in short supply, his hate was not. Some of it spilled over onto St. Cyr. He couldn't say exactly why he felt so strongly. He was usually apathetic toward stupid people. Maybe it was because he was out on a balcony playing emperor while his son was missing in the most horrible land north of hell. He could flat lay on the bullshit, there was no denying that. Major Clemson stepped from the wings and led the prayer. Another burst of hate rose into Hawk's throat. There was something about that guy, too. He fought back his emotion; he was mature enough to know that it was by and large unfounded. He knew that it was difficult for him to respect anyone but fighting men. That was probably a shortcoming.

St. Cyr turned away from the crowd, genuinely spent, as he walked back into the hall where Hawk and Carlisle stood. The Prime Minister walked up to Hawk and put a hand on his shoulder. The sergeant stared coldly into his eyes. St. Cyr dropped his head onto Hawk's chest. Hawk looked at Carlisle. "Sergeant Hawk, find my son. Please," said the Prime Minister. Major Clemson took Sir Richard's arm and they went slowly down the hall together. They entered the study and closed the door. Carlisle sighed.

From behind the door, the screaming voice of Major Clemson could be heard. He was in a most unchristian rage. "Get out! Get out, you filthy swine!" The door opened and Joe Canlon stepped out into the hall with his mouth open and his eyes half closed. He held a rifle in one hand and helmet in the other. The door slammed violently behind him.

"Uhhh...what the shit?" he grunted to the two marines looking at him.

The evening wore on and Major Clemson felt that it was better that Sir Richard forgot his sorrow in sleep. He put his cap under his arm, patted the Prime Minister on the shoulder and walked softly to the door. "Good evening, Richard," he said as he opened the door. St. Cyr didn't turn around. He remained seated at his desk. Clemson stepped into the hall and gently shut the door.

"How're you tonight, sir?" The huge and grimy bulk of Charles Larsen stood before him in the hall. Clemson tried valiantly to suppress a look of contempt.

"Fine, fine, thank you," said the officer, looking down. He stepped quickly around the guide, afraid that he might accidentally touch him, or be forced into a conversation. He certainly wasn't up to saving Larsen's soul at this hour. Larsen knocked on the study door and smiled a knowing smile at the officer's retreating back. He knew that type. St. Cyr's voice came from within and Larsen opened the door and launched his big frame into the solemn little room. St. Cyr didn't ask him to sit.

They didn't exchange pleasantries. They knew that

any time they found themselves together, it was for what they could get out of each other. "We simply must get Roger back, Charles," said Sir Richard without looking at him. He knew it was Larsen by the smell of his native insect repellant: shark oil and croc grease. "I'm losing my confidence in Sergeant Hawk. He means well, but he hasn't the background for our problems here in Malang. I want you to bring the boy back as soon as possible." Larsen grunted something like "Arrrr," a noise that an actor in a pirate movie might make.

"You have no other conflicting orders. The Americans are trying to do a dozen things at once. You must tell no one of this. Do you understand?" St. Cyr faced him. Larsen repeated his pirate noise. "Your success will probably depend upon the noninterference of these other incompetents."

"It's to be sure you can trust Charles Larsen, sir."

St. Cyr narrowed his eyes and turned away again.

At about the same time, Hawk was chewing on a tongue-numbing wad of tobacco. Canlon sat in the foxhole across from him. The rusted wire of the perimeter rattled in the winds of the darkness. Hawk had just explained to Joe that he felt morally obligated to find Roger St. Cyr, in spite of the feelings he had for the boy's father. He was the only one who could do it.

"If I go back out there, though, I'm gonna lose some boys. You know damn good and well that I am." Hawk spat.

"You can bet your ass on that. You can't take a shit out in this country without some crazy thing happening."

"There's a Jap camp out there, right around that

swamp. I'm sure of that much. The kid is there—*if* it was Japs that took him. And, you know, they did."

"Yeah? You sound pretty sure of that."

Hawk nodded and bit his tobacco. "I am. I'm gonna bet my ass on it. That don't mean nothin'. I'm gonna bet some of these boys on it, too. That's all that bothers me." Hawk shook his head. "I got a feelin' that it ain't gonna matter about that, either, what with the way St. Cry's got us boxed in here. I'll wait and see what them bastards at Regiment want us to do about marking that base, and then I'll look for the kid at the same time. If we get back, I might get Carlisle to go higher up, go around them shitbags at Regiment and get us some kind of relief or reinforcements."

Canlon lit a cigarette and took off his heavy helmet. "I hope you plan on takin' more men with us this time. I ain't shittin' you, my nerves are gone."

"Yeah," Hawk spat and aimed his bloodshot eyes out at the forest, "mine, too. I always feel like I'm late for something."

"Not me. I feel like I'm too early—for my funeral," Canlon said. Hawk smiled, but the smile left his face quickly. It was a smile of politeness. There was no feeling behind his facial expressions. He had to consciously will them.

The lonely barbed wire clattered out along the perimeter.

* * *

SIR RICHARD and Miss Asquith were in the library having a drink when Mr. Plunkett knocked on the tall double doors. Sir Richard got up and walked over to the door to let Plunkett in. They greeted one another, but Sir Richard didn't offer to let him into the room. "I thought you should know, sir, what's been going over the wireless," said the radio operator. "The Yanks been codin' their messages, sir, but I heard the sergeant in intelligence talking to the captain. They say that Hawk man done found the place of the Jap subs, and they're gonna bomb her off the map."

"Really now, Plunkett? Come in, come in out of the hall, please."

"Yessir. And their pilots have spotted some Japs out near Ranke's and the captain wanted to warn his men over there."

"You told them, of course, that I won't allow that. Ranke is a fugitive from justice, for the time being. He is in violation of national tax laws," said Sir Richard.

"Well, sir, I told them I wouldn't do it. But that Captain Carlisle came back after he talked with the Hawk feller and raised hell with me. Says I'm not the only one in town that knows how to use a radio. Now if the Hawk feller comes around, they'll be some trouble. He looks like the type of bloke what'd strike a man, if he don't get his way with things. I'm in the middle of this, sir. I wisht you'd speak for me and take some of this pressure off me, sir."

"I'll take care of everything, Plunkett. If they try to use the wireless, just come and get me, immediately. And thank you for coming by."

"Yessir." Plunkett made a sort of incipient bow and backed out of the room. As far as he knew, St. Cyr might be the king of Malang by now. He had to afford him the courtesy due that status. Sir Richard still called himself the Prime Minister, but what was he the Prime Minister of?

St. Cyr closed the door. He walked back to his chair, a concerned expression on his face. Miss Asquith was looking rather steadily at him when he sat down.

"Well, Richard?" she said. She turned her pointed chin up and looked down her tiny, well-shaped nose at him. He moved to the edge of the chair and rested his forehead on his hand. He didn't say anything, only shook his head a little. "You know what I think?" she persisted. "I think you're a coward."

"Leave me alone, Monica! Don't you realize the responsibilities I have?"

"I realize more than you think. I realize that your son is out in the jungle somewhere while you sit here moping about the fate of your precious nation. I find you revolting, Richard!" She stood and set her glass on a little end table. "Truly revolting. You have the veneer of a gentleman and nothing beneath it."

"Is that a line from one of those historical novels you're always reading?" he asked.

"No, that's a fact." She walked to the door and turned to face him once again. Her long dress swirled about her ankles. She had gotten into the imperial spirit a bit too deeply herself. She had had a wardrobe designed that was long out of fashion for a girl her age. She continued looking at him for a half a minute. He neither looked at her nor said another word. She spun around and slammed the door. He might have said something, if he had known what she planned on doing. Then again, he might not have.

* * *

IN THE EARLY MORNING HOURS, Hawk had Carlisle make certain that Plunkett was asleep or diverted. He then had the sergeant from intelligence radio Bupta. Plunkett never knew that the warning had been sent. He was expecting a more direct approach from the Americans, especially the volatile Sgt. Hawk. Bupta reported no contact.

Canlon and Hawk spent the remainder of the night in a miserable, bone-inflaming rain. It started up again around 0200. The water ran off the tattered ponchos they had fastened together, and drained into their foxhole. Consequently, they didn't get overly excited when the high wind blew the ponchos away. They were too exhausted to require very much comfort. Sleep came easily. At dawn, they were two lumps of mud in the bottom of a pool of rainwater.

"Sergeant Hawk, I want a word with you." Miss Asquith stood over the muddy hole. She wondered how anyone could survive such a health hazard. A large blob started moving at the bottom of the hole and she recognized the face of Hawk. He looked up with one eye at her sneering face. "I believe you have expressed some interest in finding Roger St. Cyr, and I want to know if you intend to pursue that interest," she said. Canlon rustled himself out of the mud, maneuvering himself to a position where he could look up her dress. Then he realized that he wasn't interested in that anyway and fell back in the mud with his eyes closed.

"Ma'am?" Hawk groaned.

"Are you going to look for Roger again?" She raised her voice this time. Stupidity annoyed her. Stupid men especially irritated her. Men were too egotistical even to *know* when they were stupid.

"Yes, ma'am." Hawk sat up. He coughed. He thought of dusting himself off a bit, but realized it wouldn't do a great deal of good. "I'm, uh, waitin' on something to develop, and once it does, we'll be going back out there. Yes, ma'am."

"I've heard that your planes spotted Japs near the swamp. That would be the logical place to look, wouldn't it?"

"Yes, ma'am. Where'd you hear that?" Hawk climbed wearily out of the hole. He could have slept a few more hours. A nagging ache surrounded his entire head. She took a quick step away from him.

"Never mind that. The word is all over town. I'm here to inform you that I'm going with you this time."

Hawk laughed. "No, you ain't!"

"I assure you that I am."

"I assure you that you *ain't*. When I go, it'll be for a couple of reasons, and cain't nothing be done with you along."

"You may say anything that you like, but of course, you cannot stop me."

Hawk liked the way she talked. She had an English accent and a kind of a lisp. But he didn't like what she was saying. "Ma'am, I don't know if you ever been out in that wilderness before, but..."

"I have. Many times. Long before you went out there. I'm an excellent marksman and an excellent woodsman. Have your man inform me of your departure time. Otherwise, I'll have you observed and merely follow you."

"You ain't goin', and that's that."

"I *am* going."

Hawk studied her for a minute. Really nice looking. "You think you're pretty sharp, don't you?" he asked.

"I'll match wits with you any day," she answered.

He smiled. "Listen—I'll walk you back to your lounge chair and you can tell me all about who put this bee in your bonnet."

"No, thank you. I don't want you walking me anywhere but to Roger St. Cyr. I'm tired of this incompetence and I shall find him with a slight amount of support from yourself. Good day." Canlon's eyes were open and he was staring at her, open-mouthed. She sneered at him and turned to walk away.

"Forget it!" Hawk called after her. She paused for a second, didn't turn around, and continued on.

"Dumb bitch," Canlon moaned. "You oughta let her come."

"Yeah," Hawk snorted, "that'd fix her ass, all right." He sat in the mud on the edge of the hole. "You watch what happens next. All them jokers are gonna come out in their knee-britches and parasols and tell me that they're goin' along."

"Let 'em," Canlon said angrily. "Let 'em die! Can you imagine that woman out in that shit? I say let 'em." Canlon had hardened considerably since Calloway's death. He had once been a restraining influence on Hawk. Now even Hawk had more common sense than did he.

"Well," the sergeant sighed, "I got enough trouble as it is, without this kind of horseshit." He opened his canteen and took a drink. "I'll knock the shit outa that goddam whore if she goes to fartin' around with me." He spat the water down into the hole.

Later in the morning, once the sun had dried him

out a little and a fine patina of mud covered his clothing, Hawk walked over to the colonial mansion. Carlisle had no news. Hawk decided to drop in on Sir Richard and clear up a few things. Sir Richard was in his study, alone. They chatted idly about Hawk's appearance, the weather and the terrain of Malang.

Then Hawk said, "Mr. St. Cyr, do you think the Japs really done this?"

"Yes. I'm positive."

"You don't think maybe somebody else might have?"

"Why, no. Whom did you have in mind? I suspected Ranke, but you absolved him."

"How about somebody here? Powers is the only one that seen the Japs. That's kinda funny. Not impossible, but funny. And you let that Starrett fella have the run of the place."

"Mr. Starrett loves the boy as much as I. I give you my personal guarantee that he is not involved in any way. I'd trust the man with my life, and often have. He was once the best barrister in London, you know. The politics of it all finally got to him. Powers...well, he has neither the brains nor the wherewithal to do such a thing."

"Yessir. What about that damn Larsen? What do you know about that character?"

"I wouldn't trust him with Tojo's life, to tell you the truth. There again, we're talking about an exceptionally dull individual. He would have to be involved with someone else, and the someone else could only be Ranke. Besides, I think we saw him about on the day it happened. Yes, I'm sure of it."

"Ranke and Larsen would make a good combination, but they didn't seem to jive. Ranke accused Larsen of doin' it, as a matter of fact. Is there anybody else that you're at odds with, sir?"

"Oh, no one capable of that type of thing. If it were someone here, wouldn't they have a purpose? Would they not have demanded something by now? No one would do such a thing for pure spite, now would they?"

Shit yeah, they would, Hawk said to himself. He couldn't make Sir Richard understand that, though. Sir Richard hadn't reached the level of forced degradation that Hawk operated on. Still, St. Cyr had a point. Not many people had reached *that* level. "No, it's the Japs. No doubt of it," said St. Cyr.

"I gotta agree with you, judging by what we've got to go on. Look here, I got something else to talk to you about. This lady friend of yours is making noises like she wants to go out into the jungle with us to find Roger. I'd appreciate it if you'd put some kind of lid on her."

"She has a mind of her own. I can't control her any more. She's had this flash of intuition, you see. She thinks she knows where Roger is. Maybe she does. Who knows about the things? It would make us all feel a little easier about it. I would like you to take her."

Hawk sat thunderstruck. He met St. Cyr's watery eyes. "Uh...but that's not possible, sir. I can't do that! You know what it's like out there."

"Oh, it's a small country, only a couple of days' travel at the widest point. Not that dangerous, really."

"Sir...you see, I almost got a half dozen armed marines raped and killed last time I was out there. A man got burnt and chopped to pieces, scared the dogshit outa my boys. It's goddam dangerous!"

"At times, perhaps. Have you ever heard of intuition, Sergeant? A situation may be so emotionally charged that a person knows about it, without having any evidence from his five senses. I believe in it. I think you should take her."

"Yessir. I gotta intuition that this town's gonna get run over by Japs. Them intuitions ain't good for much— you can tell how much good mine's done me."

St. Cyr traded a little more metaphysical banter with the marine, until at last Hawk became convinced that the Prime Minister was not entirely in his right mind. He politely excused himself and resolved to deal with the problem of Miss Asquith in his own way. No one could force him to take her, that was for sure. Or so he thought. He had another surprise in store for him later that afternoon. Carlisle came out to the perimeter, a rarity in itself, and ordered him to take the woman with him on the next patrol.

"Cap'n," Hawk shook his head, rocked back his helmet and looked at the ground, "Cap'n, you're ready for the goddam fit house!"

"Listen, let's not argue about it. I don't want an argument. I know how you feel. St. Cyr's asked me to order this as a personal favor, and I said I would. You've got to do it, or I'm going to look like an idiot."

"Well, that's what you are! Would you rather look like an idiot or have us bring her back in a snuff can?"

"Listen, let's not argue about it. I respect your opinion on the whole thing, and you're probably right. I'll take full responsibility for whatever happens."

"There ain't no 'probably' to it. I'm the one that has to watch out for her out there, and I say no."

"Treat her like anybody else. You don't have to pay any special attention to her because she's a woman. You have to do it, Hawk."

"Cap'n you have *got* to be out of your goddam mind!"

* * *

A CODED message arrived that afternoon: more Japanese were in the swamp area; three times the number previously reported. It was suspected that these new troops were being smuggled through the submarine base. This had to be checked out. The base seemed like an impractical source for bringing in troops, but the Japanese didn't always follow the rules of practicality. A build-up was under way, and its objective could only be New Oss and the neighboring refineries. Command wanted another full day's observation on the base, they wanted the demolition charges planted, and they wanted white phosphorous on the target at exactly 0700, two days hence. Carlisle excitedly relayed the message to the sergeant. Hawk took it stoically. He had been expecting it.

When Carlisle told Starrett about the attack that was expected upon New Oss, the chief advisor admitted that he had heard a rumor to that effect two days earlier. Plunkett had picked up a message from Australian intelligence. Starrett said that he didn't want to alarm anyone until the message was verified. Now it was. He didn't know any more about the exact strength of the enemy, or if or when they would attack, than did American intelligence.

Starrett then confessed something that Carlisle didn't know about. Upon hearing of this proposed attack, St. Cyr had finally agreed to call in the A.I.F. to defend the city. The Australians had been called and they refused to come. New Oss was expendable. Too many forces were needed elsewhere. They wanted to know why St. Cyr hadn't accepted help when it was first offered and available. Starrett felt the Australians were punishing Malang.

Carlisle dutifully reported all of this to Hawk. The sergeant had to start for Hollow Mountain that night in order to carry out a full day's observation. It was an awesome task, taking on the jungle at night. He would have to take the coastal route, since there were too many Japanese in the swamp by this time. That meant a rough trek, most of it through Nodu country. The latest news also meant that he had to hurry back and meet the inevitable Japanese move toward the coast. He added all of this up. He knew it was impossible. He didn't complain. He didn't say anything about any of it, until Miss Asquith showed up at the perimeter wearing her riding breeches. He really wasn't up to an argument. With all the destruction about to befall the immediate area, her welfare no longer seemed important. Nevertheless, he didn't back down. He wasn't one to allow a suicide.

"You ain't goin'," he told her. "If you're too stupid to know you'd get your ass killed, I ain't."

She gasped. "Don't you use profanity when speaking to me, Mister!"

Hawk clenched his fist. No, he wouldn't do that. He came pretty close to it, though. "You keep your goddam mouth shut! I can't look out for you. You see these men?" He pointed at the twelve selected to go with him. "Them's the toughest sonofabitches in the world, and if I get half of 'em back alive they'll be crazy for the rest of their lives. Do you understand that? I just can't fool around with you any more. Now get your ass outa here."

Miss Asquith turned scarlet. "We'll see about this," she choked in a voice filled with emotion. No one had ever spoken to her in such a manner. She turned around and stalked off.

"Let's get the hell outa here," Hawk shouted, "before she comes back." But they didn't. McGranger had left to get the explosives and the WP, and they had to wait for him. Carlisle, St. Cyr, and Miss Asquith returned to the perimeter before McGranger.

"Now the shit hits the fan," Canlon mumbled to Ned Albert. He was sure that Hawk would win out. The whole idea was absurd.

"I gave you an order, Sergeant Hawk," Carlisle said in a less than convincing tone. He sounded like an angry adolescent with a changing voice. The captain had quite an audience now; he couldn't relent.

"Then you take the patrol, Captain. I ain't goin' with *her*."

They looked at each other without speaking. Carlisle was afraid of him, and Hawk knew it. As the seconds ticked by, everyone came to know it. That's when St. Cyr stepped in. He knew that Carlisle was about to back down and go out apologizing and groveling. St. Cyr had a presence about him. He could put on a show.

"Listen to me, Sergeant Hawk," he said. "What are your objections based on here? Is it the danger? She's willing to face the danger, and let's be truthful, there's a good chance that there won't be any confrontations— now, isn't that true?"

"Oh, shut up, Richard," said Miss Asquith. "Of

course there will be confrontations. They will have to take the boy away from the Japanese!"

Hawk sighed and interrupted her, choosing to disagree with her in the process. "No, sir. It ain't the danger. It's just down right physically impossible to get over there with her, much less there and back. She can't do it. *I* can hardly do it. Shit—can't y'all see that?"

"I have a solution," said St. Cyr, totally unperturbed. "The welder down by the dock has repaired the hole in one of your landing barges with a steel plate. He says that it will probably be functional. Why don't you sail around the peninsula in it and save yourself some of the hardship? Surely even a tender creature such as Miss Asquith could go on a short boat ride."

"Somebody shoulda told me about that boat," Hawk snapped. He couldn't think of a quick reply. He was so relieved to have a landing craft, he almost forgot what he was arguing about. It seemed in that split second as if Sir Richard had successfully answered all of his objections. He knew that it had been done through some conversational trickery, but he didn't care anymore. What was the life of one woman? Who cared? It was time these bastards got a dose of the real world. "All right, then, goddammit! Get your ass over to the dock." He turned to his men and roared, "All of you, *all of you* get your ass over to the dock!"

Miss Asquith smiled and walked proudly away. She was a little afraid that Hawk was going to strike someone, and she didn't want to see any violence. Carlisle remained after everyone had left Hawk standing there. "I'm...sorry," he said.

"Forget it," Hawk snarled. "You done your part. She'll get killed, I guarantee it. What's with the King, there? He acts like he wants her dead. This ain't exactly the kind of thing you want your intended mixed up in."

"They're no longer a twosome," Carlisle said lightly. He felt better now that Hawk had forgiven him, if indeed he had. "She didn't like the way he was handling the whole thing." Maybe he felt better because he was talking about Miss Asquith.

Hawk snorted. "I'd tell that two bit bag of horse..." Then he looked over at Carlisle. "Did *she* put you up to this, Captain?"

"Well, she *did* sort of ask me to...*you* know."

"She led you on, huh? She made you think she dumped the King, and now you're after her ass?" Hawk had noticed that Carlisle was wearing his shiny, unused helmet and was carrying his dusty unused carbine. Hawk clenched his teeth and smiled a skull-faced smile. "Why, you're goin' too, now ain'tcha?"

"I thought I might. Well, see...maybe she *did* kind of lead me on, a little. But I do think that she likes me. You can tell. Isn't she the most gorgeous thing you ever saw?"

Hawk started walking toward the dock. His boots crunched heavily in the debris behind the fighting holes. Carlisle watched his swaggering shoulders retreating in the distance. "See you in hell, Cap'n," Hawk called to him without turning around. The deep voice hung eerily in the night air. Carlisle shuddered.

As the badgered party passed the mansion on their way to the dock, another quaint scene developed. All the St. Cyr servants were out on the porch to see Miss Asquith off. Hawk strolled into the middle of the great show of hugging and well-wishing.

Diana was crying. Hawk stopped. He considered

using the girl's tears in one last attempt to stop Miss Asquith. In the end, he decided that he didn't care that much about any of it. He was surprised when Diana came sobbing up to him. "Sgt. Hawk," she said, "I don't think the Japs took Roger. I think he left on his own. He...had this argument with Father, you see, about our Mother. And then...I had argued with him...and I think that he just ran away."

Hawk studied her for a moment. "Okay, kid. I'll keep that in mind." He waded through the crowd and went down to the patched landing barge. It occurred to him as he walked aboard that Diana's was the most logical solution of all. He would run away from this pack of screwballs himself, if he could.

A delay developed when Carlisle couldn't find the sailor who operated the landing craft. The captain had neglected to tell the coxswain that his services were needed that night. They never did find the particular fellow they wanted, but eventually another sailor was located and they pulled out of the harbor. The heavy waves pounded the sides of the boat, which bonged and echoed under the pressure. New

Oss harbor wasn't the most perfectly located port. It took a fairly sturdy craft to negotiate the rough water along the Malangian coast. The sharks were of such a virulent strain, the natives didn't even try to venture far in their flimsy outriggers.

Hawk leaned against the gunwales, between McGranger and Carlisle. Miss Asquith stood with folded arms on the other side of the captain. Hawk was trying to think of a way to start another argument with her when he looked over at McGranger. The boy was looking forlornly at the lights of New Oss receding in the distance. Hawk smiled and stuffed some chewing tobacco into his mouth.

"Hey, Miss Asquith, McGranger's havin' some trouble with his girl back home. She's been two-timin' him. Maybe you could give him a little sisterly advice, seein' as how you got so much experience in that kinda thing." He draped an arm over the gunwale, rather proud of himself.

Miss Asquith's head jerked like she had been slapped across the mouth. She stepped from beside Carlisle and faced Hawk. "Do you know what you are? Do you want me to *tell* you what you are?" she asked angrily.

"Not especially," he said and spat over the side.

"You are an ignorant, bullying pig! You're a big fish in a very small pond, Mister Hawk!"

"Yeah?" He spat down onto the deck of the landing craft, about an inch in front of her shoe. "It's the only pond we got, though, ain't it? I guess it's sorta like bein' Queen of Malang." Canlon was standing next to Carlisle. He nudged the captain. He didn't want to witness a murder before they got out of sight of the harbor. It was hard to say which of them was most in need of protection. Miss Asquith would have shot Hawk, had she been armed. Carlisle took the hint and seized her arm.

"I mean..." he choked, "you got what you wanted on the whole thing. I mean here you are, going along with us. Let's not start arguing for nothing." She glared at Hawk with her beautiful hate-filled eyes. He winked at her. She snapped her head away from him and stepped back on the other side of Carlisle.

After that, it got frightfully quiet along the

gunwales. The roughly running engine and the hushed parting of the waves were the only sounds to be heard. "Yeah," Canlon blurted out suddenly. Everyone looked at him as if he had flipped his wig. "Yeah, this is the way a marine was meant to travel." No one answered him. The engine caused the patched metal of the floor to vibrate against the original decking. "Yeah," he repeated, and nodded his head stupidly as he looked out into the vastness of the dark Pacific.

The voyage was brief and uneventful, making it by far the most unusual trip across Malang. The coxswain kept the barge about a hundred yards from shore and followed the coastline until Hawk told him to go ashore. The pall over the hideous jungle night was shattered by the grating of chains and the falling of the front ramp. It splashed into the water. There was no beach.

Hawk considered needling Miss Asquith with a "Don't get your feet wet" or some such rejoinder. But he had more serious things to think about. He couldn't keep up a running repartee with her. She would eventually crack, or get killed in some gruesome manner, and he might regret his meanness. She was just another problem now. The shouting and sarcasm hadn't worked. He had lost that battle. It was time to forget her.

Hawk led them through the minefield. He went into a half crouch, cradling his Thompson against his body. The enemy might have posted a guard by this time. The men moved in single file, without flankers. Flankers in the dense underbrush would have caused more noise and trouble than they were worth. The whole patrol was a risk; the absence of flankers was a minor problem. They had to spend something like thirty-six hours at Hollow Mountain. There was no sense in letting everyone know it and making the stay one continuous fire-fight.

The moon shone on the water. The coastal rocks were grey in the dim light. They crossed the higher crags and looked down on Hollow Mountain, the place of the *omat*. The waterfall gurgled from the wound in the mountain's reverse slope. The white stream that it produced flowed raucously below them. Its course curved to the west around another rock, apparently terminating by running off into the ocean again. The scene was peaceful from their lofty perspective, as if it were all encased in ice.

Hawk sighed and pushed back his helmet with his thumb. How easy it would be to just throw a smoke grenade and run. "All right," he said, "there she is. Let's keep it kinda quiet. Come here, Joe." Canlon scrambled over the sharp rocks to his side. "You wanta go in there?"

"God, Hawk," Joe looked down at the still landscape. It could have been another planet. "I don't know. How much water do you have to swim up through?"

"I don't know, fifty to seventy feet maybe. It's easy, the current sucks you right up."

"That can't be. You'd get the bends going through that much water that fast," said Joe. Joe wasn't really worried about the water. He was an excellent swimmer.

Hawk thought about what Joe had said. "Yeah, I *did* feel a little funny. The native didn't have any trouble. It ain't that big a problem."

"Well, I've done a little divin' and I can tell you that it's dangerous. The bends can kill your ass."

"Shit, I didn't order you to do it. Do you want to or not? It ain't my goddam idea."

"Okay, for chrissake, I'll go."

Hawk spread the men out on the higher rocks. They couldn't dig in, but they had a good view of the low ground.

It was a fair defensive position. It was also a fair spot in which to become trapped. A larger force below them could cut them off indefinitely. They accepted that and took up their positions. Miss Asquith settled in among them like Helen of Troy. No one thought to ask why an excellent marksman, such as herself, had come along unarmed. She would covertly raise her pants leg and remove a leech or two when no one was looking.

Hawk and Canlon doffed their helmets and shirts. Carlisle strapped the gelatin charge to Joe's back. He was the better swimmer. McGranger was to go down to the waterfall with them. From that vantage point, he would be able to rapidly relay any messages from Hawk and Canlon. Hawk remembered the guard's outpost that faced the water where they would have to surface in the mountain's interior. He hoped that since it was night, the post would be left unmanned.

Hawk ducked into the waterfall, without hesitation or another word of encouragement, and latched onto a handhold. He climbed up and reached down to grab Canlon's flailing wrist. He directed the confused hand to a spike. He pulled himself up, hand over hand, stopping periodically to touch his foot to Canlon's head, making sure that he was there. It was pitch black and cold. It wasn't until Hawk's hand touched the slide pipe that he realized that he had made a rather grave error. They wouldn't be able to find their way out in the darkness. The shaft of light that entered through the waterfall wouldn't be there when they tried to come down; there would be nothing to guide them. Canlon wouldn't know what the hell was going on, and Hawk wouldn't be in a much better position. The choices were to wait until daylight, or to go ahead and blunder about in the darkness. Neither of these was very appealing. On solid ground, he would have faced these life-threatening choices calmly. Here beneath the Pacific Ocean, he felt a charge of anger shoot through his backbone. How foolish! They could have brought a light, or possibly even delayed their entry.

He seized the pipe and was pulled up. His head broke the surface with a pop. The familiar odors assaulted his nostrils. The lighting was bright and the hum of machinery and voices echoed off the walls of the cavern. Canlon suddenly bounced up beside him. Joe sputtered and spat and coughed, generally setting up a loud unnecessary racket. Hawk clenched his teeth and ignored this indiscretion. The current bubbling along the rocks drowned out the noise. A man who had forgotten that he wouldn't be able to get out of a rat trap couldn't complain about a little noise.

One of the larger midget subs, measuring over seventy feet in length, was moored to the loading dock. Laborers were loading eighteen-inch torpedoes onto her. Three smaller craft were clustered around the boat like baby fish, awaiting their torpedoes. An even smaller craft hung on a hoist, being fitted with a warhead. This one wouldn't need torpedoes. It *was* one. The suicide sub would not return, under pain of dishonor for its pilot.

Two men were busily charging batteries. The thing that the two Americans noticed first, however, was the large number of men on the base island. They scarcely had room to move. Most of them were stripped, but

Hawk noticed that they wore the remnants of Japanese Army troopers' uniforms. Quite obviously, the men were being smuggled in for the assault on New Oss. The enemy apparently didn't care how many men failed to survive the harrowing trip through Hollow Mountain, just so they had enough to take Malang.

Canlon was petrified. He had received no preparation for this jolting sight by observing the sleepy rocks on the outside. He kept only his eyes above the chilling water. He shivered from the combination of temperature and fear. Hawk decided he had done all the observing that was necessary. He wanted to get out of there before the enemy started sending men out. He didn't want to ride the down elevator amidst a crowd of Japanese. He tapped Joe's arm and turned him around to untie the charge that was strapped to his back. The sergeant hugged the stone interior of the mountain and tried to attach the gelatin to it.

Minutes ticked by. Canlon felt like screaming. He didn't see how at least one of the enemy troops could avoid spotting them. The guard's chair was empty, but it was certain that someone would eventually sit in it, for lack of any place else to go. "What the goddam hell you doin', Hawk?" Joe whispered urgently.

"Can't make the sonofabitch stick," Hawk answered in his normal voice. Canlon swung around to the other side of him to see what he was doing.

"Give me that, you dumb plow jockey! You're supposed to put this shit under the water, so's they can't see it."

"Then do it, shitass," Hawk said impatiently. Joe snatched the charge and pulled himself beneath the water by means of the slide pipe. Canlon came up surprisingly quickly. "What'd you do, drop it?" Hawk asked.

"No, I done it right. How do we get out of here?"

"That's gonna be a project," Hawk answered distractedly. He had to get out immediately, before any of these new enemy troops surprised his men outside. "This way," he said finally and took a deep breath.

The sergeant led the way around the cave, pulling himself from one spike to the next along the surface. When they reached the far side, Hawk explained the undertow to Joe. He also told him that they wouldn't be able to see the way out and that the current would have them completely disoriented.

"Well, ain't that nice?" Joe grunted angrily. "Why didn't you tell me that before you got me into this?"

"I didn't think of it being night time," Hawk confessed.

"We can't go down this way, we'll get sucked out onto the ocean bottom if we go the wrong way."

"That's right, Hawk, and end up under about a thousand feet of water with our brains popped like a balloon. If this ain't the goddamnedest crock of shit you ever drug me into!"

"What do you think of this? We go through the hole in front of the mountain here, the same one the subs come through. Look, you can feel it right here. We'll come out on the ocean, right near the top."

Joe felt under the surface. Sure enough, there was a hole there. "But how thick is the mountain, and can we get through the currents? This wall here could be a hundred feet thick."

"Nah, it ain't thick," said Hawk. He said it confidently, although he didn't have the slightest idea of what he was talking about. He knew that Mellie had never mentioned this as a way out. That was kind of disconcerting.

Just then the Japanese started shouting angrily. The two marines turned to look at them. Someone had dropped a warhead into the water. "Shit, let's get outa here," said Hawk. The warhead could bump into something and blow up. The concussion would set off the gelatin, saving the Army the expense of an airstrike, and costing two marines their lives. This would generally be considered a fair trade in military circles, but it didn't seem that way to Hawk or Canlon. They dove under the stone outcropping.

Hawk's head collided violently with the rock. The current swooped beneath him and pressed him flat against its rough underside. He clawed his way along the surface, like a fly making his way across a ceiling. It was hard to judge how thick the mountain's wall was. He knew that his entire body length was stretched beneath it. He pulled frantically with his fingers, tearing them on the sharp rock. He dug his toes into the stone, pushing mightily. Pangs of claustrophobia fired his reflexes. The thought of being stuck to the bottom of a mountain under the ocean was an upsetting one. At last his hand reached ahead and felt the nothingness of the outside world. He pulled himself slowly through the powerful current and broke through the water and into the clammy New Guinea night.

He hugged the mountainside. The undertow wrapped around his legs and tried to jerk him back into the mountain. It was going to win, too. He couldn't resist the power of it. He looked around for Joe. A wave slapped across his head and into his ear; then he saw him. Joe was swimming along the slope of the mountain, right through the angry swells of the vicious current. Hawk didn't believe that this could be done. Joe's elbows and feet were flying like the driving rods of a dynamo.

Poor Joe. He must have panicked when he realized that he couldn't hold onto the mountainside. Hawk's fingers gave way and he flailed for another grip. He couldn't hold on much longer. He wasn't foolish enough to swim for it. All he could do would be to let go and hope that the current would carry him to the bottom where he and Mellie had first made their exit from the mountain, night or no night. But he also was pretty sure that wouldn't work, either. The current on the outside of the mountain would probably carry him out to the bottom of the ocean. The water plucked impatiently at him.

He looked over to see how Joe had fared. He had lost ground but he was still paddling, fighting it for all he was worth. The coiled strands of rippling current slacked for an instant and Joe mastered the barrier that they had erected. He reached a calm along the rocks, a few yards away. He had made it.

Hawk laughed. That goddam Joe! He could flat swim like a bastard. Swimming. Silly kid shit. If he had been a little sillier, he wouldn't have to drown here like a rat. He knew that he couldn't swim the current. Drowned in New Guinea, Hawk thought. Long way from Mississippi. Long way. He prepared to let go.

As he was about to release his feeble grip, he noticed that things were not as desperate as he thought. Joe was climbing up onto the slope of Hollow Mountain. He crawled along the edge of the rock, to a place just above Hawk.

"Gimme your hand, Hawk!" he shouted as he reached down.

"Don't pull me in, now, you dumb shithead!" Hawk lashed up at him. Joe and the current engaged in a grim tug of war. When Hawk got a hand on the side of the mountain, the tide shifted and the current lost its battle. The two of them lay breathing heavily on the steeply inclined slope.

"Thanks...Joe...you saved my ass!"

"Yeah. After...you tried to kill mine!"

"Yeah...I forgot it was dark."

"You're stupid, Hawk. You owe me one."

"What do you want me to do, kiss your ass?"

"I bet you would have about a minute ago." They laughed. Hawk sat up and nearly tumbled off of the slope and back into the water. This started Joe laughing all the more.

"Godawmighty," Hawk rumbled. Tears rolled down Joe's face; he was wracked with sobbing laughter. Then Hawk remembered the loose warhead floating about in the maelstrom of water beneath them. "Hey, we gotta get outa here! The mountain might go up any second," he said. Joe sobered immediately and jumped to his feet. They ran up to the mountaintop, caught their breath and ran and slid all the way down the reverse slope. McGranger found them huffing and puffing near the waterfall.

"What's chasing you guys?" McGranger asked.

"Get away! Get away from here," Hawk gasped. McGranger helped them to their feet and back to the other men. The mountain never did blow up.

7

HAWK AND CANLON WERE COLD AS THEY TRIED TO DRY out in the chill night air. They couldn't sleep—they were on too much of an emotional high. Dawn neared and the air strike was still over twenty-four hours away. When the time came, they would plant the RDX on the outside of the mountain at a place that approximately corresponded to where the gelatin was planted on the inside. When the bombs started falling, they would set off the RDX, which would set off the gelatin. In this way, it was almost a certainty that the walls of Hollow Mountain would be pierced. Once weakened, the bombers could finish it off. Hawk suspected that the bombers could crack the mountain easily, even without the extra charges. That was war for you. He had had to risk his life planting the gelatin, anyway.

Canlon was still telling everyone about it. You'd think that he had enjoyed the whole thing. Looking back, it was kind of funny. Hawk cupped his hands around a cigar and lit it. He sat back against a rock and looked over at Miss Asquith. "We're gonna be wastin' a lot of time here," he told her. He had noticed that she had been looking at him. He supposed that he was several shades whiter than the last time she saw him. "Too bad we can't just go after the boy," he added, when she continued to stare at him.

"We can," she said. Carlisle was sitting next to her.

"Well," Hawk answered, "if we knew where he was, we could. But there ain't no tellin' how long it'd take us to find him. There's a lot of weeds and a lot of swamp out there, you know." Hawk blew out some smoke. "Naw, we better wait til the strike's over."

"I know right where he is. We can get to him in two or three hours," she said. Her eyes were glazed with a sort of certainty.

"Yeah," Hawk smiled. He looked over to Canlon. Joe smiled.

"I'm serious. I know exactly where he is. I can lead you directly to him. He's in a Jap camp over on the western edge of the swamp."

Hawk frowned and kept a half smile on his lips. "That intuition stuff don't work out here, ma'am. We don't cross this country on hunches." His smile faded as he looked over at her. It was replaced by a serious expression. He looked ferocious beneath the shadow of his helmet. His bristly blond beard, almost the same color as flesh, made his jaw and chin seem larger than they were. His eyes were narrowed and tight with fatigue. Permanent lines of pain were etched in his young face.

"This isn't intuition—I *know* where he is. I'll take you. If we leave now, we'll be back in plenty of time for the air strike."

Hawk met her eyes. Everyone grew quiet and

watched him. "Joe," he said, "at 0650, tomorrow, put a WP grenade on the top of that rock and plant your RDX. Set off another one at 0655 and one more at 0700. If I ain't back, take the boat and the men back to New Oss without me."

Carlisle crouched in front of him. "Wait just a minute,

Hawk!" he complained. "I mean, you can't leave me with the whole thing!"

"I ain't. Canlon's in charge. Do what he tells you. Especially if you fall in the water."

"But...but...he's a *private* or some damn thing, I mean..."

"Then *you* run the show, Captain. I'm gonna go get the kid. I'll leave all the automatic weapons with y'all, in case you get in a scrape." He set his Thompson among the other weapons. "I'll take half the men. Six. Who wants to come?"

McGranger, Albert, and Shelvin had been out there; they didn't want to go again. Another good-natured corporal, Ralph Armistead, was good friends with them, and he didn't want to go either. Hawk had his pick of the others. They preferred going with Hawk to staying with Carlisle. Staying at Hollow Mountain with a base full of Japanese wasn't necessarily the safest of the two duties. Dawn lit the edges of the gloomy forest below them. The sky out over the ocean was greyish white as they prepared to leave.

Carlisle took Hawk aside. "But, listen," the captain protested again, "you can't take her out there with you!"

Hawk gave him a reassuring slap on the back and hitched Canlon's M1 higher on his own back. True love, he thought, nothing like it. "I told you not to bring her,

Cap'n. Forget her. I got a hunch that she deserves to end up out there. More than the rest of us. She knows something. She ain't no good, kid. I'll watch out for her, if I can." He raised his voice. "Move out!"

* * *

As THEY CLIMBED down the rocks, Hawk laid out the plain facts for Miss Asquith. He wasn't going to ask her any details about why she knew where Roger was. Not until he had the boy back. He did mention the raw truth, however. "You know, if we don't get back before 0700, the boat'll be gone and we won't never see New Oss again. The Nodu nation is between us and it."

"I'm well aware of that. We will be back. It isn't far. We have to get back because of Roger."

Hawk fell silent. She understood the risks and she wanted to go anyway. "Just tell me where he is. You don't have to go," he said.

"No, I *must* go."

"You do if you won't tell me," Hawk said testily.

"Leave me alone, please. I will not argue with you."

"Okay." He nodded and walked to the front of the file of men. It was better that she was along. If she was mixed up in this, she might as well pay some dues.

They followed the trail that led to Ranke's. Hawk kept a lookout for mines, though he didn't spot any. He didn't worry about Hoonoomaroo because it was daylight. If what Miss Asquith said was true, they should be back before dark. He didn't know that during their annual rape-fest they weren't as bashful about daylight attacks. Once the column was deep into the forest, Miss Asquith called a halt.

"Feet hurt?" Hawk asked politely. She pointed out a trail that branched from the main path, half hidden by foliage. The sergeant didn't ask questions. He led the way. The trail was narrow. They were swallowed by the gigantic flourishing of greenery that hung all about them. After a while, the hard-packed earth turned to mud and they began to see boot prints. Many men had been using the path recently. Hoonoomaroo didn't wear boots. Hawk stopped the patrol. He brushed aside the leafy foliage and went back to the side of Miss Asquith.

"Looks like the shittin' Japs is pretty close by. Where we goin', lady?"

"They *are* nearby. I told you that. Their camp is just ahead of us," she answered coolly.

"Well, what the shit? Are you gonna lead us right into them?"

"No, I'm not. Let's proceed a little farther and I'll show you what I have in mind." Hawk decided to go along with her until it got a little more dangerous. After another ten minutes of tense walking, she stopped him. "We can't go any farther along this trail without encountering their lookouts. Their camp is at the end of this trail."

Hawk looked up the pathway through the jungle. He rubbed a forearm across his nose. "Now what?" he asked.

She pointed to a dry gully that cut across the trail in front of them. "You see this ditch? It leads directly to the outskirts of their encampment. I told Roger to be looking for us there."

Hawk tucked a small piece of chewing tobacco into his mouth. "You did, huh?" He looked down the gully. Its bed was free of undergrowth, though it was covered overhead, making it look like a tunnel through the jungle. It appeared that it might have been kept this way intentionally by man. The Japanese were probably using it for a drainage ditch. Hawk spat. "Reckon we'll be wadin' in Jap shit before long," he said. "You men stay here, on both sides of the trail. Don't get into any fights that you don't have to. Stay hid and let anything that passes you go on by. Let's go." He took her arm and helped her down into the ditch.

The gully wound a circuitous route through the thick underbrush. Birds played in its open bed. They invariably shrieked and flew away upon sighting the intruders, who had to bend low to get beneath the riotous vines and creepers that grew from bank to bank across the top of the ditch. Hawk never considered the possibility that she was leading him into a trap. Why trap one man? Or even six? He wanted to think that Roger had run away, just as his sister had suggested, and Miss Asquith had helped him. By thinking that, he was able to prevent himself from becoming angry with her. That was better for both of them. The undergrowth ended abruptly.

A bivouac of Japanese soldiers spread before their eyes. They had erected buildings, wood and tin structures as well as the more common thatched roof huts. A quick guess told Hawk that they outmanned his garrison by five to one. Oddly enough, the first thing he noticed amidst this shocking scene was Roger St. Cyr. He was playing in the largest street of the bivouac. The street ran into the gully. The boy cast a glance at the movement over in the brush where the jungle met the ditch.

"He's looking for us," said Miss Asquith. Her voice

was a trembling whisper. Hawk thought her rather plucky, under the circumstances.

"Goddam...lookit all them Japs!" Hawk growled.

"Yes, I'm sure of it. He sees us!" Roger was shooting an imaginary gun at imaginary targets. He ran short spaces and then fell down as if he had been shot. When he got up from his last fall, he ran to the gully and vanished into the brush. His face was bright when he looked up at them.

"I've certainly been waiting for you," he said. " Did you bring your Tommy gun, Sergeant? We can get a bunch of them." The boy didn't say anything to Miss Asquith.

"No, kid...we might give 'em a break this time. Do they let you run off like that?"

"Sometimes. Sometimes they come after me. You can't get far, actually. They're all around. I think we should go as soon as possible. I feel certain that they would shoot you."

"I feel pretty certain myself. Come on." Hawk smiled and put his hand on the boy's shoulder. "It's good to see you, kid." He steered him back down the gully.

Hawk was ready for a few explanations. He had Roger himself now, and the boy could verify what had actually happened. But less than ten paces down the gully, a black and red viper squirmed from beneath the rotting leaves of its bed. Miss Asquith let out an involuntary scream. It was too loud, and of too high a pitch.

Hawk mumbled an obscenity. He heard shouts behind them. Alien, angry, guttural orders were barked from the invisible bivouac behind the curtain of vegetation. He unslung his rifle and brained the unsuspecting reptile with all his pent up fury. They heard louder shouts now and the running of many feet.

"Okay," Hawk sighed, "you two take off and get back to the men. I'll lead 'em off into this shit a ways. Here, take the rifle." He handed it to Roger.

"Won't you need it?" Miss Asquith questioned. Her eyes were glowing in the green light of the forest.

"Nah, not where I'm headed. Hurry up."

"We can't simply leave you," said Miss Asquith.

"No, we won't," said Roger.

"Look," Hawk whispered urgently, "let's do this my way, huh? We've done it all everybody else's way, so let's give *me* a chance. Now we ain't got time to shoot the shit, so get goin'."

"I'm...sorry that you and I had to be odds over all this," said Miss Asquith. He turned her around by the shoulders and said, "Hurry up!"

Hawk climbed out of the gully and crawled through the vines, threading his way between the thorny plants. The Japanese were already in the gully behind him. He thrashed about and made more noise. They kept going. They were going to follow the course of the ditch. He turned around. Another plan shot to hell. He crawled back to the gully and jumped heavily down into it. A party of three soldiers had their backs to him. They wheeled to face him, as a dozen more appeared on his other side, putting him between the two groups in the bed of the ditch. He held his hands out from his sides with the palms down.

"Hey, Jap. Sucked any assholes lately?"

The three leveled their rifles on him and approached him cautiously. The larger party covered them. He studied their faces and they studied his. It was an odd thing, seeing your enemy face to face. It wasn't a pleasant sensation for any of them. Hawk figured that he would get used to it, however. It sounded as if the pursuit had been halted. The forest was silent. Evidently, the boy hadn't been missed.

They marched him down the large road that led from the gully. He noticed that the soldiers were preparing to pull out. Scores of canoes were lined up along the muddy bank where the camp met the swamp. Several of the busy troopers stopped what they were doing and gathered around to have a look at the prisoner. A great deal of pointing, smiling and laughing followed. Hawk's steps became leaden. Each one was taking him irretrievably deeper into hell. And he had never found out what Roger was doing here, or what Miss Asquith's connection was to all of it.

He was taken to a cell of barbed wire. Its front wall opened by means of pulleys. His captors prodded him into it with rifle barrels and the growing crowd began to jeer at him. He stared sullenly back at them, measuring how each little throat would fare against his thick hands. He knew that he should be terrified.

The cell consisted of strands of barbed wire wrapped around four huge posts. The creosoted posts formed the corners of the jail. Other strands of wire ran vertically, creating a thorny cage. The four-pronged barbs were unusually long and razor sharp. It was new wire. He looked out through the squares that the wire formed, expressionless. The floor of the cage was also of barbed wire, so that a prisoner might defecate and urinate without fouling his quarters. The net of a floor was about a foot off the ground. He had to step carefully, or slip through it and cut his legs.

The cage was worthy of an animal such as Hawk. The strands of wire had been put on with boomers, turnbuckles and coffin hoists. They were so taut that even the floor strands didn't give under his full weight. The cell was perhaps twelve by twelve, with a barbed wire ceiling that matched the floor and left about an inch of head room to spare when he stood up. He sat on the netting of the floor. Getting comfortable was impossible. That had been thoroughly designed out.

The jeering finally became boring to the onlookers and they drifted away. All things considered, he had received a fairly mild reception. An English-speaking interrogating officer arrived around noon. The prisoner hadn't been given anything to eat or drink, and had been relieved of his knife, the only weapon he had on him. He watched the gully. The enemy hadn't sent any more patrols into it. They were either preoccupied with their departure or figured that the boy couldn't escape the wilderness.

"Why you out in jungle with no gun, marine?" the interrogator asked. He didn't seem especially unfriendly. Hawk remembered that American interrogators were often fond of Japanese. They must like to try out their extra languages.

"Just shittin' around."

"You be lot smarter if you tell truth. Get very hot out here these days. You get very thirsty. Soon, you be the only man in the jungle. We are leaving you here."

"Looks like I found out more outa you than you're gonna get outa me. That's Sergeant James Hawk, 6247347."

The interrogator smiled. "Maybe. But what you know will not do *you* any good. You play tough guy, like in movies. Name, rank, service number. I see movies, too. We take many movies away from marines. Marines are big men, but big only on outside. They cowards."

"Yeah, we're a pretty dainty bunch."

The interrogator lit a cigarette. He frowned. Perhaps he didn't understand this last statement. "Cigarette?"

"No, thanks. I'm cuttin' down. I heard it stunts your growth and turns your skin yella."

Fortunately, the officer didn't get the joke. He was still thinking about the "dainty" comment. "Do your forces know about this camp?" he asked this almost sweetly.

"Gosh, I don't know. I'm a deserter, you see."

"Ahhh, I see." The officer's eyes lit up. Hawk didn't think that his answer had been that clever. "You have come to be with your friends, then?"

Hawk's fiery eyes drilled into the interrogator. "Uh... yeah, yeah, that's right."

"I am sorry for the inconvenience. You are an American. We must be careful. I will send your people over and if they know you, you will be released," the interrogator smiled. He shouted at a lounging soldier nearby. The lounger jumped to his feet, startling the flies that hovered about the premises. He ran to a cistern and brought Hawk a dipper of water. The interrogator gave a short bow and walked away. Hawk looked over the top of the tarnished dipper and guzzled the welcome drink. Not a bad fellow. Things weren't going too badly. He was curious to see who his "friends" actually were. He didn't have long to wait.

"Shit," he growled. An oversized man waddled down the street toward him. Beside him walked a man with a crewcut, wearing a green undershirt and shiny black boots.

"Hello, laddy!" Larsen rested his hands between the barbs and leered at the prisoner. "Terrible accommodations you've ordered here. Dreadful lack of taste, if you ask me." Hawk didn't answer.

"You stink, Hawk," said Bupta. "You oughta take yourself a bath every once in a while." Bupta's voice was low, lingering and nasal. It angered Hawk. Still, he didn't respond. "What are you doing here, anyway?"

"Whatever it is, it must not be the same thing you're doin' here, Bupta," he said calmly. "Did you nab the boy?"

"Me? Nah. He was here way before I come here. You know that. You're the one that brought me and old Larsen out here. Nah, I didn't do it. Ain't you figured that one out, yet? You always were a stupid sonofabitch, Hawk."

Hawk stared over an intersection of wire and into Bupta's eyes. Bupta smiled. Hawk took a drink out of his dipper, continuing to look over it. "I hope I don't ever get outa here, Boopta." He swallowed his water and made an "ah" sound, as if it were very good water indeed.

"Why's that, Hawk?"

"Because what I'm gonna do to you is too nasty for even me to see." He dropped the dipper through the wire and walked away from them to sit in a corner of his cage.

"Now don't start worrying about that, laddy," Larsen laughed. "You won't be getting out of this little set-up. They're taking off for New Oss and they're going to leave you all by yourself. Oh, you might get a little rain to drink, and the odd rat or snake to eat. You won't be going anywheres, but you could live a long time, a strong young fellow such as yourself. Don't go feelin' sorry for y'self now." Larsen waved his arms through the wire.

Hawk raised an eyebrow. "Don't cut yourself on that bobwire, Larsen," he advised. Bupta laughed and rubbed his smoothly shaven face. "C'mon, Charlie, let's get outa here," he nudged Larsen. "These cages stink too bad for my liking." As they walked away, Hawk wrapped a hand around the wire beneath him and gave it a testing pull. There was no slack. The interrogator appeared before the other two were out of sight.

"So, you are not friends?" The officer smiled. "You stay here. Sorry." He said it sincerely.

"It's all right." Hawk shrugged.

"Cigarette?" The prisoner shook his head. His interrogator walked away. The number of undisciplined crowds of men moving toward the canoes increased. The push on New Oss had begun. That's one fight I'll miss, Hawk mused. But he had another surprise, before a half of the Japanese Army had departed.

Once again, the interrogator, Larsen and Bupta strolled up to the front of the cage. Bupta and Larsen smiled cheerfully. The Japanese was serious. Hawk prepared himself for a little more jovial taunting. He watched the face of his captor. The officer ordered three soldiers bearing rifles to stand before the cage.

Here it comes, he thought. They're gonna blow my guts out. The officer ordered the cage opened. The creaking pulleys lifted the door. Yep, he got to thinking about it, and figured killing me would be nicer. Bupta and Larsen took a cautious step back as the wall opened. They hadn't expected this, either. Hawk tensed his muscles for a leap across the cage and through the door.

"Where is the boy?" the officer asked Bupta. He and Larsen looked quizzically at one another. "Well, he's here somewheres, ain't he?" Larsen asked. His voice trembled when he addressed the little officer. "I see," the interrogator said sadly. "Get in, please." He motioned toward the cage.

Hawk sat in the corner of the cell, interestedly watching all this with the barbs digging into his back and rump. The turn of events that troubled Larsen and Bupta wasn't the only thing he observed. He noticed that there were wire-cutters tooled into the Japanese bayonets.

"Wait a minute," Bupta half pleaded, half ordered, "what do you think you're doing?"

"Please," said the Japanese officer, embarrassed that there might be a scene. The enemy was so cowardly and had no sense of honor or self-respect. "Get in, it doesn't matter about the boy. We have no further use for him. Nor for any of you. Get in."

"Now hold on," Bupta complained angrily. The officer nodded to the three soldiers. They lowered their rifles and pointed the bayonets at the two men, leaving the two men with little choice but to back into the cage. The heavy wall fell shut and the three soldiers ran swiftly to join their comrades by the canoes. The interrogator went to the cistern and got Hawk another dipper of water. At least that one had behaved honorably.

"I must go now," said the officer. "May you live for ten thousand years." He drew his sword and sliced the ropes that operated the pulleys, making certain that the door would never be reopened. Then he left them to their fate.

Hawk took a thirsty swallow of water. He looked over the dipper at his new cell mates. "Y'all want some water?" he asked.

Bupta smiled nervously, that same, infuriating smile. "Nah, no thanks, Hawk. Thanks, but we ain't thirsty yet."

"You drink it, laddy," Larsen insisted. The two of them stood at the opposite end of the cage, by the door, as far away from him as they could get. Hawk sighed and lowered the dipper. His chin muscles contracted and tightened his lips.

"We tried like hell to get you out, Hawk," Bupta explained. "And it made them mad. I told them, you can ask Larsen, I said we wanted you out of here or they could just lock us all up. I told Larsen we's gonna end up in here. Those damn Japs."

"Shut up, Bupta, do you think the lad's a fool?" Larsen snapped. He turned to Hawk with a worried look on his face. "As the God's honest truth, laddy, I came here to get the boy for Sir Richard, and that's all...you see..."

"Yeah," Hawk interrupted him. "But, you know, now I gotta divide all them rats I was gonna eat three ways. I figure in about thirty years this wire will rust and I'll get out of here. But what about all my rats? You look like you could hold a lot of rats, Larsen."

He stared at them and they stared at him. They measured one another like the killers that they were. Bupta was well-muscled. He had the self-inflicted muscles of a man who does regulation calisthenics every day. Larsen was older, with greater weight and strength. He lacked the endurance of a younger man, but in a twelve-by-twelve cage, endurance wouldn't be much of a factor. Bupta licked his lips and put his back against the door. He glanced at Hawk's lean, compact body, with the snake-like veins twisted across his biceps. Hawk's strength had been bequeathed to him at birth and enhanced by plowing the fields and clearing the forests of Mississippi. They were hard, permanent muscles. He was comfortable with them.

Hawk smiled without baring his teeth. He dropped the second dipper of water and it splashed through the wire floor. Troops continued to walk by and cast curious glances at the American prisoners. Hawk closed one eye to keep the brutal sun out. The other watched Bupta.

Bupta squinted. The bright silver of the sunlit wire and the scintillating of its barbs hurt his eyes.

"We gotta do something quick, while he's sittin' down," Bupta mumbled to Larsen.

"Mmmph," Larsen agreed. There was no reasoning with Hawk. Larsen knew that type of man. He was familiar with these situations. They usually happened in bars among violent types after a few drinks. Larsen was no stranger to violence. It was better to go ahead and get it over with. No sense in being queasy about it. They had him two to one.

Bupta pretended to be looking through the door. He turned around quickly and aimed a kick at Hawk's head. Hawk had been patiently awaiting something like this and he easily slipped the boot over his shoulder. Bupta fell through the floor, the wire cutting a deep gash into the back of his calf.

His right foot went through the wire wall where Hawk was sitting, tearing open his pants and the shin beneath. The fall caused him to lose his balance and he reached out at the floor to catch himself. As he did so, the long barbs implanted themselves deeply into the heel of one hand. The sight of the living blood was frightful.

Bupta sucked his breath through his teeth when he realized what he had done. He remained still to minimize his injuries. Hawk stood, then took several cautious steps on the wires of the floor in the direction of Larsen. The guide was an experienced brawler, but even so, he chose an unusual method of attack. He lowered his bullet head, hunched his apelike shoulders and dove forward at the marine's chest. Had he landed, he would have winded Hawk and ground him into the wall of the cage. He had a good fifty pounds on the sergeant.

Unruffled, the Hawk met his lowered face with a vicious right uppercut. The snapping blow parted Larsen from several of his rotten teeth, straightened him up and caused him to fall backwards onto the spiked floor. Bupta, sweat pouring from his face, had meanwhile managed to extricate himself from his predicament. The burning in his legs, the bright red flow of his blood and the meat hanging from his hand all told him to give up the struggle, but he knew he couldn't. None of them could.

Larsen rolled over, repeatedly slashing himself in the process. He got quickly to his feet before Hawk could come close enough to stomp him. All three were now standing. They maneuvered for position. The odds were against Hawk, but he had drawn first blood. He had another advantage, too: whereas their desire to stay alive was paramount, his desire to see them dead overrode his own instincts of self-preservation. They rushed at one another, all swinging powerfully and at the same time.

Hawk's fists landed like hammers, snapping back first one sweaty head and then the other. But their combined weight overwhelmed him. He had no room to get out of the way. They came pounding at him, and though the punches didn't hurt, he lost his balance under their numbing force. His boots slid through the net floor, tearing his pants, but sparing his flesh. They towered over him, the two of them still standing on the wire. He had lost mobility, having his legs surrounded by the wire, but his feet were planted firmly on the earth and the stability felt good.

The two combatants above him began kicking savagely at his face, trading legs, so that it seemed that four boots were bouncing off his head and shoulders at once. He dodged and weaved, only to run into another of the ever-present boots. His own feet shuffled in the yellow dust beneath the cage, stirring up such a fierce cloud of the fine powder that the cell seemed to be on fire.

Finally he let down his guard and accepted the punishing boots. His hair flew as they rammed his face. He found his target at last and lashed out awkwardly with both hands, catching Bupta's leg. He pulled at the leg and spun him around. Bupta fell against one of the side walls, grabbing madly at the wire to catch himself. He couldn't slow his momentum, however, and ripped his face against each successive strand of wire until his head ultimately collided with one of the strands of the flooring. Both his hands and face were severely torn. "My eyes!" he screamed.

Larsen threw himself on top of Hawk, bending the sergeant at the knees and flattening him under the great weight. Hawk's legs were left tangled in the flooring and his head was thrust through one of the squares. A barb stabbed into the back of his neck and he lay there while the pain saturated his entire body. Larsen knew that he had to capitalize on this. He climbed up Hawk's body, pounding at him with his massive fists. His weight caused the barbs of the floor to knife into Hawk's back. The pain doubled the sergeant's strength; he seized the dirty long hair of the guide and pulled him into the wire, slicing off a portion of his nose. Blood gushed from Larsen's face into Hawk's eyes, momentarily blinding him. They both had their heads jammed through the wire to the outside of the cage. They looked into each other's wild and disbelieving eyes. Hawk's vision was clouded with Larsen's blood.

Bupta got to his feet and stumbled across the cage. One of his eyes was gone; he would not be denied his revenge. He emitted maniacal howls with each breath he took. He stood bleeding over the two struggling men. Hawk caught glimpses of him. One side of his face was shredded. Bupta latched onto the wire with his hands to steady himself, and put his boot outside of the cage and onto Hawk's forehead. Hawk roared like an animal. He pushed Larsen's face away, put the guide's chin in his hand and forced his neck up against the next strand of wire above him.

Larsen bellowed in anguish. Hawk's neck could no longer withstand the pushing of Bupta's foot. He let his neck go limp, neutralizing the effect of the pressure. Bupta recognized the fact that he couldn't kill his victim in this manner. He got on his knees and grabbed a handful of Hawk's hair. He pulled his head forward, cutting the front of his throat on the barbs.

Hawk had to let Larsen go. The throat wounds could easily kill him. He stabbed Bupta's remaining eye with his thumb, thus ending his role in the melee. He pulled himself from beneath the screeching Larsen, scraping strips of flesh from his back and sides as he did. The guide moaned and tried to rise. The three of them were red with blood from their scalps to their boots. Hawk crawled weakly away, aiming a desultory fist at Bupta's defenseless ribs for good measure.

The sergeant was sure that he had the upper hand at last. But he didn't know the extent of his own injuries. For all he knew, he could be seconds away from death. The flow of adrenalin had drowned his concern for his vital signs. Blood was dripping steadily on all sides of his neck. He was certain of one thing: no one was hitting him. Then he had the opportunity to notice the commotion going on outside the cage. Several of the former Japanese guards were shouting at their prisoners, in an effort to make them stop fighting. Hawk didn't know how long this had been going on. One guard was thrusting his bayonet through the wire, and with one of these thrusts he lanced Hawk's thigh. The marine was too exhausted to move quickly enough to avoid it.

On his hands and knees now, Hawk lashed at the bayonet with his bare and bloody hand like a crazed animal. He caught the naked blade and refused to let go. The guard tugged at the rifle. The Japanese was small, but he had a two-handed grip. Hawk snatched the muzzle of the rifle with his other hand and kept it pointed away from himself. The guard feared that the prisoner was going to take his rifle away. He fired. The bullet slammed into the back of Larsen's head with a horrid slapping noise, spewing his brains along the wire, where they hung and dripped.

Hawk grabbed the bayonet's handle, oblivious to the danger of the muzzle, and finally slipped it free of the rifle. He swung it indiscriminately, at the helpless Bupta, the dead Larsen and the unreachable guards. With great relief, the guard pulled his rifle away from the frenzied prisoner. Hawk fell flat on the floor, resting his head on his arm. The bayonet dropped under him to the ground. The guards screamed passionately at him. The curses slowly died away. He looked up and they were leaving, still yelling and shaking their fists. They were among the last to board a canoe.

As Hawk lay there, bleeding and breathing heavily, he heard a voice. "If you live, my friend, it will be with two corpses. Your foolishness will cost you dearly." It was the interrogator. Hawk looked up slowly and squinted at him. When he didn't say anything, the interrogator walked away. Hawk watched him get in the last canoe. The camp was deserted. He groaned and did a push up, and rested upon his knees. Dozens of punctures perforated his body. He had a deep cut where his neck met his chest, it burned but it wasn't painful—yet. The most painful wound was in the back of his neck, which had been ground into the wire over and over again. He touched it with his fingertips. Amidst the wet, lacerated flesh, it felt as if the bone had been laid bare. *"Ommph"* he grunted. "Won't touch that again." His thigh was getting slightly stiff from the bayonet thrust. Not bad, he judged. I'll be all right, if I don't get a bad infection.

He looked at the two red bodies hung askew on the

wire. "I'm a lot better off than those two pieces of meat. Reckon I won't die of starvation any time soon." It only dimly occurred to him that he wasn't exactly sure of why he had killed them, other than the obvious reason, the fact that they were sonsofbitches. Blood continued to flow from his neck and thigh and oozed from his other wounds. He still felt no life-threatening weakness. "I'm all right," he wheezed to the vacant camp. He rested his elbows on the wire and looked it over. He could hear birds calling in the forest. "Kinda spooky."

He looked for the stolen bayonet, spotted it on the ground and picked it up. He flexed his hand. Damn, that stung! A cut ran across his palm. He studied the wire-cutter, then looked up at the camp once again. "Yeah, kinda spooky." He released a lock on the blade of the bayonet and folded it back toward the handle. It folded like a pocket knife folds, only backwards. The wire-cutter was opposite the cutting edge. It closed upon a groove in the handle. Hawk put a strand of wire through the groove and closed the blade. The wire sang like a violin string. It parted and danced in a defeated coil against one of the corner posts. He stepped through the wire, his knees buckling as his boot touched the ground. He admitted to a little dizziness. "Just out of breath," he said. His hand went involuntarily to the back of his neck.

"Goddammit! I said I wasn't going to do that!" He began walking. Sure, he was hurt. He wasn't going to grant his injuries any solicitude, though. If they wanted to kill him, they wouldn't get any help from him. If you're moving, you can't be hurt too bad, he thought. He stopped at the cistern and leaned over it. The water at the bottom was green. He pulled the wooden bucket up, and poured it over himself. When he opened his eyes, he saw Roger and Miss Asquith running toward him. He blew the water from his mouth.

"They left. Are you hurt badly?" she asked.

"Why ain't *you* left?" he asked weakly.

"We nearly ran into a lookout. We were cut off and had to hide in the jungle," she said.

"We saw what happened," Roger said. "You gave them a terrific beating! I was frightened for you. Are you too badly hurt?"

"Naw. Couple scratches. That wasn't a beating, kid, that was a killing. What's that sorry bastard Bupta doing here?" He pulled up another bucket of water. Miss Asquith tore a strip off her shirt and bathed his neck.

"Perhaps you should know what Roger was doing here first." She winced as she washed the back of his neck.

"Yeah, maybe I should, since I killed two men and nearly got my goddam head cut off, for some reason." His chest still heaved from the exertion of the fight.

"You taught them a lesson, Sergeant Hawk. What a terrific battle!" Roger said enthusiastically.

Hawk went to one knee and put his hands on the boy's shoulders. He looked into Roger's large, innocent eyes.

"You know, Roger, it's a...a awful thing when a person dies. It's a sad thing. Them people don't come back. It's worse when you're the cause of it. They're gone forever. The ones that are left will always remember that person. When somebody dies, it ain't nothin' to celebrate," Hawk explained, trying valiantly to remember his own pre-1942 morals. "You...you gotta understand that. You remember when your mother died? Them two fellas had mothers." Roger looked down quickly. "Even a goddam Jap's got a mother. You see, there's a mean streak in human nature. Sometimes people get to feelin' like they're a little better than other people and they just got to start pushin' 'em around. That's when it gets down to havin' to kill somebody. That don't make it right. But if good folks is gonna get by, sometimes they gotta do away with the bad, because, well...the bad ones ain't never gonna leave you alone. It's like evolution. You ever hear of that? We all come from animals, but we ain't all doin' it at the same time. And you can't be glad about somebody dyin', or you take a step back, you turn bad and things never get no better. You see?"

Roger looked up. His eyes were red. Tears streaked his small face. "I...I believe I *will* see my Mother again," he cried. The boy put his arms around Hawk. Hawk knew that he had cut too deep. Roger hadn't learned anything, except that his mother was dead. Hawk held him.

"Sure, you will, kid. We'll all be together when... when we pass on. We're only separated for a...a little while. Look here," Hawk pushed him away and smiled his tragic smile, "you can't start that cryin' stuff. Do you wanta make an old marine sergeant cry? We gotta long way to go, you and me. We can't get soft about everything that comes alone, can we? That's what they want us to do. They think that just because they're bad, we can't take it. We can take it, though, can't we, kid?"

Roger sobbed harder. The tears came faster. "Yes, sir."

"Goddam right. Shit on 'em!"

"Shit on them!" Roger held him again and sobbed

louder for a minute, until at last, he regained control. Miss Asquith went down on one knee and turned Roger toward her.

"Roger, would you mind terribly if I spoke with Sergeant Hawk for a few moments, before we leave? I think I owe him an explanation." The boy nodded. "Would you mind lying down over by that house? Perhaps you can have yourself a little nap." Roger left them.

Miss Asquith spoke slowly. "As you know, Richard was having trouble getting support for his nation from his friends in Australia. The Yanks, Britain, the Dutch— they all refused to recognize him. He was vulnerable to being thrown in prison without some sort of recognition. He became desperate, and he considered Japan. It wasn't treasonous, after all, Malang is an independent nation and is free to make any alliance that it wishes." Hawk squinted in the hot sun and looked at her from beneath unsympathetic brows. He leaned on the cistern.

"Of course, he didn't trust them, and I'm sure they didn't trust *him*. They both knew that any alliance was simply for convenience. He resisted contacting them for quite a while. But then, he began having trouble getting support from even the citizens of Malang. Ranke was becoming popular, being a rough and tumble outdoorsman and all that rot. Richard devised this plan. He would let the Japanese have Roger as insurance of his loyalty to them. They needed Malang's oil, or so he thought, and he needed their military support. So he let them have him. He didn't tell Roger about it. The poor boy thought it was a real kidnapping."

"Didn't we all?" Hawk interrupted. "That St. Cyr's a real nice fella!"

"Yes," she answered quietly. She didn't look at him as she continued. "As you can see, the kidnapping helped unify his popular support in New Oss. The kidnapping generated a great deal of sympathy, and he put on a brave facade through it all."

"Was Starrett and Powers in on it?"

"No. Mr. Starrett is much too wise a man to concoct anything like that. And he loves Roger. Only Richard and Mr. Plunkett, and later myself knew about it. We repaired your landing barge soon after it was damaged and hid it away. We came over here to tell Roger what had been going on. I persuaded Richard to do that, as soon as I learned of the matter. We told Roger not to worry. I felt better about it after that. Sergeant Bupta looked in on Roger for us and sent messages back to New Oss by means of runners. Richard had offered to make Bupta the commander of Malang's militia. He had no one experienced in military matters. Richard arranged an 'accident' at the refinery, and the town was virtually deserted when the Japanese came and took Roger. This almost backfired. He wanted some witnesses, he just didn't want a number of them large enough to stop the kidnappers. As it turned out, only Powers saw it, and not everyone believed him. Bupta helped get the Japanese through your lines. When Richard saw that you didn't believe Powers, he tried to involve Ranke."

"So Bupta was fartin' around with Japs," Hawk said, looking over at the grisly cage that contained his remains. He felt better about what he had done to the sergeant.

"Yes. And it all went well, until just a few days ago. We became alarmed about the Japanese buildup. There was no need for an ally to bring in such strength. Richard was in no danger of being arrested by the Australians. He questioned the Japanese colonel. The colonel was very straightforward about it. He admitted that he had no intention of honoring his agreement. He was going to take New Oss and its oilfields for Japan. He said he need not support a puppet government when the Greater East Asia Co-Prosperity

Sphere could govern Malang directly. Sergeant Bupta wasn't told of this disagreement."

"I think he got the general idea," said Hawk.

"You see, the situation had become drastically altered. Roger was no longer among friends. He was the prisoner of a deceitful enemy. Richard refused to tell anyone what he'd done. He continued with his plan to rally sympathy among the townspeople. He depended upon you to defeat the Japanese. He even called in the A.I.F. at the last."

"Is that right? That left out one little detail," Hawk said. "The kid was still over here. If we won he'd be in bad shape, and if we lost, he'd be in worse shape."

"Yes. That's when I came to realize what a truly deranged man Richard is. Roger was of secondary importance to him. He said that the Japanese wouldn't harm a child, and that he had more important things to consider. I felt compelled to do something. I had no alternative but to try a rescue myself. I sent Mellie with a message for Roger. He knew I was coming."

Hawk turned toward the cistern and splashed himself again. "Not exactly *all* by yourself," he corrected her.

"No."

Hawk noticed Roger staring at him. He winked at the boy. "Come on," he told Miss Asquith, "we oughta get outer here." He gestured for Roger to return. "Your daddy's a real character, ain't he?"

"Yessir."

"Bad situation." Hawk stared down into the well. He could see a reflection of himself. The apparition was intimidating. The sunlight glanced off of the water and sent golden shadows rocking gently across his face. "You came after him," said Hawk to her. "That counts for something."

"Yes, I hope so. And you came, merely because it was the right thing to do. I know that you don't care much for me, but I must say that I admire you," she said in a low voice.

Hawk stood up straight. "Let's go. I gotta blow that base and get back to the landing craft before morning."

He didn't mention having to get to New Oss before the Japanese. It didn't seem that would be possible. Air recon was keeping a close watch on the enemy movements. New Oss wouldn't be surprised, but surprise or no, they would still be in trouble. Hawk was sure that he would be part of at least some of that trouble.

They followed the gully back to the trail. By following it, they would have no trouble finding the six marines who were left near it. They didn't find them, however. They found only one American, and he had been beaten to death. A quiver of Hoonoomaroo arrows was strewn across the matted jungle floor. The brush had been flattened for several yards, as if there had been a major struggle. Hawk looked around. It was getting dark.

He turned the dead marine over. His weapons and all the weapons of the others had been taken. A grenade was in the dead man's web belt. Hawk lifted it off the belt, straightened its pin and dropped it into his pocket. Miss Asquith whispered, "Hoonoomaroo," at one point, but otherwise none of them spoke. All three understood the gravity of the predicament. It was night in the land of the Hoonoomaroo. They had one rifle with one clip in it, a woman and a little boy. Hawk picked up three helmets and they each put one on to protect their eyes. Roger wanted to wear only the liner, due to the great weight of the steel pot, but the two adults made him wear both parts of the helmet. They were certain to cross paths with the Hoonoomaroo; it was only a question of where and when. The fact that the rabid natives had overpowered six marines didn't give them any confidence about what the outcome would be. Hawk knew that the tribe would be more aggressive than at his first meeting with them. They knew now that marines weren't invincible.

The three of them moved wordlessly along the trail, hoping that their silence would protect them. The method seemed to work, until they reached the main trail that led to Hollow Mountain, when they heard the first familiar whoop of the unseen savages. It came from behind them, from somewhere along the smaller trail. They had been followed all along.

Hawk's neck was so stiff now that he could barely turn his head. Even in the fullness of his strength, properly armed and with a substantial number of fighting men, this land could easily have taken his life. Here, tonight, its full barbaric splendor was brought home to him: the Hoonoomaroo, with their violent and macabre ways; the even more vicious Nodu, thriving in the disease-ridden morass; the man-eating Cahwey, also somewhere out there; the Japanese, curiously at home in the backwoods; and the modernized tribes, like Mellie's, contending with all of it, fighting to survive against the sheer horror. Death stalked a man at every breath.

And yet Hawk belonged here. He had come all the way out here to kill two white men, and he would go on surviving, or else be forced to abandon the boy and woman to a stone-age nightmare too frightening to let the imagination dwell upon. Five of his men were out there with the Hoonoomaroo tonight. They were probably still alive. He peered calmly down the black void of the trail. In spite of the centuries of civilization behind him, he was the most savage of this jungle's denizens. He had chosen this life, he had made himself into what he was, he had been forged in blood. The others were evil through ignorance, or accidents of nature. He was just evil.

A whoop trilled in front of them. Two more ululated from behind. Tympanic, satanic, the morbid and mesmerizing music of the Hoonoomaroo burst from the darkness. Hawk led Miss Asquith and Roger forward. His face, his movements betrayed no emotion and none of the pain that wracked his body. He asked no mercy, and God help anything that asked it of him. The other two trembled, forcing each step from their paralyzed limbs. Miss Asquith couldn't stifle a whimper. Her grip on Roger's arm was hurting him. A single torch landed in the trail in front of the Sergeant. He kicked it aside with an obscenity, refusing to break his stride.

Roger screamed, a pitiful little boy's scream. A large and gnarled grey hand had him by the ankle.

Hawk fired into the jungle at the side of the trail. An ash-covered body wearing the conical dung headdress fell at Roger's feet. It thrashed in repulsive death throes. Hawk didn't finish the native off. He needed the bullets. Miss Asquith squealed when she saw the Hoonoomaroo's talisman on the end of his stick. Other disembodied hands reached out from the jostling leaves. Rage obliterated the searing pain in Hawk's neck. He ripped the bayonet from his belt and hacked at the hands. Torches landed before and behind them, firing the night in orange light. The beastly horde of Hoonoomaroo glided into full view.

Miss Asquith crouched, clutching Roger to her. She turned her wide and incredulous eyes from one alien monster to the next. They stood in zombie-like silence, staring from their eyeless heads at the cringing prey. The trail behind the three was crowded with tribesmen for as far as the eye could see in the flickering light. Two score more were gathered in front of them. One of their number spoke in a dreadful monotone. It was impossible to tell which one was speaking, for their mouths were invisible.

Hawk had seen this procedure before and knew what to expect. He even felt he understood what the speaker was

saying. He reached for his grenade. He knew what to do this time. No sense fooling around.

The Hoonoomaroo weren't as rigid in their operations as he thought, however. They could be flexible and crafty when it came to getting something that they wanted badly. While Hawk was watching the speaker and trying to keep an eye on the other tribesmen, several burst through the dense vegetation behind him. They latched onto Roger and swooped him up to their shoulders. The boy cried out in terror, but his rapidly moving captors had already disappeared into the endless jungle night. Miss Asquith cried out, too, when she realized what had happened. She ran to the side of the trail in an attempt to follow them. Her effort produced two unfortunate results. She blocked Hawk from following them and she received the haft of a spear across her forehead. She fell back and Hawk caught her with one arm. When he looked up, the Hoonoomaroo were gathering their torches and fading into the jungle.

Miss Asquith held her head and began to cry. The natives had vanished. They were not interested in her, nor did it seem that they were interested in Sgt. Hawk. But he was interested in them. "I'm going after them," he told her. "You can try to come with me or you can stay."

She shook her head. She knew her limitations this time. "I'm all right. Hurry. See what can be done. In...a little while, I'll go back for the others at Hollow Mountain."

He nodded and mouthed a slow "Okay." He left her sitting there on the ground and plunged into the darkness where Roger had disappeared.

Hawk could hear them. They were quiet. Inhumanly quiet, but that many men couldn't be perfectly quiet. They didn't have their music to cover the noise of the rustling leaves. He could smell them. Their odor was powerful, it clung to the forest long after their passage. The impracticality of it never occurred to him—one man rabidly chasing hundreds. He moved faster, tearing at the soft-leaved darkness, thick anger swelling in his torn throat.

Like an ocean draining toward a hole in its floor, he heard the vile concourse in front of him drawing together, bearing down on one locale. They were congregating. They were apparently coming near to their village. Hawk ripped at the shiny moonlit leaves that barred his passage. Thorny vines ripped at his bare chest and sleeves. A quietness came from ahead of him. All was still. A bird howled and it reverberated through the silent forest. Insects droned. A frog trilled. Hawk breathed heavily. He slowed. He stopped. He could no longer hear them. He heard only himself.

Something had happened. Had they heard him? Were they lying in wait? He growled. He hoped they were. He charged into the tangled nightmare of nature gone wild, taking up the same course with even greater determination. Now he saw the dim light through the forbidding screen of night leaves. Again he slowed. It must be a village. Their village, the place of their *tambaran*. He crouched and continued toward it at a speed that could hardly be called cautious. He unslung the rifle, his eyes wide and staring madly at the weakly glowing specter that winked through the trees. He knelt at the edge of the clearing. Low fires created a strange half-light.

The ghostly tribesmen moved about in weird silence. In the middle of a ring of filthy huts, the *tambaran* was under way. The crowd swayed in a grotesque rhythm, half lewd, half violent. Several held Roger off to one side. Four bodies, the bodies of white men, were strewn across the open ground. They were

naked and it appeared that they had been disembow-
eled or castrated, or both. The fifth marine was still
alive. He was tied face down on two flat slabs of wood.
He barely breathed. A long line of Hoonoomaroo were
before him.

Hawk pulled a leg up under himself, raising the
rifle. He would kill a few of them. They would kill him,
but he would rid the earth of a few. It was worth it, it
was a fair trade. Killing, how he enjoyed it, when it
served a purpose! If the pure evil that spread before him
thought it had no match, it had never met Sgt. Hawk. He
smiled. The frozen blue eyes were ablaze.

Then one of the Hoonoomaroo closest to the naked
marine cried out in an anguished voice. Hawk lowered
his rifle for a moment to see what this meant. He impatiently folded his upper lip in against his teeth like a
snarling animal. The native who had screamed walked
over to the marine's head and raised both arms in the
air. It was a signal that the victim had died. Four
tribesmen rushed over, untied him and turned him
over. Now he must be mutilated. The medicine man
made his appearance. Long bird of paradise feathers
jutted from his dung headdress. He unsheathed a
curved knife and strutted over to the dead American. As
he did, one of the men holding Roger tore the boy's shirt
open.

Two powerful, semiautomatic cracks roared from
the jungle, one close upon the heels of the other. Both
the medicine man and the Hoonoomaroo with Roger
fell like puppets whose strings had been severed. The
others looked around the edges of the forest. No panic
marked their bizarre movements. Their faces were
invisible behind their masks. Their unearthly courage

was probably due in part to their being unable to see the facial expressions of their fellows; there could be no contagious fear or mass hysteria. Hawk stepped out of the protective foliage. All the vacant eyeholes turned toward him. His slouching, confident stride took him into their midst. They watched him, the oversized masks turning as he progressed across the clearing. No one tried to stop him. His boots crunched heavily on the earth. He held the rifle in one hand. The red firelight lit the beads of perspiration on his jaw muscles. His lips were parted, his teeth clenched. His eyes were deep and clear, cutting like sharpened steel from one of the forest monsters to the next. He stopped and shifted his weight to one leg, his whole body issuing an insolent challenge. He stood over the dead medicine man, halfway between the marine most recently killed and Roger. Ghastly distortions of obscene color swam before the boy's eyes as he looked up from the carnage to Hawk's iron features.

"Come here, boy," Hawk said. The voice was low, deep, Delta-accented, serious and contemptuous of the vast horde of men that surrounded them. Roger stepped from under the big grey hand that loosely detained him and walked quickly to Hawk's side. The multitude tightened in a circle around the two of them, leaving no avenue of escape. Their bare feet stirred rancid dust. All was quiet again as the eyeless heads surveyed their prey. They recognized Hawk and they knew it would serve no purpose to speak to him.

With a loose, casual motion, Hawk lifted the lone grenade from where it hung on his pocket. He stuck its ring over the muzzle of the rifle and pulled it free with the gun sight. His thumb was light on the safety lever.

He held the bomb up for all to see. Their masks inclined slightly as they looked at it. They spoke in low tones to one another. His intensely hateful eyes mocked them. Roger looked calmly up at him. He trusted Hawk. If the sergeant chose to blow the two of them up, then that was what had to be done.

Hawk slid his thumb off the safety lever. The striker knocked the spoon forward and smacked home. White smoke spewed angrily from within the cast iron sphere. The natives grunted and began backing away. The marine tossed the grenade lazily over his shoulder.

It landed among the crowd standing between Hawk and the place where he had entered the village. The yellow flash violently knocked a dozen of them dead on the ground. Others were maimed. Hawk backed through this opening, kicking at the wounded when an opportunity afforded itself.

He held the rifle in one hand and pushed Roger with the other. By the time they reached edge of the forest, the tribe had regrouped. They approached the retreating pair in a solid front that spanned the width of the clearing. Hawk fired into them. Two fell, but he didn't have enough ammunition for that method to work.

He reached for his shirt pocket with an exaggerated motion and then held up his empty hand. Pretending to have another grenade, he made the same gesture as before toward the foresight of the Ml. They stopped, talking in loud tones this time, as if they had come back to life from some trancelike state. Several broke and ran, others moved at a more dignified pace for the safety of the forest. Hawk steered Roger into the jungle.

They ran through the underbrush. Hawk knew that

the bluff wouldn't work again. Hoonoomaroo weren't timid, they required tangible evidence of destruction before they would exhibit any caution. Hawk managed to find the trail again. Before long they had overtaken Miss Asquith.

"They're after us," Roger told her. Hawk gestured down the trail. They ran at a trot at first, then picked up the pace when they heard the noise behind them. They were coming. Had Hawk known that he had just visited only one of a dozen of their villages, he would have appreciated the great rumble of stampeding behind him. He knew they were a persistent bunch. He found out just how persistent when the three of them broke from the cover of the forest and entered the open country near the shore. When they were a hundred yards into the open, without the slightest cover, he looked over his shoulder and saw the natives following. Thousands of them, crawling like insects out of the forest.

"They want the boy!" Miss Asquith gasped. Her lungs were on fire. "They won't give up. Shoot him! Please!" She reached for Hawk and fell into the wiry grass at his feet.

"Get up," he quietly ordered, "nobody's shootin' nobody. It's just a little further." The Hoonoomaroo filled the vast open plain and closed the gap between them and their victims.

"I can't," she cried. "Leave me. They don't want me. They'll just kill me. Go on. Get Roger to Hollow Mountain." She had been weakened by making the trip into and out of the enemy camp in one day. Roger had made only one trip. He was still able to walk. Hawk handed Roger the rifle and picked her up. The ocean of dung-masked creatures walked at a faster pace, sensing the kill. Isolated whoops alternated with an answering roar from the gruesome ranks.

Hawk struggled beneath her weight. Normally, he would have been able to carry the slight girl without difficulty. Tonight, he needed someone to carry *him*. But it wasn't far. He fought his way up the rocks, dizzy and laboring to breathe. She began climbing for herself. Roger let the way and the faint Hawk fell behind. He saw them climbing below him. He turned around and grabbed for a few more inches of the slope. Hands seized him from under his armpits, and raised him upwards.

"Hey. Hawk, looks like you brought your friends along." It was Canlon and Carlisle was with him. They were right where Hawk had left them.

"Yeah," Hawk closed his eyes tightly and continued to breathe heavily, "yeah, they been askin' for Joe Canlon...Joe Canlon, that's all them Hooners can talk about."

Joe smiled. "That's because I'm such a good lookin' bastard. Want us to thin 'em out a little?" Joe wasn't worried. They had two BAR's, a grease gun and Hawk's Thompson, as well as a crate of various kinds of hand grenades.

"No," Hawk coughed. "No noise. Don't tip off the Nips."

"You goddam sure better be in the mood for love, because they're climbin' the rocks like ants," Joe warned.

"You got any extra white phosphorous?"

"Yeah, we come prepared, man." Joe fished around in a bag of grenades.

"Give 'em one of those. That oughta scare the flies off of 'em."

One didn't, but two of them did. The burning, curling, shining white explosion dispersed the most dedicated among them. The horde of zombies retreated toward the forest. Even so, it was not a panicked retreat. The marines felt certain that they would be back.

The Americans grew quiet when Hawk told them what had happened to their six comrades. Hawk couldn't worry about it tonight. He couldn't do anything without more men. He still had to blow the base and get back to the defense of New Oss. He settled down to rest.

Roger sat next to him. "Can you get me another grenade, Sergeant Hawk? The Japanese took mine away from me before we left New Oss."

"Sure. As a matter of fact, I'll get you the same one. Don't let me catch you puttin' the charge back in it this time, either."

Roger grinned.

* * *

THE NIGHT PASSED QUICKLY, too quickly for the dozing Hawk. A large moon lit the grey rocks, bathing the men in a ghostly white glow. A couple of hours before dawn, they heard explosions in the distance. Carlisle voiced the opinion that the Japanese were landing along the coast, and were coming after them. Canlon hypothesized that the enemy had had some sort of accident and had blown up their own ammunition. After they had all thought about it for a while, McGranger hit upon the truth. The Hoonoomaroo's human wave had wandered into the minefield on the eastern beach while trying to surprise the marines from the rear.

Canlon shook his head. "That shoulda killed every damn one of 'em."

Hawk raised his head and managed to say, "Goddam shame."

Miss Asquith took a great deal of satisfaction from this turn of events, making a few bloodthirsty comments. Half the men stayed up all night, and she was among them. She was too intoxicated by the day's adventures to rest. Captain Carlisle sat beside her, making small talk, in spite of being quite sleepy. He had spent a boring day in the hot sun on the rocks and would have liked nothing better than a few hours of sleep. But he also suffered from an intoxication. He wanted to spend every available minute with Miss Asquith. She was polite to him, and went so far as to make a few attempts at conversation when his own ideas ran out.

Hawk's eyes opened when the darkness went away. He lay still, too tired to move, and in no hurry to disturb his throbbing wounds. 0650 was still about an hour away. He lapsed in and out of consciousness. He heard Miss Asquith say, "Isn't he a marvelous man?" once, but he didn't know that she was referring to him. Had he heard a few derogatory remarks, he might have sat up and argued with her.

As the intensity of the daylight grew, his eyes opened wider and his brain began to function. His rural instincts roused him. The chickens were up. The nagging feeling that he was late for something forced him to sit up. He remembered the submarine base clearly now, and not just as some knotted tension at the center of his drowsing brain.

"Hey, Hawk, who's gonna mark it? I planted the RDX yesterday," said Canlon.

"You, Joe. You'll get the Navy Cross for this one," the sergeant answered. His neck was stiffer than the day before, virtually immobile. The flesh around his throat felt tight, as if a piece of it had been removed—which it had. Pain blared from behind his neck; he could feel pressure on his forehead, as if Bupta's foot was still on it. He touched the abrasion and looked down at the cuts that covered his body. He could feel each one. His leg was swollen. His hand hurt violently whenever he touched the palm to anything.

"You know, I could get shot, if the Japs come out and catch me up there," said Joe.

"They have to come out one at a time," Hawk assured him. "We'll take care of them. You try to make a guy a hero and he turns chickenshit on you."

"Okay," Canlon laughed. "Big shit! I'll do it."

"I'll do it," Carlisle volunteered. Nobody said anything. Hawk considered making a comment about Carlisle wanting to put on a show for Miss Asquith, but there was no sense in making the officer look like an even bigger ass than he already was. The sergeant could be gracious to lesser creatures. He decided to misunderstand the captain, and in the misunderstanding, afford him the opportunity to change his mind.

"Sure, if you like. It wouldn't hurt to have two people go up there. We'll need everybody here, though, if the shootin' starts."

"Well then, I guess I should stay," said Carlisle. Canlon laughed good-naturedly, without making fun of the captain. He took four WP grenades and started down the rocks. They all watched solemnly as he waded the brown stream, passed the gurgling waterfall and ascended Hollow Mountain. He reached the summit of the rock at 0652 and immediately set off one of the white smoke bombs. Hawk looked at the white water spilling from the grey rock and the stream twisting through the marl and sand. It was all kind of pretty. Soon, God willing, it would all vanish.

The marines looked anxiously at the sky. It was clear and blue without the sign of a cloud—or a plane. Canlon didn't set off the second grenade until 0700. He knelt on the broad summit, like Moses awaiting the tablets. No sign of the aircraft. Hawk got to his feet and began to swear. The other men followed his example. They spoke of the various socially taboo proclivities of the Army, and the particular wanton degeneracy of members of the Air Force. Miss Asquith lost whatever sensitivity she had had to profanity in a matter of minutes.

0705 passed. At 0710 the strike force was sighted far out over the Pacific. Carlisle began making noises like he was going to lead a cheer when Hawk told him to shut up. Canlon finally spotted the planes and set off a third WP. As he did, a Japanese soldier in a full uniform ducked from beneath the waterfall. He shaded his eyes with his hands and looked at the peak of the rock. It was covered with smoke.

"Somebody kill that sonofabitch," Hawk grumbled. The soldier carried a handgun on his hip. Hawk knew that he would never hear the end of it if the bastard took a shot at Canlon.

"I'll get him," said Carlisle. And when he did, no one

was more surprised than Carlisle himself. Hawk thought that the captain would just scare the enemy soldier away, and that would be good enough. But the officer dropped his three pronged foresight within the circular hindsight and squeezed the trigger. The Japanese pushed back on his right leg, as if he were roller skating, and slipped to the ground.

"I got him!" said Carlisle.

"Good shot, Cap'n."

"Did you see that? I got a Jap!"

"Yeah, good shot."

"I got him, just like that. What a shot!"

"Nice shootin', Captain."

"Damn." Carlisle looked to see if Miss Asquith had seen it. She had. He would be able to tell his grandchildren that he had killed a Jap. Or maybe he wouldn't talk about it. Maybe he would tell them that they shouldn't ask such questions, and they would know by the way that he said it, that he had, and that it was very serious. But he didn't feel serious. He felt giddy. Of course, the enemy soldier had been several hundred yards away, and he had never known what hit him, and he couldn't have done much about it if he had. But some men feel giddy when they shoot an animal, and some of those even boast of it! In fact, absurd as you may think, some of those who boast go so far as to chop the animal's head off and hang it on a wall. Carlisle was silly, but he was far from the silliest thing mankind has produced. Canlon heard the shot. He tossed the last WP and ran down the rock.

Hawk looked at the distant planes. "Hope them shit-bags seen that. The dumb bastard blew it too soon. The wind's blowin' the smoke and they're still a long way off.

Joe probably shit a blue streak when he heard that shot."

His concern proved unfounded. The motors of the aircraft became audible and grew in loudness. After a point, they seemed to approach much more rapidly. Excitement filled the watchers below. They ignored Joe's scramble for his life through the stream at the foot of the rock. The air vibrated with the sound of powerful engines and crackling propellers. The first stick of bombs hit the mountain like a giant machine gun. Black explosions leaped hundreds of feet into the air all up and down the slope. The ground trembled beneath the observers and Hollow Mountain disappeared behind a curtain of smoke. They heard another stick hit. By now, the RDX and gelatin had been set off. Carlisle led his cheer unopposed. The RDX had been set near the gelatin, on opposite sides of the mountain's thin wall.

Two more explosions, in rapid succession, rocked the mountain, these being louder than the sticks of bombs. Something within the base had been set off. The high wind blew the smoke out over the ocean, and the injured rock became visible, the thin crown of its roof caved in. It belched fire like a volcano. The flimsy walls of the slope fell inward, splashing into the water. Nothing within could have survived. Dive bombers swooped low over the hole that now bled black smoke. They dumped tanks of naphtha into the inferno with unerring accuracy. The heavy bombers returned and the resulting mass of explosions caused even the lower slope to split. Fire leapt from every crevice—blue, red, orange, white and yellow, but the fire was quickly over-whelmed. The ocean, a force stronger than anything made by man, ripped the mountain open from its summit to the waterfall. A mass of white water, in size comparable only to the sky itself, blew the walls apart and washed the mountain into oblivion, flooding the land behind it.

Joe beat the rising water to the top of the marines' observation point. "That takes care of that shit," said Hawk, when they all finished congratulating him. "We gotta get back and face the music. We'll need Bupta's men in New Oss. We'll need a hell of a lot more than that. If we don't hear from Regiment, that's all she wrote. I doubt if Regiment has got what it takes to stop all them Japs I seen. How many men you reckon you'll need to get back to Ranke's, Joe?"

Joe squinted painfully. "About two divisions."

"Nah, shit. You take a couple bags of grenades and you won' t have no trouble. Them Hooners lost a few last night."

"Maybe *you* wouldn't have no trouble. But when you're as good-lookin' as I am..."

"Right. Get them men and bring 'em back along the coast. The Air Force is supposed to hit the Nodu, so you ain't gonna have no trouble outa them, either. Besides that, you'll have a whole platoon with you."

Joe rubbed his big, broken nose and took a deep breath. He grunted and said, "Okay, gimme three men."

"Take 'em. See you in New Oss."

"Yeah, Hawk."

Hawk lay painfully against the wall of the landing craft. He felt as if he was still lying in the barbed wire cage, vividly conscious of each biting spike. The barge chugged against the sea on its way back to New Oss. Miss Asquith came and sat beside him. He didn't say anything. She smoothed the hair from his bruised forehead.

"Does all this mean that you ain't gonna be the Queen of Malang?" he asked roughly.

"You don't *have* to be nasty, you know," she chided.

"You don't have to answer, either."

She rested her shoulder against his. "Richard did some great things. That can't be disputed. But he was weak. Too weak, I'm afraid."

"You like 'em strong, huh?"

"Perhaps," she laughed, ignoring his belligerence.

"Ain't you heard that opposites attract? All two strong people can do is fight to see who's the strongest."

"Perhaps."

He sighed and stretched a little.

"Are you badly hurt, do you think?" she cooed.

"Not bad enough to have you sittin' this close to me." She wilted a bit with embarrassment. "See what I mean?" he said.

She nodded and rested her head on his shoulder. "Yes. You are a boor, through and through."

"Mmm hmm." Hawk was naive when it came to women. But he knew what he didn't like.

* * *

NEW OSS WAS PREPARING for its own downfall. The police, as well as the local militia, were sent out to the marine perimeter to bolster the defenses. The native population had for the most part faded into the surrounding jungles, in order to let the civilized peoples of the east and west settle their differences. News arrived that the little town of Batwan in the south-eastern corner of Malang had fallen. Sir Richard continued to lead his people with a bold flair. He had made another stirring speech to them, just before Hawk and the others arrived, assuring them that there would be either relief from or victory over the enemy. The people believed him.

The listening posts had been pulled back inside the wire. A need for them no longer existed. The sounds of the gathering Japanese could be heard all over New Oss. They eschewed stealth as they trampled the encircling jungle, seeking the best positions for their heavy weapons. Each side ignored the other as they prepared for the upcoming holocaust. Some of the timid civilians began to have breakdowns as they witnessed this madness. It was midafternoon of the day of the airstrike on Hollow Mountain.

Hawk and Carlisle made directly for the radio when they returned to the capital. They skipped the time-consuming intermediary of coded messages. Hawk called his superiors and alerted them to the situation. Regiment conceded that his predicament was severe, but that sufficient forces were not available to reinforce him. They would, however, be able to evacuate him.

"Fine," Hawk snapped rudely into the transmitter. "When?"

The voice on the wire calmly answered, "A few days. Intelligence reports that they hit the sub base today. The waters will still be hot for a while. The subs already out there will have to run out of fuel."

Hawk dropped the headset. Safe. For God's sake! What could he say? Carlisle took over. He began shouting something about the emergencies and exigencies of the situation. Plunkett sat in his chair, listening with a sort of detached interest. Hawk took the radioman's arm and without warning, tossed him onto the floor. Then he sat in the vacant chair. He was tired and needed to sit down. He could feel a mild fever throughout his body. Several of his wounds seemed already to be reddening with infection. Carlisle looked at Hawk as he set the headset down.

"I can't believe this," said the captain.

"You will."

Sir Richard St. Cyr walked into the room. Plunkett got slowly off the floor and stood beside him. "Will they relieve us?" St. Cyr asked.

"Nope," Hawk answered without looking at him.

"Then we must surrender with honor," said Sir Richard.

"We might," said Hawk. "Whatever we do won't be on your say so." He turned to Carlisle. "We gotta blow the refinery and storage tanks, that's for sure. We gotta make this place more worthless than it already is."

"You will *not* destroy the refinery installations, under any circumstances," Sir Richard told him. "Malang is just another jungle wilderness without her oil. It would take years to rebuild that complex."

"That's right," Hawk replied. "And the Japs ain't gonna be here for years."

"You will follow my orders, Sergeant. This is my country and my Army is out there defending the town," St. Cyr said. He showed no signs of being repentant about what he had done.

Hawk laughed, an ugly laugh. "He has a point there, Hawk," Carlisle intervened. "I mean, we need help from his militia and the police. There's no need to alienate him." Hawk stood with a weary groan. He touched his left hand to his right wrist and brought it suddenly across Sir Richard's face. The Prime Minister stumbled backwards, almost regaining his balance a couple of times, but finally falling down in the doorway.

"Does that alienate your ass?" Hawk snarled. "I been real nice to you, buddy. Next time I see you, you better hope I ain't holdin' a rifle. Now crawl on outa here, you goddam snake!" Sir Richard looked up, his open mouth bleeding. He tried to get up. Hawk put a boot on his shoulder and shoved him back into the wall. "I told you to crawl!" Sir Richard crawled out into the hall. Carlisle watched without interfering or speaking.

When the officer finally spoke, he asked, "Are we really going to surrender?"

"I'm against it, to tell you the truth. If they don't shoot us down, they'll haul us off to some POW camp and starve us to death. If they're gonna let the women and children go, they'll let 'em go without us. But," Hawk rubbed his feverish face, "I can't order these men to commit suicide, and that's what it's gonna take to hold New Oss."

Carlisle stared at the floor with an expression that one might have if he had just been told that his entire family had been wiped out in a plane crash. He had never faced certain destruction before. Hawk knew about such things. He had brought Roger back to *this*. He had to survive, somehow, until the evacuation.

"God! What do we do?" Carlisle asked.

"Well, the way I got it figured, we fight off their first few probes and see what develops. They might get soft. I've never known Japs to get soft, but there's always a first time. Then they might lay some kind of siege on us. We'll still be in trouble if it lasts a while; we got no medical supplies and damn little ammo or food. They'll be a lot of people hurt. But maybe we can hold out till the evacuation. It's a gamble, Captain. Will the number dead be worth the number evacuated? I'm just a sergeant, I ain't used to makin' them kind of decisions. That's for officers. It's always been my job to keep my men alive. If we give up, I doubt if any of us will make it."

"I'm going to make Major Clemson give me an order,"

Carlisle said, an agitated expression knotting his smooth features. "That's what I'm going to do on the whole thing!"

"Captain," Hawk sighed, "is that the thing to do?"

Carlisle looked at him. "No...I suppose it isn't. *We'll* have to decide, won't we?"

"Yessir."

Carlisle nodded his head and studied his feet. "If I'm going to be the one that blows the refinery," he said, "how should I go about it?" His jutting jaw was set. Hawk fought the urge to laugh at him.

"Get the sergeant major to put you in touch with a couple of men from the engineers. Y'all oughta be able to use some of these dud bombs they dropped in the air raid."

Carlisle stood. "I'll do it. It's time to stand tall. I'll do it, now." Hawk winked at him as he stalked out of the door. When Hawk sat down again, he was truly alone. He knew that he would be the one to give the order. Since fighting was all he knew, he knew already what the order would be.

He walked down to the study and stretched out on St. Cyr's couch. The attack could come in ten minutes or ten hours. He knew that he should be overseeing the defense preparations, but he needed rest more. He was finding it difficult to string coherent thoughts together. He was feverish, nauseous and weak. In the grand scheme of things, he considered these to be minor problems, but they were interfering with his normal functioning. His command would need him at his best. You're never at your best when you have to be, he thought. That was the last totally conscious thought that he had. His hand dropped limply over the edge of the couch. He half-dreamed, half-thought of how Joe Canlon had been kicked off the couch. Like a dog, he thought, like…a…

When he awakened, the room was darkened by late afternoon. He felt the presence of someone in the room, and knew instinctively that person was unarmed. He turned his head. Miss Asquith was sitting in the chair across from him. She smiled. He had heard no commotion. Presumably, the Japanese were waiting until dark, or dawn of the next day.

"Captain Carlisle has destroyed the refinery," she said. Her words were low and soft in the quiet of the room.

"Good," he said, sitting up. He rubbed his aching forehead. The sleep had helped his fever.

"Will you surrender?" she asked.

"I don't think so."

"Can I get you anything? Tea, perhaps?"

"I wouldn't mind some coffee."

"The captain had no trouble. Snipers didn't bother them. Did you hear the blast?" she asked, pausing in the doorway.

"I might have." He focused his eyes on the floor. His

nerves didn't bother him with reports of blasts unless they were within a few yards.

"Richard tried to get the militia to stop Captain Carlisle. They paid no attention. It's the end of his rule, I'm afraid." He looked up at her, neither of them commenting on the brief reign of St. Cyr. "I'll get that coffee."

She returned after a short while with a cup of coffee and a cup of tea on a tray. She sat beside him. He put one large finger through the tiny handle of the cup. "Why did you do it?" she asked.

"What? Oh, about the kid?"

"Yes, why endanger yourself in a situation that had little or nothing to do with you?"

"Well...not many situations *do*, when you get right down to it. You don't pay no attention to danger after you been doin' this kinda thing for a while."

"But you knew that you were surrounded by fools. You seemed like a practical man. I don't mean this to sound insulting, but you didn't seem like someone motivated by noble instincts."

"Yeah? Well, you can be practical and still do what's right, I figure. When you set out doin' what you think is right, you run across a hell of a lot of wrong. Sometimes it rubs off on you. I guess I could go around lookin' like a preacher and bein' nice to folks, but that ain't what gets my job done. Sometimes them folks that carries on like preachers ain't so nice, either."

"So you were just doing what was right? That's fascinating. A bit *too* fascinating, I think. I can't help but think that there's more to it than that."

"You got a bad attitude. Everybody ain't out to get something outa somebody else, you know. I come over here to kill Japs. That was mainly because I was a pretty mean fella, I guess. I didn't want to work on engines or scrape barnacles off ships. I got in the outfit doin' the killin'. I found out the killin' works both ways. I've lost a lot of friends. Most of 'em weren't fighters or killers, they just came over to do a job. I learned a lot from them. I'd be lyin' if I said I didn't like what I do. I belong here— any other kind of life would be too tame and I'd just get in trouble. I don't go around like a singin' cowboy lookin' for good deeds, but when something needs to be done and everybody's too goddam chickenshit to do it, then I goddam sure will."

"You live a terrible life."

"That I do."

"I've changed my opinion of you. There's something in you that I never thought I would find. You don't have to answer this, if you don't want. Has your opinion of me changed?"

"I never had one. Except when you was tryin' to get in my way."

"I can guess what that opinion was. You didn't consider me a gold digger, before that? Please, be honest."

"There was a lot going on. I didn't give it much thought. That's probably what I would have thought."

"Then you would have been right. I've seen myself in Richard. It disgusts me. I would like to think that this has changed me for the better. Perhaps that is expecting too much. We can't know if we've changed until a situation arises, can we?"

Hawk knew he had wasted all of the time he could afford. He had to get outside. "No, ma'am. That's for sure, talk is real cheap." He stood.

She looked up at him. "I would value your respect. It would mean a great deal to me." She reached up and gently took hold of his injured hand.

"I could say that you already have it," he squeezed her hand and gave it back to her.

"But talk is cheap?"

* * *

MEN BUSTLED up and down behind the perimeter, arranging their meager supplies in such a way as to be most advantageous. Capt. Carlisle directed the operations like an old hand. He had already decided that once he got out of this, he would transfer to a rifle company. The pride he felt when he ordered fighting men around was unmatched by any other experience. But that pride had a price, and he hadn't paid it yet.

Hawk stalked wearily along the line. He could feel the fear. No one joked. Twilight brought a dread over him. He dreaded what his men would go through. They deserved better than this. The holes were too far apart. They had to be. The wire was too thin. The holes weren't deep enough. He lit a cigar and stopped to talk with some machine gunners.

* * *

MISS ASQUITH CLOSED the door behind her with a two-part click. Diana looked up from the book she was reading.

"Hello," Diana said coolly and looked back down at her book.

"Hello, dear." Miss Asquith sat on the foot of the

bed. Only Diana's forehead was visible from behind the book. She sat at the headboard with a sheet over her. "That's very heavy reading for a child, isn't it?"

Diana rested the book on her knees and looked up at her visitor. "You didn't come all the way up to my room to ridicule me, did you?"

Miss Asquith looked down with a hurt smile. "No," she answered.

"Then why did you?" Miss Asquith moved a little closer. "I wanted to make sure that you were all right and prepared for...whatever happens. And I just wanted to make sure that we were still friends."

"Well, you can be sure that we aren't."

"I see. I want you to understand that what I did, had to be done. There is a lot about it that you don't understand—and that is probably for the best."

"What? That Father tried to save a nation and make it independent? That Roger could have helped him to do it? That you are a disloyal, selfish person? That you've been traipsing behind that brute Sergeant Hawk for the past few days?"

Miss Asquith turned red. She wasn't much more mature than Diana, in spite of a decade and the intensity of her recent learning experiences. So she didn't hold her tongue. She took up an argument that she couldn't possibly win, nor should she have won, but she did speak quietly.

"Your father did something immoral, Diana. He sold a child, *his* child, to achieve a personal goal. He made me a part of it and that's what I resented most of all. What I did, had to be done. Granted, I did it for myself, but I also did it for your brother. He was in grave danger."

"Oh, yes, I had forgotten that he was enamored with that American, too. He *is* a child, and he *is* a member of our family—we must forgive *him*, but we don't have to forgive you. When I think of all your talk of gentlemen, and honor and what a man should be, and then you turn on my father. I think you are a very unstable person, Monica. And so does Father."

Miss Asquith looked down and spoke even more softly. "I probably am. I've...traveled extensively, Diana. As you know, my family is quite wealthy—yes, reprobates have families, too. You could say that I've been in search of opportunity. I was under the mistaken impression that I couldn't survive without a great deal of security. I've met a lot of gentlemen, and your father was exactly what I was looking for. Well off, handsome, charming, and in a unique position; far from a powerless or dull life. He had the misfortune of being in a war at the same time, and that brings out one's true character. I found him, shall we say, lacking. I know that you'll always hate me for telling you this, but perhaps someday you can avoid the same mistake."

"Thank you, Monica. Your advice is priceless. When I am ready to marry, I shall wander into a dive along the waterfront and tap a Sergeant Hawk on the shoulder."

Miss Asquith stood and walked over to the girl. She put her hand on her shoulder. Then she returned to the door. "No, dear, you won't," she said. She walked into the hall with the doorknob in her hand. She closed the door with a two-part click.

* * *

THE IMPERIAL ARMY started with a mortar barrage. They refused to accept women and children without a total surrender. This was harsh, even for the Japanese. Hawk knew he was dealing with some tough warriors, appropriate for the land of Malang.

The American foxholes were spread rather well, but the enemy had had the chance to leisurely study them. As the mortars increased to a furious crescendo, the Japanese laid on the heavy artillery. New Oss erupted under one continuous explosion. The Americans dutifully returned a few mortar rounds. But the Japanese were ensconced in the fearsome jungles, with their most desirable targets hidden. The townspeople quickly broke under the horror of the massive barrage. The majority of the militia ran from the perimeter and back to the safety of the town. The Americans felt like doing the same, but through their training and experience, they knew that it would do no good. Those fleeing were like the terrified insects in a field of grass who try to avoid the path of a lawn mower. The men staying on the perimeter suffered far fewer casualties than those running through the fountains of slashing steel.

Hawk clung to the bottom of his foxhole. The earth shook and the incandescent sky breathed an unholy heat down upon him. He wanted to tell the mortar crews to save their ammunition, but it was foolish to try to get up. He had to trust their discretion. Although men whose average age is twenty have little discretion, these men were an old twenty.

He knew from past experience that the Japanese barrages didn't last as long as an American barrage would, for two reasons: they were forever short of ammunition; and moreover, they liked to get in and mix it. They weren't interested in the preparation softening that Americans sometimes spent days or weeks on. Artillery wasn't war, that wasn't fighting. They sent whole companies jammed shoulder to shoulder into the muzzle of a machine gun, screaming lustily and dying in a mountain of gore. It was a nineteenth century tactic used on twentieth century weapons. Their casualties were always several times those of the Americans, but it didn't change them. No matter how short they became on ammunition and tactics, they were always long on courage.

Hawk clenched his teeth and waited for the mind-shattering crashes to subside. He knew that when they did, the

flood of enemy troops would throw themselves upon the wire. He didn't care. He only wanted the shells to stop, or at least slow down. The Japanese had a surprise for him, however. The barrage didn't stop. It continued through the night, in a softening maneuver worthy of the most cautious American commander.

After every series of nearby bursts, Hawk assured himself that now it would end. *Now it will end. It has to end.* But it didn't. His nerve endings rose from every depth within him, leapt to the surface of his being and reached out like aching tentacles at the sounds that were all around him. The noise rubbed the tentacles raw. Flying pellets of steel swished overhead, some burying themselves in the sides of his foxhole with smoking thumps. The falling shells became the very essence of his thoughts. That one landed over there; that one landed way over there; close, too close, this time; those are landing everywhere.

He waited for his life to be turned off, as if by a

switch. Suddenly, without even knowing or thinking about it, he was so close to the eternal, he could almost envision it. The finite was *here* behind his eyelids, it was *him,* it was his disconnected thoughts. The eternal was on the other side of his eyelids—maybe twenty feet on the other side—he could feel it. That was where his consciousness would leap when the switch was flipped. It would leave the vaporized body behind and go into the void. It would squeeze through a pinhole in the finite and burst into the infinite. He could feel it. He was that close to it—the cold brink. How long a human mind can operate on this brink, wedged into this pinhole, depends upon the individual.

The others fared no better. Most of them just died. Those that didn't, proved to be the unfortunate ones. They lay paralyzed, crying, screaming but unheard, shaking, urinating and defecating. The most hardened of the fatalists, the men who had laughed at the Japanese naval guns on Guadalcanal, were begging God for mercy.

The town was spared the intensity of shelling that the perimeter underwent, but it was far from immune. Dozens of defenseless wooden structures collapsed in black flurries of splinters.

Hawk eventually got used to it. He had gotten used to everything else, why not this? It angered him. Has the human psyche any limits to its capacity for suffering? An hour before dawn, he climbed out of his hole and began checking the positions. He knew that there would be a dawn attack.

He moved alone along the winding lines. Blinding flashes assaulted his eyes, appearing brightest along the corners of his vision. The flashes lit his silhouette, creating a strobe, making him appear to be walking in slow motion. He moved through it like some prehistoric beast on the verge of the cataclysm. The determination was still there in his rolling shoulders. He still challenged the end.

He noticed the wire. A large section of it was reduced to black ashes, flat on the pulverized ground. He would get more wire. They would be coming soon. He would get some men and string some wire right in the middle of all of this. They wouldn't expect that. He could still think, but he had trouble judging. Was it a brilliant idea about the wire, or was it insane? Or was it irrelevant? If it was irrelevant, it was insane. Or...what? He threw himself into a hole.

McGranger's face, twisted by agonizing fear, confronted him. Ned Albert released the painful grip on his shrapnel-burned helmet and faced him, too. "Sergeant Hawk! Nice weather, huh?" Hawk looked blankly at Albert. He would take him for the wire-stringing. What had he just said? Whatever it was, he was still functioning at some level, if he was able to speak in complete sentences. He had even made a joke, hadn't he? God, that was a close one! Fifteen yards away, maybe. Maybe ten. Shit, who knows, it might have hit us. This might be Hell.

"Albert, I'm gonna string the wire. We gotta throw up some wire. You wanta help me?"

"Wire?"

"Yeah, gonna string some wire. You wanta do it?"

"Stringin' wire?"

"Yeah."

"String wire, *now*?"

"Yeah. Before daylight."

"Okay." Albert rolled across the hole and cringed next to Hawk. "Anybody alive out there?"

"I don't know. You're the first ones I found. Might be some buried in that shit, I don't know."

"Ain't this some shit?"

"Yeah. McGranger. *McGranger.* You wanta help me string some wire?" McGranger wasn't functioning on any level. The wire; was that a good idea? The shells soared overhead, echoing metallically, as if they were passing through a huge pipeline.

In the first light of dawn and the last darkness of the night, men could be seen stringing the bouncing coils of wire. The sheer absurdity of the maneuver insured its success. The barrage had in its early stages concentrated on the wire. It now moved steadily back and forth across the marine positions. The Japanese took it for granted that no one would be foolish enough to string wire in the midst of the fiery downfall. They knew they were wrong when light hit the smoking positions. New wire was laid over the charred remnants of the old. Gunfire sizzled from the jungle. It buzzed and sang between the men stringing the coils. They didn't seem to notice.

Hawk watched the bullets splattering off of the ground. The meaning of this registered slowly. A man fell silently onto the wire he was stringing, bounced off the coil and rolled to the ground. Hawk spat tobacco into the thorny wire. He raised his voice above the gunfire. "All right! Good enough! Piss on it! Get some cover!" The men walked peacefully back to their holes, raging volleys singing all around them. Hawk and Albert rejoined McGranger. They crouched on opposite sides of the hole, staring at one another.

Albert's eyes were propped open as wide as they could get.

"What's the matter, Ned?" Hawk asked.

"I don't know. I'm either going deaf or crazy."

A large gathering of the townspeople were in the church near the harbor. The church was a sturdy new structure made of concrete. The barrage had spared it. Of the people who had not withdrawn to the church, most were killed. Three-fourths of New Oss was a flattened pile of blackened boards. Sir Richard chose to stay in his mansion. Mr. Starrett took the children to the church in the middle of the night. The mansion had been torn in half; its entire roof was gone. The well-furnished rooms were exposed to view like a large doll house. Sir Richard cowered in his study, and didn't even come out when the barrage stopped.

Mr. Starrett had his own plan for survival, and he intended to include the St. Cyr children in it. He planned on stealing the sole operating landing craft and putting out to sea. But lesser men and bigger cowards were about in that night of terror. The welder who had patched the craft took it and his family soon after the barrage started.

Miss Asquith watched the men stringing the wire from the safety of the church. She marveled at their bravery, or their madness. She recognized Hawk among them.

8

THE HARSH SILENCE THAT FOLLOWED THE ARTILLERY barrage was only slightly relieved by the pecking of small arms fire. The numbed ears of the marines had grown used to the intense noise. When the planes came screaming over the top of the forest, it sounded good to them, until they realized they were Japanese planes.

Dive bombers, Bettys, fighters, swirling and banking over the perimeter, filled the dirty, off-white sky. They swooped low and skidded over the American positions, slinging bombs from beneath their wings and fuselages that cartwheeled and collided with the earth. It was an alarming spectacle, flesh and blood subjected to such omnipotent technology, but the sound and fury proved more terrible than the results. As the frequency of the bombing dwindled, U.S. Navy fighters barreled from out over the ocean and took on their adversaries with a passion. Hawk walked across the perimeter, through the town and down to the harbor at the height of the bombing. Most of the bombs had fallen in the hollow unmanned interior of the perimeter. Injuries were severe, but few.

Hawk walked the boards of the dock, great portions of which had been smashed into the sea by wayward shells. Looking out over the ocean, he saw no signs of what he feared most: an amphibious assault from the rear. He had no way of knowing that Japanese sea power had virtually collapsed in the region over the past twenty-four hours. He stopped at the church on his way back to check on the civilians. He couldn't do much for them. He threw open the tall double doors at the rear of the building. His belt and canteen were slung low on his narrow hips, in the manner of a western gunfighter. The crowd watched him.

Miss Asquith had one arm around Diana and the other around Roger. The night had erased whatever contempt Diana had for Miss Asquith. It had also increased her respect for Sgt. Hawk. He was the only thing between her and the Japanese. The marines were heroic figures compared to the people whimpering in the church. Heroes don't play well when things are peaceful, but they play very well when they aren't.

Miss Asquith stepped away from the crowd and approached the marine. The others in the church followed her. They wanted to hear what he would say. Bombs continued to fall on the western edge of the town.

"Will they spare no one?" Miss Asquith asked.

"Don't look like it," he answered, offering her no hope. The crowd pressed close to him, as if nearness to him would bring salvation. Nothing could have been further from the truth. "They're plannin' a big attack, I guess. I ain't never seen so much artillery. They'll take the town in the end. We can't hold 'em."

"Will there be no rescue?"

"Help is supposed to be comin' here. We don't know when. They didn't give us no time. We told 'em what was goin' on. Mr. St. Cyr's house just got blown to pieces. The radio went with it."

"Is Richard...did you see whether or not..." Miss Asquith looked around for the children and then continued, "Was he in it? Is he all right?"

"Don't know. Didn't look. Not much time, you know. As soon as these planes take off, I figure they'll overrun us."

"Will you try to surrender?"

"Nah." Hawk turned away in disgust and looked out over the simmering rubble. "You can't surrender to a Jap." The people listening traded looks of despair, then drifted away in ones and twos. None of them said a word. They were ordinary people, really. They couldn't believe that this was real. Most of them were still in shock just from being on the outskirts of the target area. Hawk stepped out of the doorway and walked outside. He wanted to say something to them, but he didn't what it would be. He finally had to walk away. That's how it was, they might as well face it.

"Sergeant Hawk!" Miss Asquith ran down the church steps. He stopped and faced her. She had taken it all well, better than any of the others. A great deal of strength was beneath that superficial beauty. He recognized strength in a person, and in her case, it surprised him. He admired her. But it didn't matter much anymore. A lot of strength and beauty was about to be destroyed. "May I say something?"

"If you make it quick."

"I like you very much. I wish I could undo some of these things or make up for all the trouble we've brought upon ourselves, and you Americans. Perhaps if we both survive this nightmare, there will be other places and times for us."

"Yes, ma'am. If there are, they couldn't be no worse."

"I meant, other times together."

Hawk looked down at her, at first without any expression in his bloodshot eyes. Then he smiled his grim smile and she returned it. "You ain't missed out on nothin' by overlookin' me, Miss Asquith. You done yourself a favor."

The plane engines were droning away in the distance. The strike was over. He had to get back. He nodded politely and turned away. She ran and caught his arm. Before he knew it, she had put her arms around him and kissed him. "I'm sorry," she said, "but I should be the judge of that." He took her arms away, and squeezed her hand. He figured that she was just afraid. Women often behaved erratically. To him, fear was a mental illness. Totally unacceptable. He cursorily observed that women were more susceptible to mental illness than men. It never occurred to him that that might be because they had to put up with men. He had to leave. He walked quickly now, stepping on fuming rubble left by the falling shells.

She watched him cross the town. He was going to get killed. She wanted to tell him to be careful. She wanted to give him a reason to be careful. She knew that she couldn't. Something else kept him going, and she would never understand what it was.

Hawk noticed the sky. Now that the Japanese had

exhausted their bag of tricks, nature was about to have her turn. A high wind blew across the ground, carrying away the smoke in a cool breeze and pelting him with fine particles left by the destruction. The sky turned from off-white to a boiling purplish black. By the time he reached his hole, sheets of water were driving across the shattered landscape. He threw an old poncho over his shoulders and watched the jungle beyond the wire. He was alone.

He knew he should have surrendered, but no one had asked for his surrender. He certainly would ask no quarter. It had all been more than he expected, had unfolded too quickly. He knew that he wouldn't intentionally put his men through that shelling again. He had only planned on a little firefight, or at worst, a big firefight. He had lost more men to the artillery than he would have in a dozen probes and firefights. No need to surrender now. He had already taken too many casualties. And the Japanese hadn't suffered any. He couldn't quit without his just and righteous share of them. Pride had brought on the downfall of New Oss. St. Cyr's, Bupta's, Miss Asquith's—all had played a part in it. Now Hawk's was added to it. His was essential. His was the final and most devastating pride. He was the Grim Reaper. He would never ask to be allowed to surrender. It was a different kind of pride, a more complex madness. It was the pride of America, of the Marine Corps, of manhood—but it was pride,· the original sin, and he couldn't overcome it.

The Japanese had to ignore the weather. If they waited for it to break, all the preparatory shelling would have been for nothing. In an hour's peace, the Americans might have time to gather their wits, to stubbornly dig in and fight a proper battle. They slipped slowly out of the forest at first, bayonets poised like the teeth of a great leviathan. Then true to their tradition, they burst out screaming, bellowing their blood-curdling cries with ardent abandon, drowning the very thunder that roared above them.

The marines, also true to their tradition, waited silently for the rush. Wraith-like creatures rose from the debris-filled fighting holes. Half blinded with shock and rain, they pointed their weapons at the wire. Hawk slipped his submachine gun from beneath his poncho. The beginnings of an emotion seethed through his tortured nervous system. *Look at them! Look at all of them!* He was glad. He would get a lot of them. He teetered on both the edge of eternity and the edge of sanity at the same time.

They hit the wire like a mile-wide bulldozer. Sappers tossed satchel charges and pipe bombs into the barbed wire: infantrymen grenaded it, others dove face first, allowing those who followed to step on and over them. Teams of men raced from the jungle carrying planking. They threw the boards on the coiled wire as a bridge. Some of the men had wire cutters on their bayonets that allowed them to scoop up a strand and fire their rifle to sever it. Others had the type of cutter that had to be used by hand. They all died.

The Americans trained strong concentrations of automatic fire on the men trying the breakthrough. The marines rising from their foxholes to meet the attack were surprised and heartened by the number of their fellow survivors.

When the vanguard of the Japanese failed to breach the wire, the shouting horde behind them ran headlong into it, reasoning that their sheer numbers could stamp the wire down. They couldn't do it this time. They stumbled, became hopelessly entangled in it, struggled with the clinging barbs and were ultimately shot. Red blotches splattered repeatedly across the wet grey uniforms. The overwhelming firepower that met the Japanese at the barrier caused them to retreat to the forest, but no one expected this to last for long. After a tense fifteen minutes, they renewed the attack, charging from the underbrush.

The bright lashings of the machine guns whipped viciously across their foremost ranks. They fell in the thick mud. The deepening backwash of rainwater was red with blood. And yet, on they came, oblivious to the casualties, hurling themselves onto the wire. The Americans felt like they were on the receiving end of a stampede of panicked animals. Hawk jammed a fresh clip into his submachine gun. He saw the faces of the enemy clearly through the downpour, each twisted with a different expression and yet somehow each one alike. Some looked genuinely angry, full of blood lust, while others seemed only to be imitating anger, watching for a chance to retreat. These latter moved more slowly and watched their comrades more than their enemies. But they came on just as inevitably as the rest, died in just as large numbers and bled just as much. The wire finally surrendered. It was pounded beneath their feet, forced into collapse by the great number of dead.

Once over the barrier, the Japanese began slinging grenades. The throws were awkward, stiff-armed attempts. made on the run. The impact of the grenades was further decreased by the American minefield buried between the wire and the foxholes. The charging

Japanese ran through it as if they wanted to explode every single hidden trap. The men stepping on the mines were flung skyward, like so many corks being popped out of champagne bottles. Scarcely a mine went undetonated as the grisly reception was repeated all down the line. Rows of men were bowled over by crushing concussions or slicing shrapnel fragments. In spite of the furious carnage, the Japanese kept coming —over the wire, over the dead, through the smoking craters left by the mines, slinging grenades all the while.

Hawk watched the curtain of smoke thrown up by the exploding mines. The driving wind and rain made it dance like a cobra emanating from the muddy earth. A group of attackers burst through it, howling into his face. His finger snapped back on the trigger of his Thompson. The leaping muzzle flash blinded them. The shuddering breechblock caused the gun to shake in his grip as he moved it across the charging men. One of them fell on his face and slid forward to the edge of Hawk's foxhole. His helmet dropped inside, spilling the little ration sack of rice that had been secreted there. The man next to him had his legs knocked backwards at the knees, the trunk of his body falling heavily in the slick muck. The others turned to flee.

Hawk saw movement from the corner of his eye. One of the attackers had made it to the side of his position and jumped in. They looked at one another for a moment, both dazed by the immediacy of the situation. The Japanese soldier had his rifle pointed at Hawk and the marine had his submachine gun leveled at the other's chest. In that instant, each memorized the other's face.

Hawk didn't react first. A blast erupted from the

muzzle of the Arisaka rifle that nearly caused adrenalin to gush from the top of Hawk's head. The bullet tore through his loose poncho, passing between his arm and body without touching him. His reaction came a fraction of a second later. He wasn't depending on a single frantic shot. He held back the trigger and the submachine gun pounded round after exploding round into the smaller man's chest. His lungs were torn out, like two doors being flung open, and he doubled up to take another burst through the top of his helmet. He threw himself again and again into the side of the foxhole, as if he expected to break through the earth to safety with his shoulder. He slammed into the mud at the bottom of the hole, twitching and gasping, though he was obviously already dead. Wild-eyed, Hawk looked back out over the battlefield. The Japanese were again retreating to the forest.

He leaned against the front of the hole, his arms and weapon propped on its muddy edge. The Thompson lay in an inch of water. Hawk breathed heavily through his mouth. He looked over his shoulder at the mutilated body in the mud behind him, and then at the bullet hole in his poncho. The Japanese would overrun them the next time. A few holes had probably fallen this time, either under pressure from grenades or hand-to-hand combat. He pulled the Thompson out of the mud and stood. The wire was gone. The mines were gone. Most of the mortar rounds had been wasted. He climbed out of the hole. Heavy layers of mud clung to his boots as he trudged from hole to hole.

"Pull back!" he ordered. "Second line of defense. Pull back!" He met unpleasant sights as he peered through the rain and down into the holes. A half dozen dead Japanese lay over two men in one hole. Nearly a dozen were stacked in front of another. A single dead marine sat inside this hole, holding a machine gun without a tripod. A single, small bullet hole was in his forehead. Hawk stepped down into the fortification and pried the gun from the dead fingers. The gunner had wrapped a rag around the barrel to keep it from burning his hand. Hawk climbed back out, carrying the thirty caliber machine gun by its perforated, rag-lined barrel. "Pull back!" he screamed into the next hole.

Capt. Carlisle looked up at him. At first, Hawk thought that he was dead. Upon closer inspection, it appeared that he was only in shock. The sergeant peered down the line. Men were pulling back— advancing to the rear, as it were, since marines don't retreat. He would have to double check the holes for the wounded, the shocked and the uninformed. Little spouts of water appeared in a circle around him. He didn't hear the shots, but he recognized the spouts for what they were and threw himself down beside Carlisle. Two dead marines were in there with him.

"Whatcha say, Captain?" Hawk bellowed over the rumble of the storm.

"Dead. All my men are dead."

"Nah. Bunch of 'em are, though. We gotta pull back, Captain, now."

"This can't be happening. No one could survive something like this."

"Yeah, we gotta pull back, Captain. We'll have a shorter piece of ground to hold on the second line of defense. We ain't got nothin' to slow 'em up with out here anymore."

"Of course. Of Course, Hawk. Let's go. I'm not afraid."

"Yessir."

Hawk pulled him to his feet, as he continued, "I mean, I never thought it would get down to this. Wrestling with them..."

"Come on, Captain, we gotta get outa here."

Bullets sprayed water and mud on every side of them as they climbed from the safety of the hole. Hawk had intended for them to split up and present two separate moving targets, but Carlisle lagged behind. Hawk went back, latched onto him and pulled him along until they reached the second line of holes.

Barbed wire did not protect the second line, and only a single sparse line of mines was strewn in front of it. The major advantage of the second line was that it was an arc, shorter than the first line, and as such, able to be held by fewer men. The Japanese would have to cross a longer stretch of open ground to reach it. The arc reached from the shore north of New Oss to the shore south of it, and when it fell, the town would be open to attack. The enemy began their next charge before all the marines could pull back. Those who didn't make it back in time were overrun and killed in short order.

The Japanese had trouble finding their footing in the slippery mush. The tightened line of defensive rifles blew gaping holes in the oncoming throng. The enemy backed away this time before reaching grenade range. Hawk calculated that there were more Japanese than there were bullets. It was a question of minutes.

The storm worsened. Visibility shrank from fifty to twenty feet. Lightning bolts zigzagged between the two opposing armies. The next attack didn't come immediately. The bloodthirsty assault troops finally took into account the negative aspects of fighting both men and nature. The Japanese could afford to wait. They had time. The wind and rain swelled into a frenzy, and then gradually the howling subsided. The next attack followed.

Moving in a human wave through the still powerful wind and water, the Japanese approached more cautiously. Hawk picked the slower-moving targets carefully. It did little good. Capt. Carlisle fired into the mass of humanity, functioning properly. Hawk picked up the machine gun with the greasy rag wrapped around its barrel and depressed the trigger. A streak of yellow molten fire speared through the storm and into the attackers. Hawk rested the gyrating weapon across his knee, sacrificing accuracy for firepower. Anything to slow them up. Scalding shell casings sizzled in the mud at his feet.

The machine gun weakened the center of the attacking force, stalling the advance, but it didn't cause a retreat. The Japanese flattened in the mud, some so close that they were utilizing the marines' first line of holes. That was it.

"Withdraw!" Hawk shouted as he climbed out of his hole. "Withdraw! To the town!" He slung his Thompson, muzzle down, and backed away from the line, his machine gun trained unsteadily on the enemy. The other soaked men did the same; backing away, crouching, firing, with stricken marines falling at random along the line. Two men carried a third whose leg had been mashed to strings. The man being carried screamed louder than any noise on the field. There was no medicine, nowhere to take him. He would scream until he died.

The line of marines drew closer together as they backed down the main street of New Oss. The Japanese chased them, running to catch up more than running in an attack. The two sides traded sporadic fire. The Japanese pushed. The marines fell back. The men in front of the Japanese force were grim-faced and serious. Those toward the rear laughed and waved their arms and fired their weapons at the sky. Hawk led them all the way through the town, to the church near the waterfront.

The Japanese stopped their chase. They fanned out and searched the rubble of New Oss for snipers and hangers-on. Civilians still hid here and there amidst the ruins, though they could hardly be termed a hazard. The storm never again slackened. It whipped at the cautious knots of Japanese crouching over their rifles. Hawk took his Americans into the church under a minimum of harassing fire.

The marines positioned their weapons in the windows of the church. Concussions had knocked out the stained glass the night before. Hawk took off his cumbersome poncho and climbed into the bell tower for a look around. The Japanese scurried about the town, grenading gutted buildings and firing into empty piles of boards. It would take a while before they were satisfied that the town was clear. They probably wanted to be certain that there would no surprises from the rear when they took the church. Less than twenty-five Americans were still alive and able to fight.

Hawk nestled into a corner of the tower and watched

the street below. The tower was at the front of the church and it stood over a side street. His eyes closed halfway. Rain blew in from the far side of the open tower. The wind rocked the bell back and forth and he fouled it with a board to prevent it from ringing. He let his head fall back against the wall, his helmet crunching on the gritty stone. He was too tired and numb to feel his fever. He wondered what had happened to Joe Canlon and his forty men. They were better off anywhere than here. Three enemy soldiers advanced through the rubble of the side street. They showed little caution.

"Surprise, Jap," he growled. A villainous frown darkened his features. He eased the Thompson over the sill. The clattering burst knocked all three of them down. One was still alive, but a second burst cured this oversight. No one below had witnessed the sniping. The Japanese were going about their business. He would be able to do it again. Reduced to sniping, he thought. That was all right. Dead was dead, and they owed him a few more.

From this vantage point he could see the whole town, and far out to sea as well. The number of Japanese below did not seem as great, now they were spread out. If the storm kept up, he would be able to hold out for a little while. Little groups of the victors were seeking shelter from the rain. As long as it rained, Hawk felt there would not be any fighting. The Japanese had the town; they could be patient with the remaining details of occupation. The three bodies in the secluded street below were nearly under water now.

Heaps of limp and twisted corpses stretched from the town to the perimeter, and from there to the jungle. The shocking scene was lessened in its horror by the torrential rains. They washed away the bright and alien colors of the split bodies, burying them in colorless water. The land was painted a dull flannel grey. The wind shifted and Hawk smelled the sea.

* * *

SIR RICHARD WAS DYING ALONE OUT THERE. Hawk didn't know it, nor did anyone else. Nor did anyone know that he had sent Larsen after Roger, and that he had sent him before Hawk or Miss Asquith went after him. No one cared that he had arranged for Miss Asquith to go on a back-up rescue attempt. Word had passed around that he was a biological traitor, a man who had sold his own son. He died a disgrace to the few who knew him in this world. That wouldn't matter, however, because they weren't destined to survive him for long.

And Larsen; he had never had anyone's respect, so he had lost nothing but his life. Hawk never found out that he had killed a man trying to do the same thing that Hawk was doing, rescuing Roger. He only knew that Larsen was with Bupta and Bupta was friendly with the Japanese and a marine couldn't do anything worse than that. Of course, Larsen wasn't a marine. They might have been able to sit down and talk it over. But they weren't talkers, they were three violent people in a cage, and that's the way those things end. It probably wouldn't have mattered to Hawk if he had known the whole story. For him, if a man was a sonofabitch, that was good enough reason to kill him. Larsen should have watched who he tangled with. Hawk was no saint. He couldn't always do the right thing. Sometimes he didn't try.

After a while, Hawk climbed down and faced the crowd below. Some of the civilians were carrying the extra weapons that the marines had brought with them. The townspeople would put up a better fight, now that it was a matter of kill or be killed. Most of them talked openly of surrender. It was the logical thing to do. They were simple people, not members of the French Foreign Legion ready to duel to the death. The Japanese might allow a surrender now that their raging ardor had subsided. Hawk didn't care what they did.

He said, "I'm sorry, folks," when he came down the ladder, and they all stared at him. He ignored their stares after that. He didn't see the party of three take a white flag out of the tall rear doors, but he heard the shots when the Japanese mowed them down. One was a woman.

"McGranger, get up in the steeple and keep a good lookout," he said in a low voice. He walked over to a corner and stared out a window. Surrender. That wasn't what mattered. Paying them back, that was the important thing. He didn't understand these people. A lot of things had gone into the making of Sgt. Hawk, and surrender wasn't one of them.

Miss Asquith watched him. Grey angles of rain blew in through each high window. It was cold. She walked over to him and without saying anything, put her arm around his waist and got close to him. After a moment, she looked up and smiled somewhat apologetically. She needed him. But to him, she was one more problem. He looked down at her, still dazed by the speed of the last few hours. Violence speeds time and drives it into your consciousness. That makes it hard to forget later, because you remember it as happening much more slowly.

"It's gettin' cold," he said.

"Is there anything you can do to get us out of this?"

"I don't know. I'll try."

"There must be *something* we could do."

"Something might turn up. It sure don't look like it, though." He sighed and looked out the window again. She held him tighter.

An hour later a recoil less rifle blasted open the double doors at the rear of the church. The blasting left the remnants of the doors flapping. A mob of soaked Japanese warriors followed on the heels of the confusion and stumbled into the crowded church.

The enemy had managed to mass before the rear doors without McGranger's seeing them. The marines lifted their rifles out of the windows and turned to help the few guarding the doors. The crowd of Japanese couldn't get organized and were shot down as they bumped against one another in the vestibule. The assault ended with a pile of bodies blocking the doors.

Hawk assembled a half-dozen men with automatic weapons for a more elaborate defense of the rear. He spread them out behind various pews at diverse locations in the church. In this way they could not all be killed at once. This was no sooner done than firing started on the western side of the building. A grenade came spinning through one of the windows on that wall. It was one of the types of grenades that does most of its damage by concussion, and even that is done over only a short range. They are used for offensive maneuvers, so that attackers may follow its blast without endangering themselves. Several people were deafened and it thoroughly scared the hell out of everyone.

The Japanese burst through the double doors at the rear again. BAR's and M3's met the unwelcome entrance, cutting them down as they forced their way in. As this attack weakened, the western wall came alive with the sounds of combat. Hawk was on the eastern wall, near the ocean, which remained unviolated. He saw his men back away from the windows, firing all the while. Helmets appeared on the outside. The Japanese climbed through the western windows with quick, urgent motions. They fired down on the defenders and tossed several grenades. The marines couldn't hold the wall. Attackers jumped to the floor and began bayoneting the Americans. The men guarding the rear doors swiveled their weapons to face the new menace. As they did, more unchallenged attackers flooded the vestibule, tearing the rear doors off their hinges.

The enemy soldiers fired indiscriminately at men, women and children. The civilians ran about, screaming in panic and inviting the executioner's bullet. Some of them stood frozen in various parts of the church, in the same places they had been standing when the attack began.

Miss Asquith ran to Hawk, crying, her bravado exhausted. She wanted him to save her. In her panic, she had abandoned Diana and Roger. Diana was nowhere to be seen, but Roger stood near the middle of the church, watching in fascination as the Japanese entered the rear. The attackers were high on anger and fear, shooting everything in sight. Miss Asquith saw this too late. A bullet hit Roger in the upper leg, slamming him to the floor as one might slam the cover of a book shut. He raised his head and crawled about in a pool of blood, right in front of the rising tide of Japanese.

Hawk brushed Miss Asquith aside, leapt a pew and ran toward him. He knew it was futile as he raced before the bobbing Japanese muzzles gathered in the rear. Nothing lived in the entire rear half of the church, other than the Japanese and Roger. In the blur of his vision, he could see at least two rifles pointed at himself; he could mentally project their lines of fire and they intersected upon him. He felt the white heat of fire spewing around his head. Behind him ran Miss Asquith, probably only dimly aware that she could accomplish nothing.

Hawk threw himself down in the face of the belching fire, letting the bullets hum over the top of his helmet. He ripped the pin from a grenade and crawled madly on his elbows to the wounded boy. Before he could release the grenade's safety lever, a slug bounced off the stone floor and into his ribs. It felt as if someone had made a direct hit on the rib bone with a hammer. He groaned and gripped the grenade tighter. He stared into Roger's glazed eyes. There were no principles, only this. Miss Asquith stepped over him and reached for the boy, taking one, two, a dozen, two dozen rounds in every part of her body. She dropped between them. Hawk managed to fling the grenade over her torn remains. The rear of the church exploded. A chorus of screams followed the blast as the Japanese who were left clutched at their maimed bodies.

The automatic weapons had stopped the flow of the enemy through the western windows. For the time being, the church had been successfully defended.

Carlisle and McGranger lifted Hawk up.

"I'm all right."

"You're hit in the side."

"No. No. It's okay. Get the kid. Get the woman."

"She's dead," said Carlisle. "Come on, Hawk. We need you on the whole thing. Don't die on me, Hawk, please!" The captain left Roger lying there.

Hawk shook them loose. "Get away from me!" He fell to his knees and gathered Roger into his arms.

"I shan't be a soldier, after all, Sergeant Hawk. It's much too frightening, actually," said the boy. Hawk stared into his eyes, barely understanding his words.

"Get a tourniquet on the leg," he gasped. McGranger lifted the boy over his head, dripping blood across his face. When he looked down, he saw Miss Asquith. He touched her shoulder, then knelt with a hand on each of his thighs and rocked painfully for a moment. He eased a hand up to his bleeding ribs.

"They're coming. They're coming, again," Carlisle wailed frantically. His tone seemed to say, "I told you so."

Hawk looked across the church, his teeth and lips parted. The survivors were looking at him with imploring eyes, begging him to get up. McGranger went toward him with outstretched hands. "Get away from me!" he roared. "By God, I told you to stay away from me!" He slung his arm at McGranger and extended his bloody fingers in a gesture that ordered him to come no closer. He jerked a knee up under himself and struggled to his feet. Bullets ricocheted along the ceiling.

"Get...get away from the windows. Let 'em come in. Get back to the altar," Hawk told them. In reflexive obedience to any authority capable of voicing itself, the crowd of terrified people surged to the front of the church. They hid behind the huge marble altar and within the confines of the sacristy nearby. The marines ripped the bolted pews from the floor, dragged them over the communion rail and into the sanctuary, where they erected a hasty barricade on the steps leading up to the altar. Hawk hurled a wooden prie-dieu onto the pile of pews and fell behind the barricade. A blast blew the trumeau from between two windows. Grenades knocked the casing of the double doors inward. The attackers again flooded the smoky interior. They met an unflinching volley from behind the barricade. Row upon row of Japanese burst through the rear doors and fell upon the stacks of bodies at the rear of the church. Hawk watched in astonishment. No force could absorb such casualties and continue to be viable. Three of the enemy climbed into the choir loft at the rear, firing down on the altar from this vantage point. Ned Albert stepped up onto the barricade and threw a grenade the length of the building and deep into the loft. The blast knocked the floor from the choir and the rubble blocked the rear doors.

Hawk lay on the jumbled barricade. One hand was on the pistol grip of his submachine gun and the other was pressed tightly to his ribs. Both hands were solid red and streaked with black dirt. The pain was steady. That was all right, as long as it didn't stab or pulsate. He began to think seriously about Canlon. Another forty men might make a difference now. Last night, they wouldn't have mattered at all. They would have been killed just as easily as had the others. But the Japanese had lapsed into insanity, they were throwing themselves at the American bullets. They had to be growing weak in numbers.

He gasped. It felt for a moment there as if his breathing had stopped. He refused to die! The sawing at his innards droned on steadily. He tested his legs. They were all right. The pain wasn't that bad. He wasn't weak. Things could always get worse, and they usually did. He remembered the blind and legless machine gunner that he and Canlon had found on the Haarmeer Archipelago.

The Japanese tried a flanking maneuver, coming through the windows again. Bullets met their faces and heads. Bodies draped half in and half out of the blasted openings. Screams came from the rooms to the right. They were breaking into the sacristy. They would soon be behind the barricade. He saw Roger lying at the foot of the altar, wordless, soundless, trembling. Hawk closed his eyes and dropped his head on the wooden prie-dieu. One more fight. One more, and then he could rest.

Grenades thundered in the sacristy. The two sides traded explosives in an orgy of self-destruction. All was quiet after that. He looked up. A dozen marines were still alive behind the barricade. Two civilians were with them on the altar. They were good fighters. The rest, everyone, was gone, killed by the grenades in the sacristy. Plunkett...Starrett...Powers...Diana.

He heard a loud hissing. It came from the sacristy. What was that? He had heard that before. *Flamethrower. Fire.*

An awful way to die. He staggered down the altar steps and over to the door of the sacristy. Two of the enemy stood in the mass of corpses working over a flamethrower. They fired a short burst of flame, as if testing it. It fell on the dead. Hawk stumbled into the clouded room, and whipped the roaring muzzle of his Thompson back and forth as they fell screeching across one another. He unhooked the sling and dragged the flamethrower with him to the barricade.

The problem of the fire wasn't to be solved that easily. Another Japanese flamethrower bearer came climbing over the fallen beams in the rear of the church. He dodged his way up the aisle, going from one pew to the next, firing squirts of flame that landed in inextinguishable globs along the top of the barricade. Other Japanese came behind him, firing over his head, providing him with cover. Hawk's bloody hands tightened on the Thompson. The pain was gone, lost in adrenalin. No shot had ever been more important. He threw himself atop the barricade and held back the trigger. The clip was dry. He rolled back down and reached for a new one. None here. None there.

"Fresh out, dumb ass!" he whispered. He took a deep breath. "Shit on you, then!" He angrily threw the Thompson across the jumble of pews. On the far side of the barricade, a marine went up in a ball of feathery orange flames. The man cried out in unreachable octaves. He tried to run but was burned to a crisp before he could vault the barricade. Hawk watched the flamethrower. It wasn't more than thirty feet away, its operator crouching behind the front row of pews.

The Japanese flamethrower bearer was smiling. Hawk latched onto his own flamethrower. How did that bastard get that close and why would he want to? He looked at his Japanese-made weapon. The launcher was a long pipe with a jet at its base, a much simpler weapon than the American version. He rolled over the top of the barricade with it. A rod of gasoline spewed over his head and landed on the pews where he had been. Hawk dropped his weapon and crawled under the fiery rod. The operator of the enemy flamethrower could not see him. He was blinded by his own blast. Hawk crawled beneath the fire and leapt at him, tackling him and knocking him over. They both went down in a sparking shower of orange globules. Hawk was on top of him, forcing his elbow into the man's throat. The Japanese fired a burst of flame at the ceiling, exhibiting absolutely no concern for his own safety. Hawk jumped off of him, scrambling away as quickly as he could. The fire fell harmlessly between them. An orb of orange the size of a dollar fell on the Japanese soldier's hand and he shook it off with a high-pitched scream.

The marine saw his own flamethrower lying impotently on the floor. He ran for it. The Japanese grinned again when he saw this, and swept his nozzle and its whooshing red-orange broom behind Hawk. Hawk grabbed his own launcher and feinted back, allowing the flames to roil and slither in arches that lapped within inches of his face. He twisted the jet of his launcher and the burst shot through the leaping curtain of jellied fire set up by his opponent. He heard the scream on the other side of the curtain. His assailant had been incinerated.

The other Japanese had fled when the two dragons became embroiled in their duel. This was to their advantage, because several pews were ablaze and fire continued to drop from a drooping beam in the ceiling. They had watched the fight from the rear door, and when their man turned into a pillar of ashes, they ran from the building.

Hawk walked slowly back to the burning barricade.

Seven men, all of them marines, were still alive. Another seven had been roasted. The last of the civilians were among these. The survivors were beating at the flames with religious vestments and their own clothing. It took half an hour to bring the persistent fire under control. During that time, they heard nothing from their adversaries outside.

An hour dragged by and then two, but the expected final assault never came. McGranger and Albert went into the bell tower to scout around. They reported that the Japanese were making themselves at home in what was left of New Oss. There didn't seem to be very many of them left. About a dozen had the church surrounded, ready to pick off any of the Americans trying to escape. This was effective. There wasn't any place to escape to, anyway.

And so, that was it, Hawk thought. They weren't going to waste any more men in their furious attacks. The Americans had to come out eventually, or become lax in their vigilance and permit the enemy to get close enough to burn them out. Even Carlisle realized what they were doing and spoke to Hawk of it.

"Fine with me," he said. They worked over his bullet wound, though they didn't know what they were doing. They had no medicine, no water to waste on washing it. It was getting terribly stiff. He waved them away. "It's not too bad," he told them. He lay quietly on a pew, conserving his waning energy.

They gave Roger what morphine and sulfa they had. No one wanted to chance digging the bullet out of his leg. That night, the boy came out of shock enough to speak.

"Miss Asquith was killed, wasn't she?" he asked.

Hawk knelt beside him. "Yeah, she...uh...got shot."

"She was a nice lady."

"Yeah," Hawk nodded.

"Have you heard from Father?"

"No...uh...no, sure ain't, Roger. He'll be around directly, I imagine."

"He's dead. Diana's dead, too, isn't she?"

"Yeah."

Roger stared unblinking at the ceiling. Tears rolled down his cheeks, but he didn't sob. "I'm all alone. Sergeant Hawk." Hawk didn't say anything. He draped a poncho over Roger. It was getting cold, with the night coming on and the rain still drizzling outside.

"Nah, you got me, ain'tcha?"

"It...it still isn't as bad as when Mother died. I guess I've really been alone since then."

"Yeah." Hawk lit a cigarette. It was all that he had. "Listen, no sense in making yourself sick thinking about it. You sleep. How's that goddam leg?"

"It doesn't hurt."

"You got a lot of years ahead of you. You got time to forget this and then some. Cry if you want to, but don't give up."

"I won't ever cry again."

Hawk patted Roger's shoulder and took another look at his leg. It appeared to him that the bullet might have gone through the little limb. Either that, or he had two slugs in him. That was unlikely, but in light of all the lead flying, not impossible.

Hawk went to a corner under a window. The moonlight flowed down on him. He pulled his shirt aside. A black knot was perched on top of his rib. He took out his Japanese bayonet and fired its tip. "You might as well come outa there, you little sonofabitch," he growled at the slug. He dug into the blood-encrusted flesh. The metal slid along the top of the rib and popped out. It plinked onto the floor. Hawk let his breath out and rubbed his forearm across his forehead. The burning was excruciating. Sweat poured from his forehead. "Jesus," he whispered, "Jesus Christ!"

He lapsed in and out of consciousness for the next three days. He would get up and walk, just to prove he still could. He checked on the boy constantly. Roger grew steadily weaker, though there was no sign of infection. Hawk and the others had to watch as the scores of mutilated bodies deteriorated around them. The hideous odor became more than they could endure; they and the corpses were blanketed with filthy black flies. At the end of the fourth day, they dragged the dead into a corner and sprayed the last of the flamethrower over them.

The Japanese occasionally lobbed a grenade through a window or fired a shot into the high portals. Everyone made a half-hearted effort to duck on these occasions, and that was the extent of it. The marines could hear the Japanese walking about outside, talking, laughing, carrying on their normal affairs. After being imprisoned with the rotting dead, the men were driven slightly mad—and some of them, not so slightly. They sat in a solemn circle on the altar on the night of the fourth day and swore to the Almighty that they would never surrender. The creases deepened in their foreheads; their cheekbones jutted defiantly out of their gaunt faces as their bodies fed on themselves. Outside, like smoke, clouds blew across the face of the waning moon, as though the universe was on fire. And it was.

Hawk quit trying to remove the maggots from his wounds. He noticed that they were cleaning out the infection. He would survive. The worms of eternal death only helped him. Nothing could kill him. He began to believe that, in his delirium.

There was no indignity left for them to suffer. They had become a part of the evil perpetrated upon them—the worst part. They discussed tearing the enemy apart with their hands, of eating their hearts and drinking their blood. On that night of the fourth day, they vowed to come out, to attack like the raging beasts that they were.

Carlisle was one of those most out of control. Hawk had been in and out of this madness before, to a lesser extent. He knew his mind would recover, if his body recovered. But he also knew that Carlisle's would not. He had gone too far. He had no toughness to begin with; his life had been too comfortable, and yet he had experienced things that would destroy the hardest of men.

McGranger climbed down from the dark bell tower. "Landing craft. Landing craft pulling in the harbor," he said. "They must be ours, Sergeant Hawk."

Hawk looked at him and let his words sink in. "Probably more Japs," he answered.

"No, they're ours, I know they are," McGranger insisted.

Hawk stood. "Well, either they are or they ain't," he said. "Let's get outa here."

The miserable group rose drunkenly to their feet. Their lack of sleep made simple movements seem bizarre. When one sleeps during such a horror, his brain continues to live it, whether or not the body is active. They weren't sure if they were awake or asleep, and they didn't care. They climbed weakly out of one of the rear sacristy windows that faced the dock. They dropped heavily to the ground, stumbling under their own weight. Hawk carried the unconscious Roger. Big LST's loomed out of the darkness, mere inches away.

Rifle shots fell among them. A single rifle was firing. A lone Japanese guard had been awakened at the back of the church. They ignored the whining ricochets. Carlisle fell with a slug in the back of his head. It was better that he died.

In six days, when the A.I.F. liberated New Oss, they would find only twenty enemy soldiers. The High Command considered it a disgrace that so few Japanese had buffaloed an entire battalion. Carlisle couldn't have taken that. Had his sanity returned, he would have tried to make them understand. He would have been badly hurt. But it didn't hurt Hawk. He expected such things. They were normal. They left Carlisle lying where he fell.

Shelvin fell as they walked slowly down the shattered wharf. Armistead and McGranger stopped and casually picked him up. He was still alive. The bullets continued to smack the wood as they stumbled into an iron-walled LST; the bullets pinged on its protective covering. Hawk's last thought in New Oss was that he should go back and kill that little Jap bastard.

A Coast Guard officer asked Hawk where the rest were. He seemed shocked and surprised by the answer. Several LST's would return to the Haarmeer Archipelago empty. With a throb of its engine and a shudder of its deck, the big craft backed out of the harbor.

"I have an arrest warrant for Sir Richard St. Cyr,"

said the Coast Guard officer. "Do you know where I can find him?" he asked Hawk.

The sergeant sat at his feet on a low bench that was connected to the wall. "No...uh...ain't seen him," Hawk answered. "What's he done?" he asked with sneering smile.

"God, you name it," said the officer, leafing through his papers. "Let's see—first he conspired to overthrow the government, it says here. Then, uh, he committed perjury in order to have his wife institutionalized in an insane asylum. Then, uh, we get down to fabricating and falsifying written documents to obtain a marriage license." The officer chuckled. "It looks like he tried to claim his wife was dead, and then hired some orderly to kill her after the fact. Crazy guy. Oh yeah, I read about this in the papers. I guess you haven't seen any lately. The wife escaped and told all the papers about him. She wants her kids back."

Hawk nodded. He showed no change of expression. "No, I ain't seen the fella. There's her kid over there."

The Coast Guard crewmen ducked and cursed the fire that came from the shore. McGranger walked over to Hawk and sat beside him. The five marines watched the Coast Guardsmen curiously as the sailors moved urgently about, shouting and cringing under the intense volley.

"You know, I should have joined the Coast Guard," McGranger told Hawk.

Hawk lay back against the wall, drinking a canteen of water and smoking a cigar that one of the crewmen had handed him. His sense of taste was gone. The lack of water had destroyed it.

"You shouldn't have joined a goddam thing."

The sergeant told the officer to travel west along the coast of Malang and try to find Canlon and the others. He supposed that Joe had seen the battle at New Oss and decided to wait it out in the jungle. He hoped so, anyway. That didn't sound like Joe, but he might have gotten smart in the last few days.

As it turned out, that was not what had happened. Halfway to Hollow Mountain, they found the party. A grisly dawn lit the shoreline. The survivors of Canlon's party lay in the murky surf, their guns trained on the forest. The others were staked to trees in front of them, in conditions of mutilation similar to that suffered by Calloway. Fourteen men slunk aboard the LST when it pulled up to the overgrown coast.

Canlon took Hawk's hand and arm and shook it vigorously. He knelt beside him. "You look like shit, Hawk."

"Feel pretty good, though. They shot me fulla dope, you know."

"No kiddin'! You gonna be all right?"

"What do you mean, gonna be? Ain't nothin' wrong with me now. Where y'all been?"

"Them Nodus got us. The ones that they was gonna bomb to hell? What they done is just made 'em mad, ran 'em outa their village and down on us. We kept losin' men one at a time. Never could catch the sneaky bastards."

Canlon shock his head. "You talk about bein' scared, now..."

"Yeah? It was a little rough for us, too!"

Canlon shook his head and looked into Hawk's eyes. They looked back through a hundred fathoms of misery. "This island is one bad place," Joe said.

"Yeah. One."

Hawk got shakily to his feet and moved across the deck. He dreamily climbed up to where he could see out over the ocean. The glare tightened the leathery trails beneath his eyes. It was a big ocean, full of a lot of scores he felt he had to settle. That was the right thing to do, wasn't it?

A LOOK AT BOOK FOUR:
TIGER ISLAND

SECRET WEAPON!

The Americans are halting their all-out invasion of the island of Rechnung, and no one knows why. Rumor has it two platoons of soldiers have mysteriously disappeared, and the Japanese have a new and deadly secret weapon.

But so do the Americans. Plucked from the front lines, Sergeant James Hawk is used as bait to provoke the Japanese to use their weapon once again. And once he uncovers what the enemy has up their sleeves, there is no weapon on earth that can match his wrath.

Can Hawk successfully destroy the enemy's lethal secret?

AVAILABLE AUGUST 2022

ABOUT THE AUTHOR

Patrick Clay was born a fifth generation Texan, in Galena Park, Texas, and went to a Catholic elementary school there. He attended St. Thomas High School and graduated fifth in his class. Patrick also received a scholarship to the University of St. Thomas and graduated cum laude from there. He then graduated magna cum laude from South Texas College of Law, where he was fourth in his class and a member of the law journal. While attending law school at night, Patrick operated his own locksmith shop. During the time he waited for the bar results, he began writing fiction. He began his second novel, *Sgt. Hawk*, in February 1977, and finished it in six weeks. Patrick had a well-known agent, who tried to sell it to major publishers and television. It was finally sold to Leisure Books in 1978, and by that time, Patrick had finished *The Return of Sgt. Hawk*, which was published in 1980. *Sgt. Hawk Under Attack* and *Sgt. Hawk Tiger Island* followed in 1981 and 1982, respectively. The titles of the latter two books were selected by the publisher, Leisure Books, as they originally had different names. *Sgt. Hawk and The Firebolt* was written in 1982 when Leisure Books went bankrupt, returned the rights, and never fulfilled distribution. Patrick had by then begun a solo law practice and gave up writing. He worked in a poor neighborhood, with plenty of wonderful clients, but not much compensation. So,

Patrick became a captain in the Civil Air Patrol and was Houston chess player in 1990, more for his tournament directing ability than playing skills. After fourteen years, he gave up the private law practice, and worked as an attorney for the federal government for the next thirty years. The podcast, *Paperback Warrior*, rekindled his interest in *Sgt. Hawk*.

Patrick met his beautiful wife at Astroworld in Houston, the first year that the amusement park opened. When he began writing in 1977, he had no children, and by the time he stopped writing in 1983, he had three daughters; he now has nine grandchildren. His father, a disabled veteran, and six uncles served in the South Pacific during World War II. Patrick was named after one of them, Patrick Clay, who was on a U.S. Navy ship with four battle stars. Another one of Patrick's uncles was at Pearl Harbor when it was attacked.